"It isn't easy being Andrés Montano, is it?

"You have to be so responsible...dedicated to duty...honor-bound," said Brenna. "When was the last time you were selfish, the last time you took something you wanted...without thinking of anyone else but yourself?"

There was no hesitation in his answer. "Last night."

"You didn't take anything last night that wasn't freely given, and you were as considerate of me as any man could have been."

"But it was wrong, and it was selfish."

"Why? Because for a few hours you weren't a soldier, a leader, a national hero, but just a man?" She smiled gently. "You're entitled to that, Andrés...to feel and want and need."

He stopped in shadow and pulled her around to face him. "But not you. If I want a woman, I should find one of my own people...one who lives with war and horror and hardship, as I do. I'm not entitled to want or need *you*. You're an American. You're my prisoner."

Dear Reader,

This month we're bringing you an absolutely stellar lineup of books. In fact, I hardly know where to begin. First up is *Runaway*, by Emilie Richards. She delivers exactly the kind of knockout emotional punch she's come to be known for. This is the first of two novels about sisters separated by deception and distance, and it's a book with a very different sort of subject: teen runaways, the dangers they face and the lengths they sometimes have to go in order to survive. Next month's *The Way Back Home* completes the circle. I truly believe these two books will live in your memory for a long, long time.

Theresa Weir has written for Silhouette Romance until now, and has also tried her hand at mainstream romance adventure. In *Iguana Bay* she makes her debut appearance in Silhouette Intimate Moments, and what a stunner this book is! The hero is anything but ordinary, as you'll discover the minute you meet him, and his meeting with the heroine is no less noteworthy. And lest you think that's all we have in store, the month is rounded out by two veterans of the bestseller lists and the award rosters: Heather Graham Pozzessere and Marilyn Pappano.

Later in the year, the excitement will continue with new books from favorites such as Linda Howard, Kathleen Korbel and Linda Shaw, to name only a few. The moments are never dull at Silhouette Intimate Moments, so join us for all of them.

Yours,

Leslie J. Wainger
Senior Editor and Editorial Coordinator

Not Without Honor

MARILYN PAPPANO

Silhouette Intimate Moments

Published by Silhouette Books New York

America's Publisher of Contemporary Romance

SILHOUETTE BOOKS
300 East 42nd St., New York, N.Y. 10017

ISBN: 0-373-07338-0

First Silhouette Books printing June 1990

Printed in the U.S.A.

Books by Marilyn Pappano

Silhouette Intimate Moments

Within Reach #182
The Lights of Home #214
Guilt by Association #233
Cody Daniels' Return #258
Room at the Inn #268
Something of Heaven #294
Somebody's Baby #310
Not Without Honor #338

Christmas Stories 1989

"The Greatest Gift"

MARILYN PAPPANO ·

has been writing as long as she can remember, just for the fun of it, but a few years ago she decided to take her lifelong hobby seriously. She was encouraging a friend to write a romance novel and ended up writing one herself. It was accepted, and she plans to continue as an author for a long time. When she's not involved in writing, she enjoys camping, quilting, sewing and, most of all, reading. Not surprisingly, her favorite books are romance novels.

Her husband is in the Navy, and in the course of her marriage she has lived all over the U.S. Currently, she lives in Georgia with her husband and son.

Prologue

The prisoner sat in a straight-backed chair in the center of the room. His hands, bound tightly to the rungs behind his back, were the only thing that held him upright. His head fell to his chest, and his body sagged heavily against the ropes, pulling them tighter, deeper, into the tender, bloody flesh of his wrists.

His uniform—olive drab, with no name, no rank or unit insignia—was stained with dirt and sweat and blood. The too-large jacket was gathered around his waist with a wide webbed belt, but the weapons it normally held—a survival knife and a holstered revolver, both stolen from American shipments to the San Angelo government—had been taken from him. His black combat boots were badly scuffed, the soles worn thin.

Commander Tom Mathis of the United States Navy, commanding officer of the U.S. Military Advisory and Assistance Group, or MAAG, assigned to the small South American country, walked in a slow circle around the San Angeleno army's prize prisoner. Mathis was on a tight schedule—in a few more days his daughter was flying into the capital city of Santa Lucia to spend his two weeks' leave with him, and he had a lot to do before she arrived—but this task couldn't be put off. He had been responsible for the prisoner's capture, and now he would make the positive identification that would most likely lead to the prisoner's death.

Ignoring the stab of an unfamiliar emotion that he thought might be guilt, Mathis reached down and grabbed a handful of thick black hair, forcing the man's head back.

The prisoner's face was bruised and swollen almost beyond recognition. One eye was closed, his lip split in two places, his nose obviously broken. Dried blood and dirt were caked on the lacerations that marked his cheeks and jaw. The brutal beating he'd received had altered his appearance a great deal...but not enough, the American admitted with a grim sigh. As badly beaten as he was, there was no way anyone could mistake this man for Andrés Montano. None.

Clenching his teeth together to contain the curses, Mathis released his grip on the prisoner, turning away as the man's head rolled forward again. He walked to the Angeleno captain standing between two guards at the door and gave the man a scornful look. "I handed Montano to you on a silver platter," he said, his voice heavy with derision, "and your boys still couldn't get it right. That *ain't* him."

The young officer bristled at the insult. "You're wrong, Commander. It *is* him. He walked right into our trap, just as you said he would."

Mathis pulled a pack of cigarettes from his pocket and stuck one between his teeth, then lit it with a battered silver lighter bearing the gold rope-and-anchor insignia of the navy. "I don't know who he is," he said at last, blowing a stream of smoke into the officer's face, "but he *isn't* Andrés Montano. You got the wrong man."

Chapter 1

Let me out of here!"

Brenna Mathis gave the locked door one last bang with her clenched fist, then turned away, her expression one of frustration. She had been yelling at the two guards outside the door for the past hour, but they had never so much as glanced her way. Instead, they lounged against the wooden posts that supported the narrow porch, rifles slung with wide green straps over their shoulders, talking, smoking, occasionally laughing—and totally ignoring her.

She paced to the opposite wall—exactly seven steps—and back again, her hands in tight fists, her muscles taut with fury. Her anger wasn't producing results from the men outside, she acknowledged, but it served the purpose of keeping her fear under control. Ever since a small group of men had taken her—*taken* her? she fumed. They had *kidnapped* her!—from the Santa Lucia airport, she had concentrated on anger, on letting her temper build into pure outrage. As long as she was angry she couldn't be scared, couldn't torture herself with questions of what they wanted with her or images of what they might do to her.

The entire situation was totally unacceptable, she decided, planting her fists on her hips. Granted, San Angelo was involved in a long-running civil war, and her father *was* on the government's side. Still, Tom Mathis was the most powerful non-Angeleno in the country. He commanded an entire army; no one dared cross him. So how had these, these *criminals* managed to kidnap his daughter from the middle of the heavily patrolled, government-controlled airport in broad daylight?

Taking a deep breath, Brenna turned her attention once more to the room where she'd been locked for the past hour and five minutes. It was seven paces wide, four paces long. The walls were constructed of thick, sturdy boards, the floor of hard-packed dirt. Against one wall was a rickety cot that looked as if her slight weight might cause it to collapse, and against the opposite wall, an even shakier looking wooden bench. There were three boarded-over windows, the slats placed far enough apart to allow some light and air into the miserable little space but too close to allow even the possibility of escape. And there was the door, its small window covered with a square of wire screen so encrusted with dirt and dead insects that only the blurriest of views was possible through it.

Brenna leaned one shoulder against the wall and stared out the side window. It offered her a small slice of the village—dusty green trucks and jeeps parked in the rutted road, a few ramshackle whitewashed buildings that appeared to have been shops or businesses at one time and a church built of crumbling adobe, its steeple supporting a broken white cross.

There were men visible, too, all swarthy and armed and dressed in military uniforms, like her kidnappers. But there were no women, no children, no dogs or farm animals, as she'd seen in other towns on the trip here from Santa Lucia.

That meant she was in some kind of rebel camp. And *that* meant she was in the hands of the enemy her father had come here to defeat.

Deep inside, the fear surged, but stubbornly she ignored it. Her father must know by now that something had happened. With the intelligence network he'd set up within the country, he probably even knew where she was and who she was with. It would only be a matter of time before he found her, before he rescued her and punished her kidnappers. All *she* had to do was wait ... and stay calm. She could do that. She wasn't Tom Mathis's daughter for nothing.

She was still standing beside the window when she heard the creak of the door. She resisted the urge to turn and confront her captors and instead continued to look out, displaying an air of studied unconcern.

Two men came into the room behind her, their shadows falling distortedly across the dirt floor and up the opposite wall. "We've brought your bags, Miss Mathis," the taller man said as the other one laid her suitcase and her small nylon duffel bag on the cot, alongside her purse. "You might want to clean up before you meet with our commander."

How polite he was, she thought with distaste. Even at the airport, when he'd accosted her after she'd cleared customs, he'd been polite, going so far as to say "please" before displaying the gun he had pointed at her side. At the time he had worn the rank of a major in the National Army, but the insignia had come off as soon as they were out of the city. There was no doubt, though, that he was in command of the small unit. The men had called him by his name, Vicente, but there had been respect in their voices and in their manner.

Slowly she turned to look at the two men. She knew her hair was a mess, her face slightly burned from the long ride to the village in the hot sun, her makeup long since melted off and her clothes rumpled, but if they thought she was actually going to freshen up to meet their boss, they were sadly mistaken. If he was going to go around ordering the kidnapping of innocent women, he'd have to get used to seeing them looking less than their best. "Your commander can go to hell," she said, smiling pleasantly, "and you can go with him."

The man restrained an amused smile, sparking Brenna's temper again. "Very well, Miss Mathis. If you'll come with me..." He walked to the open door, stopping only when she spoke.

"No." She met his gaze evenly when he turned to look at her. "If your boss wants to talk to me, he can come here. I'm not leaving."

This time there was no hint of amusement in his darkly handsome face. "All right. I'll tell Andrés that you prefer to see him in your cell." With a curt nod, he turned and left the room, leaving the door open behind him.

Brenna stood frozen for a long moment, then hurried after him. "Wait a minute!" she commanded, her voice low and strained. "What did you say?"

Vicente drew a pair of sunglasses from his breast pocket and slid them into place, then gazed coolly down into her face. "That's not the question you really want to ask, is it?" He glanced toward the building where the road ended, a small wooden house with a long, narrow porch. "Yes, it's Andrés Montano," he said without waiting for her to ask. "And he's waiting to see you."

When he turned and walked away again, Brenna remained motionless. She had thought of many things in the past few hours, but strangely enough Andrés hadn't been one of them. She had never suspected that he'd played a part in her kidnapping, had never suspected that he was even capable of such a crime! Lord help her, she had never expected to see him again, not after six years had gone by without so much as a word.

But he was here, less than a hundred yards away, in the building at the end of the road. Waiting for her.

For just a moment she let herself remember, let herself feel once more the love…and the pain. She remembered the day her father had brought a young San Angeleno soldier, a student in the U.S. Navy's training program for foreign allies, home for dinner, remembered falling in love with him, remembered how her world had shattered when her father told her that Andrés was dropping out of the program to return to fight in his country's civil war. She remembered, too, her anguish when she had realized that he was going to leave without seeing her, without telling her goodbye, without offering her any hope for the future.

He had been cold that last time she'd seen him, as he'd packed his bags for the trip home. His country was at war, he'd said, and his people needed him. She needed him, too, she had insisted, but he had simply looked at her, the expression in his eyes distant and unyielding. His duty lay with his country, not her. Untouched by her pleas, caring nothing for her pain, he had finished packing and left without a goodbye, a regret or even a kiss.

But now he was here, and he had ordered her kidnapped and brought to him. Why? Surely not because he wanted to see her. He hadn't cared enough about seeing her six years ago to stay in Orlando, and she wouldn't be foolish enough to believe that he cared now.

Was it because of her father?

Slowly she began walking toward the house where Andrés and Vicente waited, her sandals filling with warm sandy dirt. Tom seemed a far more likely reason for this threat against her. He trained the government troops to defeat the rebels, and Andrés was the rebel leader. They must intend to somehow use her against her father…but how? Tom would never believe that Andrés would hurt her or allow anyone else to, so the threat lacked substance.

At the first step she stopped to empty the sand from her shoes. Only five steps, the porch and a screen door separated her from Andrés. She briefly considered the idea of staying where she was, but it would only postpone the meeting, not cancel it. If she didn't go inside, Andrés would eventually come to her.

With a sigh, she ran her fingers through her hair, wishing she'd followed Vicente's suggestion and cleaned up a bit. At the time it had seemed such an arrogant thing—but at the time, she hadn't known she was going to see Andrés. Well, it was too late now.

She climbed the steps and pulled the screen door open, letting it shut behind her with a bang. She found herself in a small room, roughly half the size of the house. Its construction was similar to the shack that served as her cell— thick, rough-hewn boards, and windows on the outside walls. The floor here was wooden, made of wide planks that looked as if they'd never seen a coat of paint.

There was little furniture—a cot underneath one window, a rickety table that seemed to do double duty as a desk, two wooden chairs and a battered metal cabinet. The table held a grimy oil lamp and was covered with a large ragged map that held both men's attention.

Brenna gave up her attempt at nonchalance and settled her gaze on the men. On Andrés. Although he was leaning over the table, his back to her, his head bent, she had no doubt that it was him. She had loved him too long to be mistaken. For months after he'd left, she had treasured every memory, every photograph of him, until finally she'd had to forget or go mad. The photographs had been burned, the memories forced into the darkest corner of her mind, and she had gone on with her life. Until now.

She stood motionless, uncertain whether to force him to acknowledge her or pray that he would forget about her completely. Before she'd made up her mind, he looked up from the map and turned, his dark eyes locking with hers.

Dear God, he had changed. She searched his face but found no sign of the sweet, gentle, laughing young man she had loved. He was hard and lean and sleek, well suited to these mountains where he lived. The gentleness was gone from his face, as were the laughter...and the love...and the life. He was as impassive, as empty of emotion, as a living man could be.

Under the force of his gaze, she took a startled step back. This wasn't the Andrés she had known—the one who had lived life with such joy, the one who had made love to her with such passion. This man was a stranger, a soldier, a warrior. He was hard and cold and...dangerous.

Yes, she admitted apprehensively, he was dangerous.

Wordlessly Andrés turned back to the map. He'd seen the fear leap into her eyes, fear of *him*, but it didn't touch him. Nothing touched him these days. He gave what little passion he had to the war, his country and his people, and saved none for himself, none for anyone else.

With one blunt fingertip he outlined a section of the map indicating the rain forests of eastern San Angelo. Aware that Brenna had never found languages easy, he spoke to Vicente in Spanish, the words flowing softly. When his lieutenant acknowledged his instructions, he carefully folded the map and laid it on top of the cabinet. Turning again, he watched Vicente leave, watched him shut the door carefully, then gestured to the chair across the table. "Sit down."

She looked as if she wanted to refuse but wasn't sure what the consequences would be. After a moment's hesitation, she came closer, sliding the chair from beneath the table and sitting in it.

Andrés stood casually, resting his hand on the slatted back of his own chair. He'd had two days to decide how to deal with her, but he had stubbornly refused to think about it. That was how he handled matters that might cause too much pain, that might force him to acknowledge the emotions he'd spent six years learning to bury. His parents, his

family, Brenna—they were all subjects he avoided. But
Esai's capture had changed that. Now he had to remember
his family's murders. He had to face the possibility of losing his last living relative. And he had to accept the fact that
the only way he could save Esai was by sacrificing himself—not his life, but his future, his only chance for ever
living a normal life again.

When he'd left Florida six years ago, he had fully intended to return someday—not to the state, but to Brenna.
He had loved her with an intensity that sometimes frightened him, and he had dreamed of the day when they could
be together again. But he hadn't asked her to wait. He
hadn't promised to return. He hadn't told her he loved her.
His future had been too uncertain, his chances of surviving
the war too slim. All he'd been able to offer her then was
maybes, hopes, dreams, and that wasn't enough. She deserved so much more.

But he hadn't given up his dreams of her. The years of
war had taken their toll: watching his people die; finding his
family—his parents, his sister and brother, his nieces and
nephews, his aunts, uncles and cousins—dead in the field
behind this house; burying the children of the village who
were executed in the sanctuary of their church simply because it was *his* village. He had lost his family, his dreams
and, somewhere along the way, he feared he had lost his
humanity. He had counted on the future, a future with
Brenna, to restore those things.

But now he had lost her, too. If his leaving six years ago
hadn't ensured that, his actions today would. She would
never forgive him for what he was doing. But he was going
to do it anyway.

Slowly he pulled the chair out, its wooden legs scraping
the floor. When he sat down, he leaned forward, his arms
resting on the table, his hands loosely clasped. "What do
you think of my country?"

The question was calculated to remind her of their past, of the many times she'd asked him eager questions about San Angelo and the village where he'd grown up. This village. Although she had never asked him to bring her here for a visit, that was what she'd wanted, to see his land and to meet his family. He saw that she remembered in the tautening of her jaw and the narrowing of her eyes. She was vulnerable, he realized, to her past memories and hurts. He could make that work in his favor, could use it to convince her that she was in danger, to convince her to fear him. That was what he needed, no matter how dear the cost.

"What do you want from me?" she asked quietly, her eyes locked on his face.

He settled back in his chair, managing a slight smile that was sinister in its innocence. "Nothing. Nothing personal, anyway. I brought you here to use. When we've accomplished our goals, I'll send you back."

There was a shadow of hurt in her eyes, there before she could stop it. She wasn't as good at hiding her emotions as he was, Andrés noted. He had already seen shock and fear and now pain in her eyes. But then, he wasn't hiding his emotions. He simply didn't let himself feel them anymore.

Brenna struggled to sound unaffected by his blunt words. "I appreciate the honesty, but I would have appreciated it more six years ago."

He shrugged, letting her sarcasm pass. "You got exactly what you wanted six years ago: an affair with one of your father's students, handpicked by the great man himself."

"An affair?" she echoed in dismay. "I lo—" Quickly she swallowed the word, clenching her jaw until she had regained control of herself. When she could speak again, she asked harshly, "What do you need me for? I can't believe women are so scarce in San Angelo that you have to kidnap tourists. I'm not much of a cook, I won't nurse your people, I don't speak your language, and I don't know anything about your war. So what do you want? How can you use me this time?''

"We have women," he replied stiffly. "We have cooks. Hector is our doctor, trained at your Johns Hopkins. We speak both our language and yours, and we are fighting our war. All we need from you is your presence."

"For what?"

"You may not know anything about our war, but you sure as hell know something about your father."

She tilted her head back and stared at the bare rafters above. So she had been right. Andrés's only interest in her was her father. He wanted to use her against Tom. She was disappointed that he could stoop so low and saddened that the once strong bonds between him and Tom had deteriorated to this. They had been more than instructor and student; they had been friends. Tom had been his mentor, and Andrés had been the son Tom had never had. Her father had loved Andrés as much as he'd loved Brenna, she reflected sadly—maybe even more.

When she lowered her head again, she studied the man across from her. Outwardly he had changed very little. He was barely six feet tall and lean. His eyes were still dark chocolaty brown, his hair still thick and coal black, his mouth still sensuously shaped. The thick mustache that shadowed his upper lip was the only real physical change. The tougher, menacing air about him, the coldness that marked those dark eyes, the hard set of his mouth—those changes came from inside.

And they frightened her.

"What about my father?"

He considered possible lies and discarded each one. He also considered telling her nothing, keeping her in the dark about her father's actions and his own plans. At last he told her the truth. "The army captured one of my men. They're holding him prisoner, and we want him back."

"So you want to exchange me for this man." She shook her head. "It will never work. My father is a soldier first, a father second. Nothing, not even family, comes between him and his duty. So whatever you have planned—"

Andrés interrupted, his voice low and cold. "He loves his daughter very much. To save your life, he would betray his duty, his country, even his honor. He would give his own life."

"To save my life...maybe." But she didn't sound convinced. Tom had joined the navy a few months before she was born, and she had come second with him ever since. She had learned to deal with the long hours, the longer absences, the knowledge that nothing in her life was as important to him as his job—not her birthdays, holidays, her high school or college graduations. Her mother hadn't handled it so well. When Tom had been deployed for the umpteenth time, missing Christmas, their wedding anniversary and Brenna's thirteenth birthday, Eileen Mathis had filed for divorce and moved herself and her daughter back to Kansas. That was where Brenna had lived until Eileen's death six years later.

"But you wouldn't hurt me," she said, forcing her attention back to the present. "I know it, you know it, and Dad—especially—knows it."

"What makes you so sure of that?"

"Because I know you." Stubbornly she ignored her earlier thought that this wasn't the Andrés she had known and loved so long ago. "You *couldn't* hurt me, because if you did, you would be no better than your President Romero and his soldiers."

Was she guessing, he wondered, making assumptions based on the character of the man he'd been six years ago? Or was her statement an attempt to convince herself, as well as him—merely wishful thinking? As long as she refused to believe he was capable of harming her, she didn't have to be afraid. She didn't have to face the reality of her situation.

But the reality was, he admitted grimly, that she was right. He could never harm her or allow anyone else to. But somehow he had to make her believe the opposite. Somehow he had to convince her so she could convince her father. "People change, Brenna."

"Not that much," she denied.

"Yes, that much and more. Do you want to know what I've been doing for the last six years while you went to your little nursing job at the hospital, while your father safely carried out his duties on heavily fortified military bases, miles away from any danger?" He didn't wait for a response from her, but continued, his voice growing harsher with each word, his eyes turning darker. "I've been killing people and defending myself against people trying to kill me. I've watched my people—the farmers, the peasants, the children—wasting away, starving because the government destroys their food so we won't get it. I've seen entire villages devastated, even their old women and infants murdered by the government's soldiers. I've buried my friends, some who were lucky enough to die in battle, others who were unfortunate enough to be taken prisoner, to be beaten and tortured before they died. I've buried my family—my parents, my sister Maria and her husband, my brother Martín, and his wife, all their children, even the babies— and I've had to live with the knowledge that they died because of me."

She felt his revulsion as easily as she imagined his grief. She knew little about wars, even though her father had spent large portions of his life fighting them. He talked to her about the beauty of the countries where he'd been, about the people, but never about the death. Never about the horror. But Andrés lived with the horror.

Slowly the anger, the hatred and the bitterness drained from him, leaving him weary. "I have no place in my life for softness, Brenna, or for memories. I do what I have to do to survive, to help my country survive. If it means killing

government soldiers, then I do it. If it means killing you..."
Slowly he rose from the chair and walked to the door,
speaking in Spanish to the man waiting there out of Brenna's
sight. He watched the man leave to obey his orders, then finally looked back at Brenna. "I will do that, too."

She didn't believe him, she silently insisted. He was simply trying to frighten her so he could get whatever it was he
wanted from her father. Even though he'd left her, even
though his life had undergone tragic changes, she would not
believe he could hurt her.

Andrés stared out the door, his back to her. He didn't
want to look at her anymore, didn't want to see the combination of hurt, fear and stubbornness that colored her eyes,
didn't want to see that she believed his threat...or didn't.
"Raúl is bringing your luggage. You'll stay here with me.
There will be guards outside at all times. You can go out, but
you'll be accompanied by them wherever you go. Our village is remote, our mountains rugged and heavily wooded.
If you try to escape, you'll probably die, unless you're found
by government troops. Then you'll definitely be killed...
once they've finished with you." He paused to let that sink
in. "We have no electricity, no running water. There's an oil
lamp beside the bed, but we have to conserve fuel as much
as possible. There's a well beside the church, and one of the
men will get water for you when you need it."

Brenna stood up, squaring her shoulders, holding her
head high. "I'd prefer to stay in the cell."

"What you prefer doesn't matter. You don't seem to understand, Brenna: you're our prisoner. You have no say in
what you do. No choices. You'll stay where you're told, eat
when you're told, sleep where you're told." He turned his
head so he could just see her from the corner of his eye.
"Don't worry about your virtue," he said, the scorn in his
voice made all the more powerful by its softness. "You'll
sleep in my bed...and I'll sleep in here."

Her cheeks flushed a heated red. When she'd expressed her dissatisfaction with his arrangements, she hadn't even considered the possibility that he intended to share the bed with her. She had simply wanted a place alone, away from him. But now that he'd brought it up, images filled her mind—warm, tender, passionate memories of long nights and incredible loving. He'd been a talented lover, gentle and sensuous, teasing, tormenting and satisfying. He had taught her what it meant to make love...to feel love...what it meant to hurt.

"I couldn't care less where you sleep," she said clumsily. But her voice was too husky, too unsteady, to give credence to the denial. Turning, she walked to the door in the back wall, pushing it open with her palm. "Is this my room?"

My room. Andrés squeezed his eyes shut. She would live in his room, would unpack her clothes into his dresser, would sleep in his bed. By the time the exchange was made and she was gone from his life again—permanently, this time—she would have left her mark on his quarters. The dresser would seem empty without her clothing, and the sheets would be sweetly scented with her fragrance, and his days would be achingly empty without her.

Slowly he realized that she was waiting for his response. *Is this my room?* He answered in a low, defensive growl. "Yes."

Brenna walked into the room, stopping in the center to look around. The floor was bare, lacking even a rug beside the bed, but the wooden planks were worn smooth from years of hard wear. The walls were bare, too, broad expanses broken only by the windows that provided light and air.

It wasn't much bigger than the cell where they'd first held her. Even the few pieces of furniture made it seem crowded. There was a bed, barely a double, its head- and footboards fashioned from iron rods that had once been painted white. Now only flakes of the paint remained. Beside the bed was a small nightstand that held a grimy oil lamp and a book of matches. The slab of wood beneath the lamp was warped, its finish chipped and peeling, like the dresser across the room. Three drawers wide and two high, it had an awkward, squat shape, but it was functional. The same could be said of the mirror above. The wooden frame was badly worn and warped, and the silver backing had scraped off in large patches, but it reflected an image.

At least the windows weren't boarded up, Brenna noticed with relief. If they were, she would probably develop a screaming case of claustrophobia before suffocating from the heat. She walked to one side window and saw a soldier, obviously one of her guards, sitting under a tree, a rifle cradled across his lap. Curiously, she checked the opposite window and found a guard there, too, seated where he could watch both the side and the back of the house.

She really was a prisoner. The realization sank in fully for the first time. It wasn't a mistake or a joke or a bad dream. She was a prisoner, watched by armed guards who took orders from Andrés Montano, once her lover, now her captor. Once he'd held her in his arms. Now he held her life in his hands.

I do what I have to do to survive. If it means killing you, I will do that, too.

Dear God, what was she going to do?

In the outer room, Andrés continued to stand at the door, staring out. There was little activity in the village this afternoon. For the rest of the camp, it had been business as usual. A shipment of weapons and medicines was scheduled to arrive at the nearest army post today, and a large contingent of men had gone to relieve the government of the badly needed supplies. The men who remained knew there was a prisoner—how could an American woman go unnoticed in an armed rebel camp?—but they didn't know who she was or what she meant to him.

She meant *nothing* to him, he insisted. She was a means to an end, a desperate solution to a desperate problem, and he couldn't allow her to be anything more. Besides, what would be the sense of letting himself care now? She certainly wouldn't want anything to do with him, not when he'd ordered her kidnapping, not when he'd threatened her life. Considering their present, they had no chance for a future. So he would use her and, when the time was right, he would return her. In the meantime, he would keep her safe. If anything happened to her while he held her...

God, he didn't need this new burden, he thought wearily. Wasn't it enough that he was responsible for the people's fight for freedom? They had placed their hopes, their dreams and their lives in his hands, and in six years he hadn't disappointed them. Since he'd taken leadership, after his brother Moisés was executed by government soldiers, he had devoted his life to their cause.

But he was tired now. Tired of the war. Tired of the fighting, the killing, the suffering. Tired of seeing his country devastated, families destroyed, lives wasted as if they meant nothing. Every day he prayed for it to end; every day he prayed that he wouldn't have to hurt another person, wouldn't have to kill anymore. But every day his prayers went unanswered. Now it was Brenna he had to hurt.

Heavy footsteps drew him out of his thoughts, and he realized that Vicente was standing a few feet in front of him. Having Brenna in camp was going to be hell on his concentration, he acknowledged with a faint smile, and in this job, he couldn't afford to let his thoughts wander. In this job, inattention could be deadly.

Andrés opened the screen door and stepped out onto the porch. He accepted the two bags Vicente offered and laid them on the floor inside the door.

"Raúl says you've posted guards here." Vicente's tone was clearly disapproving. "He says you're going to keep her here."

Andrés made no response.

"You know that's not necessary. She'll be safe in the cell."

Safety had little to do with his decision, Andrés silently acknowledged. Being close to her, being able to see her and watch her and talk to her—those were the important things. Storing up memories for a long, lonely future.

But that was *his* secret. Making certain that his voice would carry into the back room, Andrés responded to his lieutenant's remark. "I'm not concerned about her safety. I want her here where I can keep an eye on her."

"You don't trust her?"

He snorted with disgust. "She's Tom Mathis's daughter. Would *you* trust her?"

Vicente ignored the question. "Do you think he'll agree to the terms?"

"If he wants her alive, he will."

"*Will* he want her alive?"

It was a harsh question, softened only by Vicente's bewilderment. Over the years they had come in contact with many soldiers who had valued their own lives but no one else's, not even their families'. Like Vicente, Andrés was at a loss to understand them. He would have given his life to save any one of his relatives, and he would do so for Esai, too. He would even do it for Brenna, he admitted, and so would Tom. "He'll want her alive," he said confidently.

Vicente shifted on the steps, staring down at his booted feet when he asked the next question. "What if Esai is already dead?"

The possibility had haunted Andrés from the moment he'd seen that his cousin had been captured. If Esai was dead, it would be *his* fault, and Tom's. Tom had devised the trap—no one else would know enough about Andrés to use the bait they had used—and Andrés had fallen into it. Vicente had suspected a trap, and Esai had been positive, but like a fool, Andrés had insisted on going to the meet-

ing. But instead of a quiet private meeting between him and
Tom, there had been more than three dozen soldiers waiting at the cantina. And instead of capturing Andrés, the
soldiers, confused by the fight and careless of the family
resemblance, had taken Esai. If they killed him, it would be
one more death on Andrés's conscience. One more sorrow
for him to bear.

He opened the screen door and walked inside, pausing to
pick up the two bags. When he straightened, he looked at his
lieutenant and friend, his expression somber. "If Esai is already dead," he said in his empty, emotionless voice, "then
Brenna will also die."

In the bedroom, Brenna sank down onto the edge of the
mattress, barely hearing the protesting creak of the bed-
springs. Andrés's words were intended, she knew, for her to
hear, and they left her with a curious mix of pain and
numbness.

Did he really mean what he'd said, that if this Esai had
died in prison, she would also die? She didn't want to believe it, but some tiny part of her did. The Andrés she had
loved couldn't hurt her, but the one who led his people in
war against their government, the one who had seen his
family executed, the one who had lived for six years with
death and hunger and pain—*he* could. To that Andrés, she
was the daughter of his enemy, a weapon, a bargaining tool
that could save his friend Esai's life. And if it cost *her*
life . . . well, this was war. He'd seen many people die.

But she wasn't going to be one of them, she vowed with
fierce determination. Her father would find her; he would
rescue her, and the men who had taken her could join their
friend Esai in prison. All of them—including their leader.

The image of Andrés in prison made her shudder. He
wouldn't handle prison well. He believed in freedom, had
spent the past six years of his life fighting for his vision of
freedom. Prison, especially the primitive prisons run by
Romero's government, would destroy him.

Maybe she could reason with him. She could make him see that his plan would never work, could point out its flaws in a calm, rational manner and—

He walked into the room then and met her gaze when she looked up. In that moment, staring into those dark, cold, empty eyes, she lost what little hope she'd found. She couldn't reason with this man who looked at her as if he'd never seen her, as if he had never known her or held her or loved her. She couldn't be calm or rational with this man who held total power over her life and seemed completely willing to use it.

He set the bags he carried onto the floor, then silently emptied two drawers for her things. She watched him move the familiar items—drab green T-shirts, even drabber thick socks, neatly coiled webbed belts and a handful of brass buckles badly in need of polish. Her father had an identical, though larger, supply at home.

"Who is Esai?" From the conversation she'd overheard, it was clear to Brenna that Esai was the prisoner her father had helped capture, but surely Andrés didn't go to such lengths to help every one of his men taken prisoner. Esai must be someone special, someone important. Knowing who might help her.

He looked up from his task, his gaze meeting hers in the mirror. The expression on his face was guarded, giving away nothing of his thoughts. For a moment she thought he would ignore her question; then he slowly turned to face her. "Esai Villareal is my aide, my friend and my cousin," he said flatly. "He is the last relative I have, and he is a prisoner of the National Army."

She remembered what he'd said earlier about friends unfortunate enough to be taken prisoner, to be beaten and tortured before they died. At home in the United States, she'd heard such stories, but the American government discounted them as so much propaganda, and so did her father. Would he support a government, Tom had asked her,

that brutally tortured and murdered its people? And she had
accepted his response. Now Andrés had made her wonder,
and she resented him for it. "Your cousin is an enemy of the
government," she said coolly. "He belongs in prison."

For a long moment he stared at her, the emptiness in his
eyes growing even deeper. "You were always naive, Brenna,
a typical navy brat. Your country, your military and your
father could do no wrong." His derision was sharp and
wounding. "It was amusing when you were twenty-three
and protected and innocent. You're nearly thirty now, and
you're still naive—but now you have no protection. Now
you have to rely on me."

Amusing. He'd found her amusing! Brenna bit hard on
the inside of her lip to hide the anger and embarrassment
that simple word caused her. All that time she'd been in love
with him, and he'd thought she was *amusing*. "Rely on
you?" she scoffed. "I tried that before, and look what it got
me. Do you think I'd actually depend on you for anything
again?"

He felt the knot of pain that formed in his chest and
spread its icy fingers outward. He waited until its power di-
minished, until he was certain it wouldn't show in his voice,
before he answered her. "You have no choice. Without me,
you're dead."

She gave a careless shrug. "Idle threats, Andrés."

Slowly he walked toward her until he was standing so
close that his trousers brushed her legs. Involuntarily she
looked up at him, and he raised his hand to her face, gently
stroking her cheek, her jaw, her throat. There he tightened
his grip just slightly, not enough to hurt her, just enough so
she could feel his strength, so he could feel her heartbeat,
throbbing violently beneath his callused fingers. "Not
threats," he said in a soft, silken voice. "Facts. Tell yourself whatever you want to hear, whatever you need to believe. But it doesn't change the facts. The facts are that I
could kill you right now, and nobody would lift one finger

to stop me. The facts are that your father engineered Esai's capture. He has my cousin, I have you. If they kill my cousin, we'll kill you. The facts are..."

He eased his hold but didn't release her entirely. Her skin under his hand was hot and flushed and smelled of some sweet, spicy Oriental fragrance. "I can do to you whatever they do to him. I can beat you, starve you, torture you and murder you. I understand that, and so will your father. The sooner you accept it, the sooner we can complete our business, and the sooner you'll be out of my way." He let his hand slide away, a millimeter at a time, until his fingertips were free. "Those are facts, Brenna," he said, the softness, the silkiness, gone, replaced once more by the cold harshness. "Not threats."

She drew a deep breath, still feeling the pressure of his fingers on her throat. "I don't believe you," she whispered. "You couldn't have changed that much. You couldn't do those things."

He walked to the window and looked out at the guard posted there before facing Brenna again. "A few hours ago you would have denied that I could ever be involved in your kidnapping. You would have denied that I was even capable of it." He was making guesses, but the startled look that flashed across her face confirmed that he was right. "And you were wrong. Bringing you here was my idea. Using you was my idea." An idea that he would pay for for the rest of his life.

She stood up, holding her shoulders back, her head high. Her expression was defiant, her manner bold, but he recognized both as a bluff. She was playing Tom Mathis's daughter now, relying on her father to give her courage. "I'm not afraid of you, Andrés."

He smiled then, a gesture so icy, so frightening, that it made her shiver. "You should be, Brenna." Then he clarified that with a promise. "You will be."

He passed through the door and closed it behind him, then leaned back against it, his eyes closed. He was making progress: she wasn't truly afraid of him yet, but she *was* starting to hate him. It would all come in time—fear, disgust, derision, hatred—and it would end in destruction. Not hers, as he had threatened, but his own.

Chapter 2

Things will look better in the morning.

That had been Eileen Mathis's favorite saying whenever Brenna was upset. Crises ranging from being excluded from a friend's tenth birthday party to facing another Christmas without her father to not being asked to the prom by that special boy she'd been dating—all had been handled with a hug and a kiss and a "Things will look better in the morning." And they always had.

Until now.

Last night she had gone to sleep in an unfamiliar bed in a strange place in a foreign land, a prisoner with two armed guards outside the windows and a third one, Andrés, sleeping in the next room. She had assured herself that when she awoke things really *would* be better. She would be in her own bed at home, or maybe in the guest room in her father's quarters, and she would find that the whole thing had been a bad dream—the kidnapping, Andrés, the death threats, all of it.

But it was morning, and she was awake, and she was still in the same dreary little room. She was still lying in the bed with sheets that smelled faintly of Andrés, there were still armed guards outside the windows, and she was still a prisoner. So much for favorite sayings.

Soon she would have to get up and face the day. First on her list, after visiting the primitive bathroom facilities she'd been escorted to last night, was to find a place to take a bath. She thought longingly of the hot shower and luxurious shampoo she could have had at her father's house, but she would gladly settle for a tub of cold water to wash away yesterday's grime. But for the next few minutes she lay on her back, one arm folded beneath her head, and stared at the ceiling.

So far, for captivity, it hadn't been so bad. The food last night had been pretty awful, and the mattress was a bit lumpy, and the lack of air conditioning and indoor plumbing was something of a nuisance. Still, she hadn't been tied up or mistreated or locked up with other prisoners or rats or anything like that, and she hadn't been assaulted or terrorized or starved. Except for Vicente's brief show of the gun at the airport and Andrés's words, she hadn't really even been threatened. All in all, for a prisoner, she had it pretty good.

Andrés. Not surprisingly he'd been in her dream last night, a strangely jumbled version of the old and the new. Darkly handsome, with that wicked mustache, as he looked now, yet gentle and sweet, as he'd been six years ago. Alternately threatening and loving, enticing and frightening.

The dream, confusing and bewildering, was a perfect reading of her own feelings. Old love insisted that Andrés could never hurt her, while logic forced her to acknowledge that if he could kidnap and threaten her, he could hurt her. Memory kept searching for the signs of the man she remembered, but reality found nothing—no gentleness, no loving, no humor or softness.

There was no place in his life for softness, he'd told her. No place for memories. Was that how he survived—by shutting out all the tender emotions that would make him vulnerable? Was that how he dealt with the pain and the horror, the grief and the loss, the guilt and the dying?

On a smaller, less important scale, she could relate to what he'd done. The only way she'd been able to deal with losing him six years ago had been by banishing him from her life—all thoughts, all memories, all mementos. Everything that she could destroy, she did. The rest was forced back, locked away in her mind.

With a sigh, she swung her feet to the floor and stood up, deftly wrapping the top sheet around her. There were no curtains on the three windows, a fact that certainly wouldn't disturb Andrés but made her awkwardly aware of her over-populated surroundings. From the duffel bag she took a change of clothing, then quickly, clumsily, got dressed and discarded the sheet. She found the small zippered plastic tote that contained the necessary toilet items, slid her feet into her sandals and opened the door that led to Andrés's office.

As suddenly as she'd walked into the room, she stopped. She had expected to find Andrés, maybe Vicente or maybe no one at all. But circled around the table in the middle of the room were Andrés and Vicente, along with eight other men who all turned dark, unfriendly faces her way. They stared at her, and she stared back, chilled by the emptiness in some faces and the outright hostility in others.

These were Andrés's senior officers, she assumed, and she had blundered into some type of strategy session. Several of them were only boys, no more than twenty, maybe twenty-two. Several others were in their sixties, with white hair, lined faces and gnarled hands, while the rest appeared to be in their thirties and forties. They were all silent, all grim and weary, all wary of her.

Andrés looked at her, his expression as blank as the others', hiding the fleeting pleasure that seeing her brought. She looked startled and uncomfortable in this roomful of soldiers. The hardness of the men emphasized her own delicacy. In black shorts and a white blouse that left her arms and long legs bare, with pale golden skin and light brown hair, and soft, innocent brown eyes that darted uneasily from man to man, she looked like a child guiltily interrupting a meeting of adults.

The silence had gone on too long. Andrés took a step back from the table and asked, his voice carefully hard, "What do you want?"

She moved a little closer. "Do they speak English?" she asked, gesturing to the men with a wave of her hand.

"Only Vicente."

She found an odd sort of relief in that. She might be forced to ask for everything she wanted or needed, but at least she could ask with some semblance of privacy. "I want a bath." A soft rumble in her stomach sounded then. "And breakfast."

"Breakfast was served over two hours ago." He had considered waking her when he'd gone into the bedroom this morning to get clean clothes, but she'd been sleeping so peacefully, so enticingly, he'd thought, feeling a true physical ache. The desire to stand and look at her, to touch her, to lift the covers and slide into bed beside her, had been so compelling that he'd grabbed his clothes and rushed from the room, nearly slamming the door on his fingers in his haste to get away. If she was hungry enough, he had decided darkly, she would learn to awaken in time for breakfast, but he wouldn't tempt himself again. Once had been more than enough.

Brenna shrugged. Her hunger could wait until lunch. Considering the quality of last night's dinner, she was sure she hadn't missed much. "What about a bath?"

He stared at her until his vision blurred, until she was only a haze of colors—black, white, soft brown and dreamy gold. There was a stream nearby, but allowing her to bathe there naked, in the open, visible to curious eyes, was an invitation to trouble. Someone would have to go along to watch her—not to make certain she didn't try to escape, but for her own protection—but to whom would he trust such a job? Not one of his men. Hell, not even himself. "I'll have Raúl bring some water to your room."

She looked blankly at him. "You mean I get to take a sponge bath? How generous of you."

Her sarcasm made his smile evil. "There's a stream not far from here. You could go there. But let me warn you: you're the first woman my men have seen up close in weeks. Months, for some of them. More importantly, you're an American woman. Every one of those men has lost family in this war. Their wives and daughters have been raped and tortured. Their children have been killed, their homes destroyed, their lives devastated. Do you think they don't understand the role your country has played in this? Do you think they would pass up the chance to do to an American what the Americans have been doing to them for so long?"

Her gaze faltered, but continued to hold his for a long moment. She was angry with him for making her feel a shiver of fear, for making her aware once more of the hostility some of the men clearly felt for her. She was angry, too, because she had to give in. He was right, and there was nothing she could do about it, but she sure as hell wouldn't be gracious about it. "There aren't any curtains in my room. I have about as much privacy there as I would at the stream."

He shrugged carelessly. "Do the best you can."

"What about my hair?"

She was deliberately pushing, Andrés realized. She had given in to him on the bath; now she wanted something in return. Give and take, compromise, the supporting structure of an equal relationship. But they weren't equals; she was his prisoner, and she had to take his orders.

He shifted his gaze to her hair. It was combed back from her face, its color a shade too dark for blond, its style half curled, half frizzy and all sexy. Slowly he looked back at her and shrugged. "Do the best you can."

Temper flared, its heat coloring her face, and she opened her mouth for an angry retort. But before she could get it out, Andrés had lifted his hand for silence. "One more warning about the men, Brenna," he said softly. "Don't argue with me in front of them. Most of them value your life only because I do. Don't make me look foolish to them, or you might lose even that small importance in their eyes."

She breathed slowly, her jaw clenched, her hands in tight fists. At last she pulled her eyes from his and returned to the door. "I'll wait for Raúl in my room," she said, her manner stiffened by wounded pride.

She closed the door, not with a slam as she wanted, but with a quiet click. Andrés felt the faint beginnings of a smile that quickly faded away. It wasn't going to be easy having her around, he admitted, but at least it would be different.

He returned to the men, picking up the conversation where Brenna had interrupted.

Yesterday's mission had gone well. No one had been injured, and now they had the medical supplies that Hector had been asking for daily, along with a new stock of weapons and ammunition. Practically all their supplies were gained from unexpected raids on army convoys. The men took a certain perverse pleasure in knowing that weapons, medicines, clothing, blankets—even food—were supplied to the rebels courtesy of the National Army and the United States.

Benedicto was the first, during a lull in the talk, to bring up the topic that had them all uneasy. The old man had been a soldier his whole life, first in the army, then with the rebels, and was one of Andrés's most trusted advisors. "What about the woman, Andrés?" he asked.

Andrés exchanged glances with Vicente. "What about her?"

"You should have discussed it with us first." That came from Reynaldo, the youngest of Andrés's leaders. He had just turned twenty last week, but he had killed his first Angeleno soldiers when he was barely fifteen. He was experienced, ambitious and hotheaded.

"Are you questioning my judgment, Reynaldo?" Andrés asked, his tone almost gentle. He filled different roles for all of his men—a father figure to the youngest ones, a trusted friend to the ones more his age and a wise, patient son with the elderly. He had yet another role to play for Brenna, the tough, cold captor. The man who would kill her. It was the hardest thing he'd ever done—harder, even, than leaving her.

Reynaldo's face burned with shame. "Of course not. But she's an American, and her father is a powerful man. Having her here will bring the army to our camp."

"As long as we hold her here, Tom Mathis will make certain the army doesn't come close," Andrés explained. "He won't do anything to risk her safety." He looked around the circle, his gaze settling on each man's face for a few seconds. "Anyone else have anything to say?"

They all remained silent, dropping their eyes from his, except one. "We don't threaten women, Andrés," Javier said quietly.

Andrés knew without asking that they were all in agreement on that. No matter how much they hated the Angeleno army, no matter how much they despised the Americans who trained and supported and supplied them, they were honorable men. They didn't threaten innocent women. Not even American women. Not even the daughter of the American they hated most. "The woman is my responsibility. Whatever has to be done, I will do it. Beyond protecting her, I won't involve anyone else in what happens with her.''

It was the only reassurance he would offer them, and the men accepted it because they respected their leader. Andrés waited a moment for further questions, then turned back to the business of war.

Brenna lay on her back on the lumpy mattress, her head hanging over the edge, staring at an upside-down version of the room where she'd spent the past twenty-four hours. She was bored and desperately wanted to get out for some fresh air, a little exercise and maybe some friendly conversation, but that last part kept her inside. So far, the friendliest conversation had come from Vicente. The looks those other men had given her were as *un*friendly as they came. She didn't need to venture outside for hostility; she could get all that she could handle from the next room, from Andrés.

He'd been arrogant during their meeting this morning. Granted, he'd been arrogant six years ago, too, but then it had been tempered by good humor. This morning he'd been playing commander in chief of the rebel troops, demonstrating his power, but she hadn't been impressed. Well, maybe a little.

She rolled onto her stomach, her hair falling into a finger-combed tangle around her head. She *had* been impressed when Raúl had brought the water, and had also brought three rough, yellowing sheets to tack over the windows for privacy. And although Andrés had denied her the pleasure of a bath, there had been plenty of water to bathe and to shampoo her hair. Of course, that might have been Raúl's doing, not Andrés's.

She gave an exasperated sigh. She had been here little more than a day, and she was bored, frustrated and impatient. She wished she was back home in Orlando, or even in Santa Lucia—anywhere away from here. But she had only three chances of leaving here: if Andrés freed her, if her father rescued her or if she escaped.

Andrés had warned her about the risks of attempting to escape yesterday afternoon, but she'd given it no serious thought, in any case. She was a stranger in a strange land where she didn't even speak the language; she knew nothing about survival, about weapons or protecting herself; she didn't even know what part of the country she was in. She had no idea how to go about planning, much less executing, an escape. She was a helpless woman in a situation controlled by men. That wasn't a pleasant image, she admitted ruefully, but it was accurate.

And Andrés wasn't going to free her, not after going to all the trouble of kidnapping her. Vicente and the other men must have been in grave danger, walking boldly about the airport. No, if she had been worth that risk, he wouldn't suddenly change his mind and let her go.

That left waiting for her father to rescue her. Surely he knew by now where she was. He was a bright man, so Andrés would be his first guess. Army intelligence had to know where he made his camp—wasn't that what intelligence was for? Maybe even right now they were preparing a rescue attempt.

She was certain that would be Tom's preference. That would sit better with his conscience than the trade that Andrés wanted. Freeing a prisoner of the government merely to gain *her* freedom would be a betrayal of his duty to the United States and to San Angelo. Rescuing her would be so much more acceptable, so much more honorable. He could beat Andrés at his own game, could keep his prisoner *and* free his daughter. He could prove that he was the better soldier, the better strategist, and he could do it without compromising his professional principles.

It was only a matter of time. He wouldn't leave her here long, she was certain—not because, as Andrés suggested, he believed that she would be harmed, but because he knew his daughter well. He'd been with her those months after Andrés had left her. He'd seen for himself her sorrow, her heartache and, even then, her love, and he had blamed himself for introducing them, for encouraging their romance. He wouldn't force her to stay with Andrés for one minute longer than necessary.

Restless and edgy, she jumped up from the bed and paced across the room to the dresser. Her duffel bag lay where Andrés had left it yesterday, plopped on the floor beside the ancient piece of furniture. In spite of his obvious intention that she unpack her clothes and put them into the drawers he'd emptied, she hadn't done it. When her father came for her, she wanted to be ready to go on a moment's notice.

Curiously she opened the dresser drawers. Two were empty, and two held Andrés's clothes—all working uniforms, she noticed with a quick glance. When she had known him in Orlando, he'd usually worn the dress blues or working khakis of the National Army, complete with showy medals, ribbons and insignia. Off duty he had quickly adapted to American style—jeans, shorts, sneakers, sports shirts and the more casual T-shirts. There was no sign of any of those things now. When he'd left the army to take up the rebel cause, he had left behind those influences as surely and as easily as he'd left her.

The fifth drawer held documents of some sort—some official looking, some neatly typed, others written by hand. All of them were in Spanish. She scanned a couple, identifying the very few words she knew, then put them back and turned to the last drawer.

It was nearly empty, holding only a single sheet of black paper. She picked it up and carried it to the window, taking advantage of the afternoon sunlight to study it. It was an old-fashioned photo album page. The holes on the left edge of the heavy paper had been torn where the page had been ripped from the album. Held in place with sticky black triangular corners were four snapshots, pictures of Andrés's family. Pictures she had seen so many years ago in Florida. Pictures of dead people.

She felt oddly uncomfortable with the photographs, as if she were somehow intruding on something private. She started across the room to return them to the drawer, but stubbornness mixed with curiosity stopped her. If Andrés hadn't wanted her looking at the pictures, he should have moved them when he moved his clothes, she thought defiantly, and turned her attention back to them.

There was his father, stern and weary, worn out from a lifetime of backbreaking work, and his mother, the strong lines of her face softened by her loving smile. There was his older brother Moisés and the younger one, Martín, both as handsome as Andrés, both standing with their wives and children, and Maria, the youngest, with her husband and their baby. And there was a picture of Andrés as she had known him—smiling, happy, without a care in the world beside the family he loved. The family that was dead now.

"They should have killed me, too."

Brenna started, her gaze flying from the photographs to the man a few feet in front of her. Absorbed in the photos and the memories they stirred, she hadn't heard the door open or Andrés walk across the room. She stared at him for a moment, listening to her heart thud in her ears, slowing her rapid breathing. When her system was operating normally again she made an automatic admonishment. "Don't say that."

He shrugged. "Maybe they did. The body still lives, the heart still beats, the brain still functions . . . but considering everything I've lost, I might as well be dead." Hearing his words echo in the sudden silence, he gave a stunned shake of his head. He had come in here to tell her that she would have dinner in the office with him, not to make morbidly personal pronouncements. It was seeing her with the photos that had caused him to speak so honestly. The images of his family captured forever on paper in happy poses, countered by images of them, burned forever into his brain, in bloody, violent death.

He looked from the album page to her and saw the dismay darkening her face. Before she could say anything he might not be able to handle, he gave a low mocking laugh. "You look so shocked, Brenna. You shouldn't be. You see enough people die, you kill enough people, and after a while you stop feeling the shock or the sorrow or the fear. You know that someday it will be your turn to die, and you don't care." He shrugged indifferently. "It's one of the hazards of war."

"You chose to fight this war," she whispered, her tone accusing. "You could have stayed in Florida. You could have finished your training. You could have—" Realizing what she was about to say, she bit off the words, but her flushed face gave her away.

"Stayed with you?" he finished for her. "If I had stayed there, your father would have had me married to you and applying for citizenship and a commission in the U.S. Navy before I knew what hit me."

And would that have been so bad? She didn't need to ask. The derision in his eyes made his opinion on the matter achingly clear. He had preferred a war over a life with her. "My father loved you."

"Your father loved controlling me. He pulled the strings, and I jumped. He told me what to do, and I did it. He thought he could get everything he wanted from me."

Helplessly she dropped her eyes to the photographs again. "And what did he want?" she asked in a quavery voice as she studied the love clearly evident in the long-dead faces.

"An admiring student. A respectful officer. The obedient son he'd never had." He paused, making his voice colder, harsher, for effect. "And an acceptable husband for his only daughter."

She didn't believe him. Oh, it was true that Tom had pushed them together from the start. He had admired Andrés, had respected and liked him, and of course he'd thought a relationship between the two of them would be perfect. But Andrés was talking as if that were *all* that had brought them together, as if he had dated her only because Tom had wanted it. As if he had made love to her only because Tom had wanted that, too. That couldn't be true! And yet...he had left her, and he hadn't even planned to bother telling her goodbye.

She forced back the tears that were burning her eyes. She wouldn't give him the satisfaction of seeing her cry. Any tears would have to wait until he was gone and she was alone once more. "And you were willing to be what he wanted until the war broke out here. How fortunate for you...and for me."

Her last sentiment had the impact of a sharp-edged dagger slicing through him. He wanted to tell her that he was lying, that he had loved her then, that leaving her had, until now, been the hardest thing he'd ever done. But he said nothing and let her believe the worst.

"So you came back here to fight your little war—and to get your family killed."

For a moment she stood frozen, hearing the words as if someone else had spoken them. She was shocked that she could be so cruel, but judging by his lack of reaction, he wasn't. He already blamed himself for their deaths, she realized and was ashamed that in a petty attack based on hurt feelings she had reinforced his guilt.

He took the black page from her hands and glanced at it for only an instant before returning it to its place in the bottom drawer. "Yes," he agreed softly as he came back. "I got my family killed, with the army's help...and your father's."

Brenna turned pale. She wouldn't believe that her father had anything to do with the deaths of those children. He was a good, honorable man. He wouldn't hurt an innocent man, would *never* hurt a woman or a child. "You're lying," she whispered. "They died because of the war, not my father!"

Andrés's look was bitter. "Don't you think I would change the truth if I could? They died because they were my family, and they died because Tom couldn't forgive me for disappointing him and hurting you. Ever since he came here, he's fed the government's fear of me, convincing them that I'm the biggest threat they face. Stop *me*, he says, and they'll stop the war, and they believe him. They killed Moisés and his family six years ago. Two-and-a-half years ago they came back for the others."

He took her arm and turned her toward the window, forcing her to look outside. "They gathered them in that field. First they killed Maria's baby. She was two years old, and her name was Luisa. They dragged her screaming from her mother's arms and shot her in the head."

Brenna shuddered with revulsion, horrified by his words as much as by the empty, lifeless tone in which he spoke.

"When all the children were dead," Andrés continued, "they turned on my aunts and uncles, my cousins, Maria and her husband, Martín and his wife. My father was last. They made him watch while they killed every member of his family, and then they killed him." His voice grew low and hoarse. "They died because they were my family, because your father convinced Romero that I was dangerous, because his soldiers enjoy killing. They died because in this country the army can get away with it. We don't have the freedom to protest, or the means to punish them, or the strength to stop them. We can't elect our president or our congress, and we can't have a say in our laws. Our people are poor and sick and hungry. They're dying from too much work and too little food, while our president, placed in power by *your* government against the will of the people, grows fatter and richer every day. Yes, people are dying because of our war, but they were dying before, and if we lose, they'll continue to die, because our government and your government don't give a damn about them.''

Brenna could see his reflection in the dust-streaked window, could see his fierceness, his bitterness. If everything he said was true he had good reason to hate her father, and hatred could make carrying out his threats against *her* that much easier.

But she couldn't believe him. The United States spoke out vehemently against this kind of human rights abuse; they didn't support the people committing it! They simply didn't know it was happening. As for her father... he was just doing his job. As a career military man, surely Andrés could understand that if he wanted to. Tom didn't make policy; he simply followed orders. And as angry as he'd been over Andrés's leaving, he wouldn't use his military authority to gain satisfaction in a personal vendetta. He wouldn't!

She turned and found herself too close to Andrés for comfort and, with the windowsill behind her, she had no place to move. Ignoring the heat from his body and the faint musky scent of him that filled her nostrils with each breath, she said quietly, "I'm sorry your family is dead, but my father isn't responsible."

The anger, fear, shock, disbelief—all the emotions he'd seen pass through her eyes earlier—were gone, replaced by simple compassion. He drew away as if it might wound him and, to chase it from her, spoke harshly, derisively. "Like I said earlier, tell yourself whatever you want to hear, but it doesn't change the facts. Your father *is* responsible. He volunteered to come here to train Romero's army to win, to destroy us, to kill anyone who dares to disagree with government policy."

"According to you, killing is one skill they were already well trained in," Brenna reminded him.

He muttered a curse as he turned away. "Why should I expect you to even try to understand?" he practically growled. "You're an *American*, the daughter of an American military officer."

"You didn't find Americans and the American military so distasteful when you were living in Florida," she reminded him with a sniff. Folding her arms over her chest, she leaned back, settling her hips against the narrow wooden windowsill. "You know, when Dad finds out where you're holding me, he's going to come after me."

"You think so?" He shook his head slowly, feeling almost regretful about letting her down. "Tom already knows where you are."

She didn't believe him. If her father knew where they were holding her, he would already be here or, at the very least, on his way with a squad of heavily armed soldiers. But Andrés didn't look as if he expected such an attempt. Why? What did he know that she didn't? How could he be so sure that her father wouldn't try to rescue her, that he would prefer to compromise, to give up his prisoner, his pride and his honor? "How do you know?" she asked suspiciously.

"Because we told him. As soon as Vicente picked you up at the airport, we sent a message to Tom's office telling him where you were and with who." He stood at the end of the bed, rubbing his hand back and forth over the iron footboard. Flakes of white paint clung to his fingers before falling unnoticed to the floor. "We also told him that we would contact him tomorrow, so you and I will drive into town in the morning and call him. You can tell him you're sorry you missed him at the airport. Tell him how eager you are to see him, how you hate being here with us."

"I see. And I suppose it wouldn't hurt if I sounded scared out of my mind, would it?" she asked sarcastically. "This is your big plan? You're going to put me on the phone and I'm supposed to plead with him to do whatever it takes to free me? And just like that—" she snapped her fingers "—he's going to get your cousin out of prison and hand him over?"

He was totally impervious to her mocking tone. "That's the general idea."

"And what if I refuse to speak to him? What are you going to do then?"

"You don't have to speak to him." He watched the skepticism slide over her face. "A cry, a scream, a moan, any sound that your father can identify as a woman in fear—or pain—will do."

He looked as if he had no doubt of his capability to coax such sounds from her. Could he? Brenna wondered, aware of the fear shadowing the edges of that question. Of course he could ... but *would* he?

She wanted to say no, but then she wanted to believe a lot of things that didn't seem to be true. She wanted to believe that she had meant something to him six years ago, wanted to believe that he'd started the affair because he'd cared about her, not because her father had engineered it. But according to him, she was wrong there, too.

Yesterday she had wondered if the Andrés she had loved still existed. Now she wondered if he had *ever* existed anywhere besides her dreams.

He was watching her, waiting, solemn and grim. She looked up at the face that was so familiar and yet so strange, to the eyes that were so cold. "All right," she murmured, her voice weak but sure. "I'll talk to him. Now, would you go away and leave me alone?"

That was what they both needed, to be left alone. The less he saw of her, the better off he'd be. But, perversely, now that she wanted him to go, he wanted to stay. She'd sounded so weary and looked so ... disillusioned. As if he had shattered her dreams. But he could only cause her more pain if he stayed, pain that he would have to share with her. "You'll eat your dinner in here," he said, his tone harsh and empty again. "Breakfast is served at six. We'll leave for town around eight o'clock tomorrow."

Brenna heard his words but paid them little attention. She heard the door close behind him, but that didn't register, either. Shifting positions slightly, she stared out the window. The sun was starting to set, its fiery rays coloring the forest to the west. The few buildings she could see from this window were already in shadow, the dimming light camouflaging their cracked windowpanes and sagging porches and rotting boards.

She was tired, she realized, with the kind of weariness that goes beyond the physical. She was tired of this room, tired of hearing about the war, tired of being threatened. Most of all, she was tired of dealing with Andrés. That was the hardest part.

When the door opened again sometime later, she was still standing at the window. It was Raúl with her dinner. He spoke no English, but he seemed pleasant enough. Smiling broadly at her, he gestured for her to sit down so he could give her the tray, but she shook her head. "Put it over there," she said with a wave of her hand, not caring that he didn't understand.

Still smiling, he waited, so she crossed the room and patted an empty corner of the dresser. "Set it here...uh, *aquí*."

He obeyed and left with a soft murmur. Brenna looked at the food without interest. It was the same as last night's dinner and today's lunch: a bowl of thick stew containing few recognizable vegetables and lumps of brownish-gray meat, a slab of bread that managed to be both chewy and hard at the same time, a cup of bitter coffee and a piece of fresh fruit.

With a sigh, she settled on the bed, listening to the springs squeak. If there was anyone in the outer room besides Andrés, she would find some way, through gestures and her very basic Spanish, to tell them to take the food back. She knew they had precious little of it, and they didn't need to waste any of it on her. She could survive on fruit for the few days it would take her father to get her out of here.

She wanted to go home. She didn't know what had possessed Tom to invite her to San Angelo or why she had accepted. She should have realized that sometime during the trip, Andrés would show up, if not in person, then in her memories; after all, it was *his* country. She should have stayed in Orlando, where she'd learned to forget him, where she knew she would never see him again as long as she lived.

But she hadn't been able to pass up the chance to spend time with her father. In the six years since Andrés had left Florida, she and Tom had grown apart. He'd worked harder, longer hours, finding all sorts of things to keep him out of the house they shared near the naval station. Since he'd volunteered three years ago to head the MAAG, she hadn't seen him once. He'd taken little leave, and none of it had brought him to the United States. He had called periodically, but often through the Military Affiliate Radio Service, or MARS, station, with the calls patched through ham radio operators. There was no privacy with such arrangements, no chance to discuss anything personal.

So when he'd asked her to fly to San Angelo to spend two weeks with him, she hadn't given any thought at all to Andrés or the war or anything else. She had accepted immediately, excited by the knowledge that her father finally wanted to see her.

Now she wished she'd never left Orlando. The two weeks with Tom were ruined. As soon as he saw her, he would put her on the next plane to the States and never, ever consider letting her visit again. And just as he'd blamed himself for her broken heart when Andrés left, he would blame himself for her kidnapping, and he would withdraw even further from her.

And once she got home she was going to have to deal with Andrés all over again. It had been difficult before, when only her heart had been broken. Now she had to deal with the disillusionment of knowing that he had never cared for her. With the wounded pride of knowing that he had used her, that he had made a fool of her.

Worst of all, she was going to have to deal with the shame of knowing that she had let him do it again.

Andrés finished his breakfast and moved the plate to the step beside him, then laced his fingers around the coffee cup. It was battered aluminum, taken from some army mess kit the men had picked up on a raid. If the coffee was ever hot, holding the cup this way could cause a fair burn, but he'd never known Manuel's coffee to be more than tepid or his food to be more than just barely edible.

He wasn't looking forward to today's trip. Vicente would stay here, taking over command of the camp until their return, while he and three of his best men escorted Brenna into town. He wished he could trade places with Vicente, but the phone call was too important to leave to his lieutenant. Still, Santiago, the nearest town with phone service, was a good three hours away. That meant six hours in the close confines of the truck with Brenna. He wasn't sure he could bear it.

A rotund figure sat down on the step below Andrés, drawing him out of his thoughts. He smiled a weary greeting to Hector, the doctor whose sick bay, such as it was, filled the building behind them. "How are your patients today, Hector?"

The doctor gave a cheerful shrug. "Better than they were yesterday. We woke them from a sound sleep, fed them and told them to go back to sleep, just like they do in the big American hospitals." He laughed as he mopped the gravy from his plate with a biscuit, then narrowed his suddenly sober gaze on Andrés. "I hear that your prisoner is a pretty American woman."

Andrés simply shrugged.

"I also hear that she's a nurse."

Knowing what was coming, Andrés spoke to head him off. "She made it pretty clear that she doesn't want to nurse any of our wounded."

"And I heard you made it clear that she's a prisoner and must do what she's told to do." Hector's smile was sly. "So what if you told her to help in my clinic?"

"If I forced her to help you, she could do more harm than good."

The doctor considered that while he chewed his food. Washing it down with a swallow of water—he couldn't abide the cook's version of coffee—he shook his head in disagreement. "She's a *nurse*."

Andrés was amused by the serious tone of Hector's voice. "You say that as if it means something. She's also an American and a prisoner. She's our enemy."

Hector was vehemently shaking his head this time. "Nursing is a difficult job, Andrés. You don't go into it for the money or the hours or the benefits, or for any other reason except that you want to help people. Politics don't enter into it, either. Your American didn't decide to become a nurse and to care only for American patients."

"She didn't decide to come here and be a prisoner and care for Angeleno patients, either," he pointed out.

"So you don't trust her."

Andrés was trapped, and he knew it. He would have trusted Brenna with his life. He knew she could never do anything to hurt another person, especially a patient. She was exactly as Hector had described—she hadn't cared about the money or the hours, about the lack of respect or the degree of difficulty. She had simply wanted to help people.

Hector waited for an answer, then smiled. "So you do trust her. Ask her if she would like to help out. And if she says no..." His voice trailed away.

Andrés chuckled. "And if she says no, you want me to give her an order? To a woman who doesn't take orders very—"

The doctor bluntly interrupted him. "She's *very* pretty. No wonder you want to keep her in your quarters."

Looking up, Andrés noticed that everyone in the area was looking in the same direction: toward his house. He turned his head and saw Brenna coming their way. Her arms were folded over her chest, and her expression was a passable attempt at a scowl. But the closer she got to the men, the more intimidated she seemed to become. He saw her search the group seated on porches, low walls and the ground itself around the building that held Manuel's kitchen. He saw her gaze settle only briefly on him, then move on without the slightest hint of recognition. So that was how she wanted to play it, he thought with regret.

Catching Vicente's attention, Andrés gestured toward her with a slight move of his head. His aide nodded, left his seat on a rough-hewn bench and met Brenna where she stopped. He led her back to the bench, got her a plate of food, then sat beside her.

"She's angry with you," Hector said, barely able to keep the amusement from his voice.

Andrés shrugged as if her feelings meant nothing to him. Picking up his dishes, he stepped around the doctor and to the ground. "I'll think about letting her help you." He left his dishes on a table outside the kitchen, then headed for his office.

He'd told the men to be ready to go at eight. It wasn't even six-thirty yet, but he was anxious to leave. To get Brenna away from all those men? his sly subconscious suggested. To get her into the truck where she would be forced to acknowledge his presence?

Yes, he admitted. Even as he was destroying everything that had ever existed between them and the hope for anything in the future, he was aching to be with her, to look at

her and talk to her, and he was jealous of anyone else who
looked at or spoke to her.

Maybe his luck would be good. Maybe Tom Mathis had
already figured that they wanted Esai in trade for Brenna
and taken steps to arrange it. Maybe, if he was very lucky,
the exchange could be made in a matter of days, and she
would be out of his life—forever this time.

With a sigh he pulled a key from his pocket and opened
the padlock on the metal cabinet. The cabinet was normally left open, and he'd had to scrounge for the padlock
when Brenna had arrived, so he could store his weapons
there. He didn't expect her to make an escape attempt, but
he saw no reason to leave guns lying around to tempt her.

He withdrew a sheathed knife, a .45 caliber semiauto-
matic pistol with its holster, several clips of ammunition and
an M-16 rifle. The sheath and the holster slid onto his belt,
the knife on the left side and the pistol on the right. He left
the rifle on his desk, its green sling dangling over the edge.

There was nothing left for him to do but wait and think
about the long trip with Brenna—and his first conversation
in six years with the man who'd once been as close as his
father, the same man who had spent the past three years
trying to kill him.

My father loved you, Brenna had insisted last night, and
the feeling had been mutual. He had admired, respected and
loved Tom Mathis more than any other man in his life except his own father. He would have done anything to keep
the older man's approval ... except turn his back on his
country. If anyone had known, while he was still a student
at the naval station in Orlando, that he would be taking the
rebels' side in the newly declared war over the army's, he
would have been branded a traitor—tried, convicted and
most likely executed. Not even Brenna had known that his
brother was the rebel leader, that his family was working
with them, that he himself was beginning to share their sentiments, their concerns, their anger.

Even when he'd chosen to drop out of school and return to San Angelo to fight, everyone still believed that he was a loyal Angeleno, serving his government and the army in which he'd made his career. The Americans had sent a supply of weapons and ammunition back with him for delivery to the army. It wasn't until they learned that he and the shipment had never arrived in Santa Lucia, that instead both had ended up in the rebel camp, that they'd found out the truth about him. Then he'd been branded a traitor, and Tom Mathis's love had turned to hatred in its most destructive form, the kind that fed upon itself and eventually destroyed everyone it touched.

To distract himself, he unfolded the map to the portion that included his village and Santiago and studied it. There were a half-dozen different routes connecting the two, one direct, the others twisting, winding mountain trails that only the locals knew well. He and Vicente had discussed the possibility of Mathis setting up an ambush and decided it wasn't likely. If the prize was anything less important than his daughter, Tom would strike, but he loved Brenna too much to risk her safety—Andrés had complete faith in that. Besides, it would take a massive operation to cover so many roads, and their contacts within the army hadn't reported any unusual troop movements. As for a strike in the town itself, Santiago had always been a rebel stronghold. No stranger could enter the town unnoticed or act unwatched. No, for Brenna, Tom would play by Andrés's rules. Until she was safely back in the States, he would follow orders.

Then he would devote all his energy and hatred to tracking down Andrés and killing him.

But at least Esai would be alive.

Soon it was time to go. He picked up the rifle and went outside as the three men he'd chosen to accompany them drove up in an ancient green pickup. Vicente was standing on the steps, and Brenna sat beside him, arms on her knees, chin on her arm. Andrés clasped his lieutenant's outstretched hand when he passed him. It was a ritual in a place where no goodbye was casual, when any trip out of the village might be the last a man made.

Brenna slowly stood up, brushing dirt from her shorts. She didn't want to get into the truck, didn't want to find herself sitting so close to Andrés, and most of all she didn't want to talk to her father. She didn't want to know that, because of her, he was willing to betray his duty. But Andrés took her arm and pulled her along, giving her no choice but to follow. He lifted her onto the seat, then pushed her aside so that he could climb in beside her. Immediately she moved away from him, settling herself exactly between him and the driver, as far as possible from both of them.

She focused her attention on the truck, ignoring her companions. It was at least thirty years old, and they'd been hard years, judging from its condition. Most of the gauges were broken, along with the windows; only the windshield was all there, although cracked in several places. The seat cover had originally been fabric, but it had rotted and ripped away, so now they sat on hard, crumbling foam that provided inadequate protection from the springs below. There were holes in the floorboard—small ones beneath her tennis shoes and a bigger one between Andrés's boots. It caused him to sit with his feet wide apart, his leg uncomfortably close to hers.

Uncomfortable for *her*, at least. It didn't seem to bother *him*, she noticed with a scowl. He was leaning back in the seat, one arm out the window, the other along the seat behind her, the rifle nestled between his right leg and the door. She didn't seem to have any effect on him at all.

Maybe that was because this time no one was ordering him to have an affair with her. She ducked her head and closed her eyes against the pain. Had Andrés read more than was intended into her father's actions, or had Tom known exactly what he was doing when he encouraged their relationship? Was that why he'd felt so guilty when it had ended—because, if not for his prompting, Andrés never would have started the affair or broken her heart?

A bump in the road lifted her off the seat and deposited her against Andrés who, she noticed with annoyance, had casually braced himself against the jostling. When she hastily tried to slide away, he moved his arm from the back of the seat and settled it around her shoulders, holding her in place.

"Let go of me," she said in a quiet, threatening voice.

He would. As soon as he'd savored the pleasure of her body against his, shoulder to shoulder, hip to hip, thigh to warm, shapely, bare thigh. It had been years since he'd held a woman, years since he'd been intimate with one. He had discovered that when his life was constantly in danger, sex was one of the many things he could do without for months, even years, at a time. He had also discovered that, after making love with Brenna, sex with any other woman had lost its appeal.

And if he didn't let go of her soon, he warned himself wryly, she would see proof of that. He withdrew his arm and let her scoot away, taking advantage of her brief distraction to shift positions himself. He had never found reason in the past to be grateful that the uniform trousers he wore were baggy. Now he did.

"How far is this town?" Brenna asked, sounding sullen and ill-tempered.

"It's about fifty miles from the village."

That didn't sound so bad...except she'd be willing to bet this old truck wasn't going one-tenth of a mile faster than fifteen miles an hour. Andrés confirmed that for her with his next words.

"It will take us about three hours to get there."

"And three hours back? *Six hours?*" She heard the dismay in her voice and knew he'd guessed the reason when he almost smiled. It was barely a twitch of his lips beneath the mustache, and it faded almost immediately, but she recognized it. She'd seen his mouth form too many smiles to forget them.

Six hours in this truck beside him, so close that if she relaxed at all they would touch. So close that if she breathed deeply she could smell the musky scent that was his. So close that if she tried she could forget that they were enemies, forget that he was her captor and she was his prisoner.

Six hours. She sighed heavily. She didn't know if she could stand it.

Chapter 3

Santiago was a small town by Brenna's standards—less than five thousand people—but according to Andrés it was the largest town in their district. It was also the only one with telephone service. Strengthening San Angelo's primitive communications network had been one of Romero's great plans when he'd come into power nearly twelve years ago. Telephones, Andrés said with a shake of his head, when the majority of the people in this district worked for below-poverty level wages on the big coffee plantations or struggled with subsistence farming to feed their families. When ninety percent of them had no electricity or running water, when for every mile of paved road, there were fifty miles unpaved and unimproved.

The driver parked in an alley between a general store and a cantina. The four men sheltered Brenna as they moved down the alley and through the back door of a building that served as the town's church. The weak glow of the electrical lights in the sanctuary competed with the brighter, lively glow of the candles at the front.

Brenna wasn't surprised that the priest knew all four men by name, and he wasn't surprised to see an American woman in their midst. Was he a part of their plan, too? she wondered. Didn't his religious background lead to any protests at all about the kidnapping of an innocent woman?

"This is Father Hidalgo," Andrés said, drawing her to his side. "He used to be the priest in our village—until the children were killed and the women were moved."

She looked sharply at Andrés. He knew just the right words to say to bring a response from her. Like telling her about his sister's baby last night, and now this. "So he's one of you."

"Yes. So appealing to his religion for assistance won't help you. Besides, he speaks no English." He gave rapid orders to the three soldiers who had accompanied them from the village, and they dispersed in different directions. Tugging on Brenna's arm, he followed the priest into the back of the church, to a tiny office where the phone was.

There was a wooden chair, straight backed, its lines softened by the intricately embroidered pillow it held. Andrés gestured for her to be seated while he dialed the series of numbers that would connect him to her father. Although he spoke English as well as the American sailor who answered the phone, he chose to speak in Spanish, deliberately preventing Brenna from understanding the conversation.

She couldn't understand the words, but she could tell from his manner the exact moment when her father got on the line. He muttered a few harsh words, then thrust the receiver at her.

She stared at it for a long moment, then lifted her eyes to Andrés's face. It looked hard and mean and angry because he knew she wasn't going to obey his silent command. For a long time she continued to look at him, even when the anger turned to contempt; then finally she looked away.

This time he spoke in English. "Your daughter has some foolish idea that if she doesn't talk to you, our plan will fail.

I can't make her talk, but I *can* make her listen. Explain the facts to her, Commander.'' He pulled her to her feet and held the phone to her ear. When she jerked her head away, he grasped her chin, his hold almost tight enough to bruise, and forced her to stand still and listen.

"Brenna?"

The sound of her father's voice almost made her cry, but, still staring into Andrés's cold eyes, she stubbornly refused to give in to the weakness of tears. More stubbornly, she refused to speak.

"Brenna, for God's sake, talk to me!" Tom's plea sounded frantic. "Listen to me, honey: this isn't the same man you used to know. You're dealing with a very dangerous man. Don't play games with him. God, Brenna, *don't* make him angry! You do what he tells you, do you understand?"

Andrés could hear every word her father said, Brenna saw, but he showed no satisfaction at Tom's apparent fear. He showed no emotion at all but anger.

"Damn it, Brenna, answer me!" Tom shouted.

The sound made her wince, and it also made her answer. "Hello, Dad," she said calmly. "How are you?"

He gave a great sigh of relief. "Are you okay, honey? Have they hurt you?"

"Don't worry about me, Dad. I'm fine." Her gaze locked with Andrés's, dark and challenging. "Sorry I missed you at the airport."

"Honey, listen to me. About Montano—"

"He's behaving, Dad. Don't worry."

"Brenna, he's a dangerous man," he repeated, giving each word added emphasis. "He's a thieving, murderous outlaw. He's seen and done things that even I can only imagine, and it's changed him. Don't argue with him, don't fight him, and don't give him—"

She interrupted again. "I'm not afraid of him, Dad."

"If you had any sense, you would be! Damn it, Brenna!" Tom broke off, swearing long and loud. "The man is a killer! Life means nothing to him, and because of me, yours means even less!"

Shivering at the ominous tone of her father's voice, she at last looked away from Andrés, turning her back on him. She nervously wet her lips. "He's not going to hurt me—it's just a bluff. So don't listen to him, and don't do what he asks. Don't compromise your honor because of any threats he's made against me, because he's not going to carry them—"

Before she could finish, Andrés reached over her shoulder and pulled the phone from her hands. Slowly she turned to look at him. He was livid, the lines of his face set in a mask of rage, his dark-ice eyes damning her. He gestured curtly for her to move away, then conducted the rest of the conversation in Spanish.

Brenna walked to the tiny window high in the outside wall and stared out sightlessly. The conversation had used up all the defiance in her, and now the thought of the fury she would have to face when Andrés got off the phone made her tremble. She folded her arms over her chest and hugged herself tightly.

She wasn't sorry she'd defied him, in spite of the dread now filling her. She had surprised him. He had expected her to break down when she heard her father's voice, had expected her to obediently say the right things—that she was afraid, that she wanted Tom to do whatever necessary to free her. Would he punish her now because she hadn't?

She wasn't afraid. She'd told her father that; if she repeated it often enough to herself, maybe she would start to believe it. But right now she *was* afraid, because her *father* was afraid.

Under different circumstances she would have found that idea totally astonishing. Her father, who'd spent all of *her* life in the navy, who had fought two years in Vietnam, who had seen action in Grenada, in Central America and for three years here in San Angelo, was afraid of Andrés Montano. That had been terror in his voice, an emotion she had believed foreign to him. But there had been no mistaking it. Her father was afraid for her life. Afraid that Andrés would kill her.

Had she misjudged him so badly? Her head said yes. Her father wouldn't be so worried without good cause. But some part of her—her heart, she admitted bitterly—couldn't quite accept it. She was so confused, so bewildered by conflicting feelings and differing opinions. She didn't know what she believed or felt or thought anymore.

Tom was shouting again. She could hear it even across the room and glanced over her shoulder to see Andrés holding the phone away from his ear. Whatever he'd said to her father had succeeded in enraging him, which seemed to be precisely the response Andrés had wanted. After six years, the roles they had played so well in Florida were reversed. Instead of Tom being in control, Andrés was. Instead of Tom giving the orders, he was obeying them. Her father was being forced to learn that, this time, the student was the instructor.

A moment later Andrés hung up the phone, ending the call in midtirade. He walked slowly to Brenna, and she turned, just as slowly, to face him. Now she *was* afraid, he saw with some satisfaction, if not of him, at least of his temper. But, with more courage than he would have expected from her, she met his gaze, waiting for him to unleash the full force of his fury on her.

He raised his hand, pointing one finger at her as if in accusation, and opened his mouth, but the words wouldn't come. In frustration he closed his eyes, and the muscles in his jaw clenched tightly as he dragged in a deep calming breath; then he looked at her again. "Damn you, Brenna...."

She watched him, both frightened and fascinated by the power of the emotion that gripped him. She had once, only once, seen her father so angry that he couldn't speak, and it had taken him days to get over it and treat her normally again. Andrés, now clenching his hand in a white-knuckled fist, looked as if he might never get over this.

"Get out of my sight." Each word was distinctly spoken, tautly controlled, as hard and shivery as ice.

Under his relentless damning gaze, Brenna turned and walked out of the office. The priest immediately followed.

Andrés walked to the window where she had stood. Whispering a curse of frustration, he slammed his fist against the stuccoed wall and felt the pain, quick and sharp, spread up his arm, then fade.

He had never wanted to hurt a woman, but for a moment there he would gladly have given a few years of his life to feel his hands around her throat. She was so foolish, so arrogant, so damn stubborn ... and so admirable, he admitted with a rueful grin. She had displayed a courage that was lacking in most of Romero's men and many of his own. She had deliberately defied him, all the while daring him with those soft brown eyes of hers to stop her. And he had stood there. Helpless.

He wondered if Tom Mathis knew how incredibly brave and how incredibly foolish his only child was. He doubted it. He didn't think Tom was a man to appreciate what it had cost Brenna to look him in the eye and say what she had said. But *he* did. God help him, he knew, and it made him love her just a little bit more.

Grateful for the reprieve but still trembling, Brenna walked down the narrow hallway and into the sanctuary, the priest close behind. If she tried to leave she knew the soldiers would stop her, so she stayed away from the doors and instead concentrated on the building.

At last she sat down on one of the wooden pews. Each
bench was long and massive, made from some native wood.
She liked the roughness that characterized the church—the
pews still bearing the marks of the tools that had shaped
them, the thick swirls of plaster that covered the walls, the
uneven stone floor, the distorted glass panes in the windows. She liked the silence, the cool air, the dim lighting, the
smoky scent of candle wax. She liked the peacefulness.

Years had passed since she'd been in a church. Ten years
ago, in a tiny farm town in Kansas, she had sat beside her
father while the minister who had married Tom and Eileen
performed the last service her mother required. The next
week she had sold off everything that could be sold, gave
away or packed the rest and moved to Florida to live with
her father while she finished college.

There she'd met Andrés.

His boots sounded heavy on the smooth stone. She saw
them come to a stop beside the bench where she sat, but she
didn't look up at him. She knew he was waiting for her to
join him so they could go, but she didn't move. Finally he
prompted her, his voice sharper than ever.

"Say a prayer before we leave. You're going to need it."

Slowly she rose and faced him, but her eyes didn't reach
higher than the top button of his jacket. "I'll say a prayer
for you," she said deliberately. "A prayer that when my father kills you, you die quickly...and with only a little pain."
With that, she pushed past him and walked to the back
door, waiting there without so much as a backward glance.

Andrés stared after her, then gave a shake of his head and
turned to the priest. They spoke quietly for a moment; then
he followed Brenna. The three soldiers were waiting outside, and they quickly made the return trip to the truck.

The drive back to the village seemed longer to Brenna.
The two men in back talked quietly back and forth, but the
driver remained silent—she hadn't heard him speak all
day—and Andrés... She dared to look at him from the

corner of her eye. Andrés was dangerously quiet, staring out the window at the forest. He braced himself against the sharp curves, the steep climbs and descents, and the ruts that jolted them from side to side, but otherwise he seemed to be off in a world of his own.

She was on edge, wondering when the anger she had touched off would break his tight control and explode around her. After an hour passed with no word, then another, she began to relax. Yesterday he had warned her against arguing with him in front of the men; maybe he was taking his own advice and saving his rage for when they were alone.

Andrés was aware of Brenna, but only in an oddly detached manner that allowed him to acknowledge that she sat beside him and nothing more. He forced himself to channel his anger into a more productive outlet, concentrating on the conversation with Tom, replaying it in his mind, hearing again his old friend's fear, his impotent rage, his fury at knowing he was helpless to save his daughter unless he followed Andrés's orders to the letter.

He hadn't given Tom those orders yet. There had been no talk of Esai at all. Andrés had deliberately refrained from mentioning his cousin, making any demands, offering any trades. Instead he had made threats. He had explained to Tom what would happen to Brenna if he didn't cooperate—in detail after excruciating detail. He would let him worry a few days more, then contact him again with the terms of his deal. By then Tom would be half out of his mind with fear. He would be willing to agree to anything to get his daughter back safely.

It was a dangerous play he'd chosen. Tom Mathis was a doting father, which made his actions predictable. But he was also obsessed with destroying Andrés, which made him totally unpredictable. Andrés was betting that the father's love would overcome the soldier's hatred. Either way, his own life wouldn't be worth much; it was only a question of

whether Tom would come after him now or wait until
Brenna was safely back at home. But Tom knew her safety
could be guaranteed only if he followed orders. If he tried
to rescue her and punish Andrés, she could be wounded or
killed. Innocent civilians caught in the crossfire were a tragic
but common occurrence in San Angelo.

When they drove into the village it was after two o'clock,
and there were few people about. Brenna climbed down
from the truck and bent over from the waist, stretching taut
muscles, soothing aching joints. When she straightened
again, she looked warily at Andrés.

She was waiting for him to blow up, he realized, but the
long trip back and the grim thoughts that had filled his mind
had drained the anger from him. Now he only felt tired.
"Manuel saved us some lunch," he said brusquely. "Let's
eat."

After the meal Andrés dismissed the driver. The other
men, Brenna realized at last, were the two who'd sat outside her windows for the past two days. She could remain
outside, take a walk, get some sun, Andrés told her in
English and the guards in Spanish, but they would remain
with her. If she tried to escape they would stop her.

Brenna looked pointedly at the fully automatic rifles they
carried. He didn't say they would shoot her, but then, he
didn't say they wouldn't, either. Without a word she turned
and walked away from him, the two men following close
behind.

He'd caught her looking at the men's weapons, and now
he gave a shake of his head. She was too angry to realize that
the guards were there for her own protection. Although the
village itself was relatively secure, there were men in the
mountains who owed their allegiance to Romero and his
army, and others who had no allegiance to anyone save
themselves. There were also the animals that made their
homes here, some harmless, some deadly, and there were the
mountains themselves, treacherously steep in places, im-

penetrable in others, and dizzyingly alike to strangers. If she wandered far from the village, she could get hopelessly lost, and it would cost valuable time to find her.

He gave another sigh. José and Diego understood their orders. They would watch her and keep her safe. Now he had work to do.

Brenna walked slowly along the street, ignoring the two guards, studying each of the buildings. If she was forced to make an escape attempt, she reasoned, it couldn't hurt to be familiar with every part of the tiny town.

This village that had no name, where Andrés had grown up the second son of a poor farmer, had never been prosperous. There was only one street, wide and sandy. The buildings that lined both sides were spaced at uneven intervals, and most were elevated, with a small porch and a flight of fragile-looking steps leading up. Some had once been shops—faded signs still hung over the doorways—but most appeared to be houses, as simple and plain as Andrés's. Some had once been whitewashed, but most were that soft gray that unprotected wood takes on after long exposure to the sun and rain.

The church was the only obviously different structure in town. Built of adobe, it gave the impression of strength, of steadiness, but the dried mud was starting to crumble away in places. Its steeple was small, its cross broken but still recognizable.

The church had served as their school, too, Andrés had told her long ago. When the children could be spared from working in the fields, they were taught to read and write by the priest. His father had placed a high value on education, and Andrés had done well with his lessons, so the priest had arranged for him to attend a regular school in Santiago. From there he'd gone on to the university in Santa Lucia— it had been free to any resident who qualified—and then he had joined the army.

She knew his past as well as she knew her own. About that much, at least, he'd been truthful. No, it was only the present and the future he had lied about.

She walked through the gate in the low stone wall that surrounded the church. Behind her, both men hesitated, exchanged glances, then followed. Patches of grass grew in the yard, tall and in need of cutting. The brown-planked doors in the center of the building were closed, secured with a board that formed a crude lock. The dirt in front of the doors had been undisturbed for so long that it had a thick, crusty surface.

The building had been abandoned from its original purpose, but unlike the shops that now housed soldiers, it hadn't been converted for other use. It was empty, neglected, forsaken. With a chill running down her spine, she remembered Andrés's words about Father Hidalgo: He used to be the priest in our village until the children were killed and the women were moved. Were they killed here? By soldiers? Sometime she would ask . . . when she was sure she could bear the answer.

Turning, she saw her guards waiting just inside the gate, looking oddly uncomfortable. She walked between them, back onto the road, and once more turned away from Andrés's quarters. She passed the tiny cell where they had first held her, and a few more houses, then was at the edge of town. She stood there for a few moments, wondering where else she could go to avoid Andrés. But there was nowhere, so she turned back to retrace her steps.

After passing Manuel's kitchen with its unappetizing aromas, she came to a stop in front of the next building, her attention caught by the man sitting on the steps. He looked like all the others—dark hair, dark eyes, dark skin—but he was different, too. It wasn't just the extra weight he carried, and it wasn't the embroidered white shirt and khaki slacks he wore, while all the others dressed in olive-drab or camouflage uniforms.

Slowly she smiled. He was different because he was look-ing at her. Oh, the others had looked, especially when she'd come out of Andrés's quarters this morning in shorts and a tank top, but they had quickly glanced away. This man not only continued to look, but he met her eyes. Andrés and occasionally Vicente were the only ones who'd done that.

"Good afternoon."

And he spoke English. Her smile widened. "Hello."

"You are Andrés's American."

She raised one brow at that description, but he didn't no-tice.

"I'm Hector Escobar."

"Brenna Mathis." She moved closer and extended her hand. He leaned forward and shook it, then settled back again.

"You're the doctor, aren't you?" The round, smiling man went up more than a few notches in her estimation.

"Yes, and you are the nurse."

"I see."

"See what?" he asked innocently.

"Friendliness comes with a price tag around here." She sat down on the bottom step, folding her legs beneath her. "You wouldn't happen to be shorthanded, would you, Dr. Escobar?"

"Short everything," he replied, his voice and expression dramatically woeful. "Medicines are hard to get, supplies are hard to get, help is hard to get. Only patients are easy to find."

She didn't doubt that. The only thing the rebels and the army seemed to agree on in the news back home was that a lot of people were dying. "I suppose I'm the first registered nurse you've seen since you came here."

"That's right."

"And I just happen to be stuck here, not two hundred feet from your clinic, with nothing to do all day."

"And bored, too," he said with an eager nod of his head. "You would have to be bored to take such an interest in the buildings of our village. But if you spent a few hours each day working with our patients, maybe you would forget to be bored."

The humor that had made her smile only moments before faded. "Have you talked to Andrés about this?"

"Yes. He says that you don't want to care for enemy soldiers." He frowned, remembering Andrés's certainty on the matter, then brightened again. "And I told him nurses have no enemies. A patient is a patient."

She *had* told Andrés she wouldn't nurse their wounded, and at the time she had meant it. But at the time she hadn't realized what it meant to spend an entire day in a small room with nothing to do except eat her meals. She hadn't realized what it meant to be always within a few yards of Andrés, to be able to hear him speak if she was quiet, to be able to see him if she went to the door.

Maybe it would be interesting to help Hector Escobar with his patients. At least it would give her time with someone who spoke her language and didn't seem to scorn everything about her. It would keep her too busy to devote all her free time to thoughts of Andrés, as she was doing now. And, most of all, it would allow her to feel useful in a way that, unlike the phone call this morning, was good and decent.

Slowly she rose from the step and brushed dirt from her shorts. "All right, Dr. Escobar," she said, her voice even and with only a hint of challenge. "Show me how you practice medicine down here."

She spent the rest of the afternoon in the house that was now the doctor's clinic. It was the largest home in town, he told her as he gave her a tour, and had once belonged to the village's leading family. Unfortunately, they were dead now, and the surviving relatives had given the building to him for his patients.

His patients suffered from a variety of illnesses—gunshot and knife wounds, infections, burns, broken bones and malnutrition. There were more than a dozen of them, and they lay on cots, four or five to a room. Sterile conditions were impossible under the circumstances, but the doctor did his best to keep the place clean. The wood floors were swept several times daily, the meager bedding washed as often as possible. Even the screens that covered the open windows were cleaned regularly.

Hector introduced her to each of the patients, translating back and forth as easily as he breathed. He introduced her as a nurse from America, here to help him, and not as their leader's prisoner. She was grateful for that small shred of dignity.

By the time the patients had been fed their dinner and settled for the night, Brenna had learned that Hector wasn't married and that he had spent more than ten years in the United States, attending school and setting up practice. He had given it all up to return to San Angelo and offer his services to the rebel forces.

"Why?" she asked bluntly, sitting next to him on the floor with the dishes that held her dinner. "You could be making a hundred grand a year in the States, easy, and have a much better, much more secure life. Why give all that up to come back here?"

"Because my people need me."

She'd heard that response before—from Andrés some six years ago—and she didn't accept it any more easily now than she had then. "What is it about you people and this debt you feel toward your country? What has this country given you? You became a doctor, but you did that on your own, in *my* country. Why do you feel you owe this place anything?"

"It's my home," Hector said simply. "These are my people, and I owe them my life."

"Why?"

He eyed the untouched bread on her plate. "May I?" At her nod, he took it and, with some struggle, broke it in half. "It surprises me that you ask. You Americans make such a big deal out of patriotism. You pledge allegiance, wave your flag and claim to be the greatest country in the world, 'the land of the free and the home of the brave.'" He stopped to take a bite of bread. "We love our country as much as you love yours. Our people are as brave as yours...but we're not free. That's why we fight. So that we and our children and our grandchildren can enjoy the freedom that you have had for more than two hundred years."

"But others can fight. You didn't have to give up your new home and your practice to come back here."

"Others *can* fight, and do. But they can't heal the sick, and they can't mend the wounded. They need doctors as much as they need fighters. We must all do our share. Don't you see—"

"Don't waste your breath trying to convince her." Andrés closed the screen door behind him, then leaned back against the doorjamb. "Not all Americans are willing to die for their country. If the United States goes to war, she can send her father off to battle, and that's the extent of her responsibility. She'll never have to fight, never have to pick up a gun to defend herself, let alone her country. She'll never know what it's like to see entire cities of her countrymen slaughtered like pigs by a butcher. She'll never understand the true meaning of duty or obligation or honor."

She forgot the outburst that she'd been dreading most of the afternoon and rose slowly to her feet, ready to anger him again. "You enjoy it, don't you, the power that this war gives you? Half of your countrymen believe you're a saint, and the other half tremble when they hear your name. You're no longer just a minor lieutenant in the president's army—you're Andrés Montano, the great leader, the hero of the oppressed. You can do whatever you want. You can kidnap an innocent woman, frighten a powerful American officer—you could kill me—and nobody would stop you."

She bent and picked up her dishes, then walked to the door, stopping in front of him. "That's how your President Romero started out, isn't it? No one would stop him. Then it got to the point where no one *could*. Interesting, isn't it?"

The silence following her departure was filled with tension. Hector started to speak, but a warning shake of Andrés's head stopped him. He didn't want to hear anything more.

After a moment he wheeled around and went outside. The sun was setting, its last rays unusually bright before fading away. He watched it, then searched the long street for Brenna. She was easy to spot, walking purposefully toward their quarters, trailed by José and Diego. She didn't go into the house, however, but veered to the right and into the clearing behind it.

She sat, with her knees drawn up and head bowed, on a crumbling stone wall that separated the yard, such as it was, from the field that had once grown enough crops to support its owner's family. Andrés watched her for a moment, then approached the guards, speaking quietly to them. After taking the rifle from one, he waited until they left before joining her.

Her gaze started at his face, then moved lower to the rifle, the pistol and the knife. She gave a puzzled shake of her head and turned away.

"You don't like weapons?" he taunted.

"I'm not used to them. Lazy, irresponsible Americans like me rarely see armed men, except for the occasional policeman. We certainly don't hang out with men who carry guns everywhere they go."

He sat down beside her, but she was positioned so that all he saw was her back. "What kind of men *do* you hang out with, Brenna?"

She shivered in the swiftly dimming light. Once she would have believed that her answer mattered to him. Now she knew it didn't, and never had. At the first twinge of pain, she directed her thoughts into other, safer directions. What kind of men did she see? "I go out with doctors, technicians from the hospital . . . occasionally even patients." She was satisfied with the answer, the kind that he usually gave: partly true, partly not. She had gone out with a doctor, a lieutenant commander from the Naval Hospital in town, and she had once dated a lab technician from her own hospital. It was even true that she'd had a few dates with a patient she'd met in the emergency room. But the lies were in the plurals. There had been *one* doctor, *one* technician, *one* patient. Three men, three casual dates, were all she'd found the courage to deal with in the six years since Andrés had left.

He sat motionless, his face as blank and hard as the stones that made up the wall. He had known there would be men— a woman as pretty and warm and generous as Brenna wouldn't be alone for long—and he had known that hearing it would hurt, but he hadn't expected this kind of deep, raw wound. He wanted to ask more—had she made love with them? Had she loved them?—but he didn't dare. He could only bear so much before his control shattered, and everything that he'd struggled to bury inside for years would burst out and destroy him.

"Well, life isn't so simple down here," he said, and his voice sounded rough and rocky. "We don't go on *dates*. We just try to stay alive."

Then, finally, she looked at him, but her face was in shadow. "You chose this life for yourself."

Even the simple accusation in her tone hurt. He shook his head slowly. "No. I can think of a thousand lives I'd rather live than the one I've got."

"So quit."

"And where would I go? What would I do? My government wants me dead. Your government considers me a criminal. I wouldn't be safe anywhere."

"And you wouldn't do it anyway, would you? Even if you had a place to go, a place that was safe, you wouldn't go. You wouldn't leave your people."

"No," he said quietly. "I wouldn't."

Silence fell over them with the same steady stealth as the darkness. Brenna saw the stars appear above and watched the moon, just a glow behind heavy clouds. At last she gestured to the field spread before them. "What are the rocks for?" She had noticed them when she'd sat down, irregular clumps of rocks, a half-dozen stacks here, a dozen there, still more over there. The field had once been tilled, and it didn't seem logical that the farmer would have left so many rocks there.

"They're markers."

"For what?" Then she quickly looked over her shoulder at the house. She realized it was the field he had shown her from the window last night.

"For graves."

She shuddered and huddled tighter in her cramped position. "You mean the soldiers buried them where they died?"

"No." He turned his back on the field and the memories it held. "One of the men in the village was sent for me. I got here the next day...and I buried them."

When he'd told her the details last night, she hadn't realized that he'd seen their bodies. How horrible it must have been for him, she thought sadly, because if there was one thing he had loved more than his country, it had been his family. He had been so proud of them, so full of love for them. Even the brief time he'd spent in Florida had been too long away from them; he had missed them terribly.

Without thinking, she turned and reached for his hand, squeezing it tightly between hers. "I'm sorry, Andrés. God, I'm sorry."

He looked down at their clasped hands. It had been a long time since anyone had offered him comfort—there was so little to give, and so many who needed it. It was amazing what the simple touch of a human hand could mean.

And the simple touch of *this* hand ... He closed his eyes to hide the surge of emotion. Given the time and the desire, she could heal all his wounds. She could give his life meaning and make it worth living again. She could give him hope and a future and love. She could give him back his soul.

But she didn't have the time or the desire. She was touching him now only out of compassion for his sorrow. The only passion she felt for him was that of anger, of outrage and something very close to hatred. In this moment she was soft and giving, but soon she would remember that she was his prisoner, that he had threatened her life, and the softness would disappear.

He had destroyed any chance of a future with her and had ensured that their present could be filled only with the darker emotions. There was no place for gentleness, for remembrance. No place for need or hunger or desire. God help him, there was no place in their lives for his love.

He withdrew from her before she could withdraw from him—pulling his hand away, standing up and slinging the rifle over his shoulder. Brenna was left sitting on the wall, her hands suddenly empty. They tingled from contact with him, and they ached to touch him again, to hold him and force him to feel something good for her. But it would be an impossible task. He'd made his feelings for her clear from the beginning, and nothing she could do would change them.

She got off the wall, and they walked, wrapped in painful silence, across the rough ground to the house. As they passed Diego, Andrés returned the rifle, then climbed the steps behind Brenna. He stopped in the office while she continued into her own room. She closed the door quietly behind her; then he heard the whispery rustle of clothing being removed, of the sheet being pulled back, the protesting squeaks of settling in.

He stood in the center of the dark room, his head bowed, the desire low in his belly as strong as anything he'd felt in the past six years. When he'd decided to bring her here to trade for Esai, he had thought he could live with the consequences. He had already lost so much—his family, his hope, his humanity. But this—this had cost him much more than his future. This time he'd lost his soul.

When Brenna came out of the house for breakfast the next morning, her guards were waiting at the bottom of the steps, their attention on the road, not her. She followed the direction of their gazes and saw the trucks parked there, the group of men preparing to leave, and a shiver passed through her. They were going out to fight, to risk their lives. Some of them would probably come back wounded. Some of them probably wouldn't come back at all.

The men were unusually quiet as they checked their weapons and supplies, as were those who would be left behind. She searched each small band for one familiar face. When she found it, she wished she hadn't. Andrés was talking to Vicente and several of the men she'd seen in his office that first morning. Instead of the usual green utilities, he wore cammies, and a soft cap, called a utility cover and made of the same camouflage fabric, concealed most of his thick hair. Its bill was pulled low and, with the aviator-style sunglasses he wore, left his face in shadow.

She told herself that he was simply giving instructions to the men who would lead the troops today, but she knew it wasn't true. He was going with them. The knowledge made her heart thud painfully in her chest.

When Andrés finished speaking he dismissed the other men. Only Vicente remained. Once again he would stay behind and handle the day-to-day routine of running the camp. If any emergencies came up, he would deal with them. Andrés knew his friend was fully capable of that. His only concern was Brenna.

"If I don't come back," he said, his mouth barely moving beneath the mustache, "make the exchange as planned."

"If you don't come back, we've lost a great deal of our bargaining power," Vicente replied, his voice equally soft. "The name Vicente Morales means nothing to Commander Mathis. It's *you* he's afraid of."

"You'll still have the winning hand, because you'll still have Brenna." He saw her standing on the porch and immediately looked away. "He'll still be willing to trade Esai to get her back."

"You stay and handle it. I'll go with the men in your place."

Andrés shook his head. His aide hadn't yet guessed that he'd chosen to go along on this mission because of Brenna, because he couldn't bear spending one more day in the village with her. Because he couldn't handle one more night in the same house with her, listening to the soft, restful sounds of her sleep, afraid to close his eyes because of what he might dream. "Keep her safe."

"I will."

"Don't leave her alone at night. Move into my office until I return."

Vicente knew what that request had cost, and he nodded solemnly. "Take care, my friend."

Andrés shifted the rifle on his shoulder, then once more looked at Brenna. She was walking toward him. He considered turning away as if he hadn't seen her, but that wouldn't be fair to either of them, so he stood his ground, waiting for her, half wishing she would snub him and walk on by, half praying that she wouldn't.

She didn't. She stopped a few feet in front of him. This morning she wore a white T-shirt, emblazoned with pink flamingos and the name *Florida* in flowing neon-green script, and tucked into white shorts. The stark white was softened by the pale gold of her skin and the tumbled honey brown of her hair.

"Where are you going?" Her voice and expression were blank, but she couldn't control the look in her eyes—fear, not of him, but for him.

"We have work to do." He paused. "Do you think we got our reputation as thieving, murderous outlaws by sitting around our village all the time?"

She didn't acknowledge his sardonic echo of her father's insult. "What are you going to do?"

"We're going to kill some loyal Angeleno soldiers."

"And maybe get killed?"

He shrugged carelessly. "It happens."

"What if it happens to you?"

Behind the dark glasses, his eyes narrowed. Slowly he pulled them off and leveled an arrogant, mocking look on her. "Why all the questions, Brenna? Are you worried about my safety? Afraid that I'll die?"

Dear God, yes. She was furious at her own weakness, but she was sick inside with a kind of fear she'd never known—fear that he could die, that she would never be able to see him or speak to him again. But she didn't tell him that. Instead she shoved her hands into her pockets, then clenched them into fists that he couldn't see. "You're my ticket out of here."

"And here I thought your concern was for me, not yourself." He replaced the glasses. "Don't worry. Vicente can negotiate with your father as well as I can."

Brenna bit her lip, torn between anger and worry. She wanted to tell him to take his sarcasm and his arrogance and go to hell . . . and she wanted to plead with him to stay here where he would be safe. The worry won out. Regardless of what he was now, six years ago she had loved him, and she didn't want to see him hurt. She took a step back, and another; then, just before she spun around and bolted, she murmured, "Be careful . . . please."

Andrés stared after her for a long time, unaware of the others around him. It wasn't much, but it was the best incentive he'd had in years to stay alive.

Reynaldo's shout jolted him out of his reverie, and he turned to see that the men were climbing into the trucks. He said goodbye to Vicente, tossed the pack that held his supplies into the nearest truck and climbed up after it. The last thing he saw as they drove out of the village was Brenna, on the steps of the clinic with Hector, solemnly watching him. Dear God, he silently whispered as they turned the bend that cut her off from sight, let me survive this one.

In the middle of the tiny village, a similar prayer was being offered. Don't let anything happen to him, she pleaded. Bring him back safely.

Chapter 4

She wasn't meant to play the dutiful woman waiting at home while the men went off to battle, Brenna wryly acknowledged early Friday morning as she sat down on the steps of Andrés's quarters to eat breakfast. Even though she had spent yesterday helping Hector, the time had passed interminably, made longer by frequent trips to the door to look down the long, empty street. The knots in her stomach hadn't eased at all until late last night, allowing her to sleep for a few hours, but they were there again when she woke this morning.

Her concern seemed the most natural and at the same time the most unnatural response in the world to Andrés's absence. Why should she worry when she knew his life was in danger? She no longer loved him, her rational side argued. She was being held prisoner by him, her own life placed in danger by him. She shouldn't care one bit what happened to him, whether he came back alive or wounded or even dead.

Unfinished business. That was the only acceptable explanation she could come up with. Andrés's leaving six years ago had been so sudden, her heartache so complete, that she'd never really dealt with the ending of the relationship. She'd had to focus on survival, on forgetting him and not loving him and getting on with her life, and maybe, she admitted reluctantly, some feelings remained.

When Vicente joined her on the steps, she murmured a quiet good morning. She had tried to talk to him yesterday, had asked him how long the men would be gone, where they had gone, what they were doing. He had been polite—he was still the most courteous "thieving, murderous outlaw" she'd ever met—but he hadn't answered a single question. She didn't know if the answers were secret—though after all, who would she tell—or if he simply didn't have them to give.

She stacked her empty plate, bowl and cup together, then leaned against the railing, her fingers laced loosely in her lap. "Do you think they'll come back today?"

He looked up, his dark eyes wary. "Maybe."

"What happens if they don't?" she asked, her tone challenging. "What if they never come back?"

He studied her for a long time, seeing through her questions to her real concern. "He will. He always does."

"Not to me," she murmured, her thoughts distant. When she realized what she'd said, she looked up and saw him looking oddly at her. She assumed he knew about her earlier affair with Andrés—he seemed to know everything else about his leader—and she saw that he was curious, but thankfully he didn't ask any questions. "What happens to Esai and me if he doesn't?"

"The exchange will be made as planned."

"Will my father deal with you?"

"He'll deal with whoever has you."

That sounded like Andrés's sentiments, not Vicente's, Brenna thought, and there had been a noticeable lack of confidence when he'd voiced them. "I don't mean any offense, Vicente, but I don't think my father would be as concerned with you as he is with Andrés."

He shrugged. "It doesn't matter. All that really matters is you. If your father wants you back, he'll negotiate with me or Andrés or whoever happens to have you. He'll do whatever he's told by whoever's in charge."

Grimly she acknowledged his correctness. "I hate you all for this. My father has always been a man of honor. Now, because of you people, he has to violate that honor."

Again he shrugged. "It was the only action we could think of to save Esai."

"I understand the prisons here are bad, but surely his cousin could survive a few months or even a few years in them."

Vicente gave her a look that was part censure for her naiveté, she supposed, and part pitying...for her ignorance? "The government of Eugenio Romero does not keep prisoners," he said slowly. "They would beat him, and then they would torture him, and if he didn't die from his wounds or from starvation, then they would kill him."

"But they claim—"

Vicente interrupted her, his voice still low and soft. "Claims mean nothing, Miss Mathis. They claim that *we* killed Andrés's family. They claim that we torture our own countrymen. They claim that we rob and rape and murder for money, for pleasure. For *pleasure!*" He spat out a curse, vicious and hate filled. "Esai was taken prisoner in Andrés's place. If we do nothing, he will die in Andrés's place. The army doesn't care, and your father doesn't care, and maybe you don't care...but it would destroy Andrés. After everything else that he's lost, everything that he's borne, knowing that his cousin died because of him would kill him."

Brenna sat silent for a long time, holding Vicente's gaze. "What exactly does my father have to do with it?"

The passion in his eyes, dark and deep like Andrés's, faded and was replaced by impenetrable shadow. "Your father is a powerful man. He can help us, if we provide the right incentive.''

And *she* was that incentive. The knowledge left a bad taste in her mouth. ''Andrés said that my father 'engineered' Esai's capture. How was he involved?''

''I can't explain what Andrés meant by his statement. Ask him when he returns.''

''*You* said that Esai was taken prisoner in Andrés's place. What did *you* mean?''

He looked away from her, his mouth set in a stubborn line.

She gave it a long moment's thought before reaching a conclusion, but it was too impossible to believe. ''You think the soldiers were trying to capture Andrés when Esai was taken prisoner, don't you? And you think my father was somehow behind it. Is that it?''

Slowly Vicente got to his feet. ''I have work to do, Miss Mathis,'' he said in his polite and impersonal English. ''Save your questions for Andrés. Maybe he cares enough to debate the subject with you. I don't.''

Brenna watched him go, then shook her head. They blamed her father for Esai's capture, and that was why they had kidnapped her. But she didn't believe it. Tom was an instructor, training Romero's army on gathering and interpreting intelligence and teaching them unconventional warfare methods. He was simply showing them how to fight their own war, not fighting their battles for them, and certainly not capturing their enemy leaders for them. It was a mistake, pure and simple. Because of his position as commanding officer of the advisory group, because he was the most visible and most vocal American in San Angelo, and because of the rebels' enmity against Americans for their assistance to Romero, he was an easy target, there to take the blame for anything that went wrong in the rebels' fight. The army's trap to capture Andrés had failed and netted his cousin instead, so it was easy, even natural, for Andrés and

Vicente to blame Tom, even though he couldn't have been involved.

She picked up the dishes and carried them to the kitchen. The building was one large room, all of its windows open. The tables inside held stacks of mismatched dishes, made of metal, plastic and crudely fired pottery. There were also boxes of food—fresh fruits and vegetables, canned vegetables and meats, heavy bags of flour and cornmeal—all donated by people who supported the rebel cause, and crates of C rations, donated to the Angeleno army by the American government and taken off their hands by the frequent raids. The room was used mostly for storage; Manuel cooked outside, with big pots over open fires and strangely shaped brick ovens. The dishes were washed outside, too, by boys who couldn't be more than fourteen or fifteen. If the war continued the way it had for six years, soon they would graduate to carrying guns and fighting alongside the men, and their menial tasks here would pass to other children.

She left the dishes on a table with others from the morning meal, then wandered over to the clinic. The patients would already have eaten—Hector saw to that before he ate his own meals—but there would be bandages to change, medicines to be given, housekeeping chores to be done.

The day passed slowly. Four of the patients were well enough to return to their own quarters, and Brenna gathered the bedding from their cots after they were gone, adding it to the laundry pile in the back room. Doing large quantities of laundry by hand was the one sick-bay task, she thought ruefully, that she wouldn't volunteer for without an order. Her own laundry was going to have to be done in another day or so, but at least it consisted of nothing bulkier than shorts.

After dinner Hector sent her back to her quarters. She sat on the steps, watching the sun go down, feeling the darkness settle over the village, then pulled herself up and went inside. She was tired, she thought as she undressed in the

shadowy room, pulling on the bright yellow tank top that
served as her nightshirt. Maybe tired enough to sleep tonight in spite of her uneasiness about Andrés's absence.

She *did* sleep, but she was awakened only a few hours
later by voices in the outer room. Even in her drowsy state,
the fact that one of those voices was Andrés's registered, and
she rose quickly from the bed, stepping into the khaki shorts
she'd discarded earlier.

There were half a dozen men in the lamp-lit office, talking quietly back and forth. Andrés leaned against his desk,
his left hand pressed to his right shoulder. He wore the same
clothes he'd worn yesterday; he hadn't shaved or bathed and
seemed almost too weary to stand, but to her he looked
wonderfully handsome.

It was true that absence made the heart grow fonder, Andrés thought, light-headed from exhaustion, hunger and
pain. She was more beautiful now, sleep softening her
brown eyes, than she'd been even yesterday, and he wanted
her more now than he ever had. But he didn't reach out for
her, didn't make any move at all. He managed a smile, but
instead of sardonic, it was merely tired. "Sorry to disap-
point you, but I came back pretty much in one piece." Except for the chunk of flesh missing from his shoulder, neatly
nicked out by a razor-sharp knife.

Her gaze shifted to his shoulder and the fresh blood coloring his fingers, and her heart began pounding. Ignoring
the other men, she hurried to him and gently lifted his hand
away. The dried bloodstain on his jacket was enlarging as
the renewed flow, bright and red, seeped into the fabric. She
was trembling badly inside, but her hands were steady as she
swiftly unfastened the jacket buttons. Steeling herself for the
worst, she peeled back the shirt, then gave a sigh of relief.
The knife wound had been painful, but it didn't seem to be
serious. If it had included the artery, he would have bled to
death in a matter of minutes. There was still the possibility

of muscle damage, she acknowledged, but that couldn't be determined until a thorough exam had been made.

She bent her head and closed her eyes for an instant, whispering a silent prayer of thanks, then drew away. "You need to see the doc—"

"Hector is very busy," he interrupted. "Why don't you go and help him?"

She nodded once. "At least sit down before you collapse."

This time the nod was his, but he didn't move. When she, too, remained still, he walked around the desk, pulled out the chair and eased himself into it. The look he gave her was challenging, and she met it with an even, bland gaze. Having won one tiny victory, she left the office and hurried barefoot to the clinic.

There were only three new patients, but they were all seriously wounded. Brenna worked alongside Hector, cleaning wounds, suturing them, repairing the damage caused by bullets tearing through fragile flesh, realigning broken bones. When they finished hours later, two of the men were resting quietly. The third one was dead.

Hector removed his surgical gloves and dropped them into an overflowing trash can. "When they brought these men in they said that Andrés has a minor wound." There was none of the usual friendliness in his voice. She had never seen him look so somber, so weary.

"Yes, a knife wound in the shoulder." She tossed her own gloves after his, then wiped her arm across her forehead. She was tired, drained. Seeing a patient die always affected her that way. But this time there was guilt, too. She was sorry the man had died, but God help her, she was glad it was him and not Andrés.

"Take whatever supplies you need and treat it, will you, while I take care of this one." He pulled the sheet over the patient, covering the massive chest wound that had killed him, covering his face.

Brenna moved stiffly to the cabinet and made her selection of gauze bandages, adhesive tape, antiseptic, antibiotics and scissors. "What is his name?"

"Ricardo. Ricardo Aleman."

"I'll tell Andrés."

When she returned to the office everyone had left except Andrés, Vicente and the old man, Benedicto. Brenna laid her supplies on the desk without looking at any of them, then bent over Andrés and unhooked the wide webbed belt at his waist. "Vicente, would you get me some hot water and some drinking water?" she asked, laying the belt with its weapons on the table and opening the remaining buttons of the jacket. There had been more packages of sterile surgical gloves in the clinic, but the supply was limited, so they had to be saved for serious injuries. For a wound like this, she would wash her hands with boiled water and antiseptic scrub.

"How are the men?" Andrés asked, cautiously shrugging out of his jacket.

She hesitated, aware that all attention was on her, and her eyes dropped to her limp, motionless hands. "The two younger ones are all right. Ricardo Aleman is dead."

There was a moment's silence in the room; then Vicente left, the screen door banging softly behind him. The old man, although he spoke no English, understood what she'd said, perhaps because death was a common occurrence for them. Because some of them had to die so that others could live. He spoke softly to Andrés, then pushed himself to his feet and shuffled out the door.

The wound on Andrés's shoulder was still seeping. She would clean it, she decided, and pack it open with a wick made of gauze to allow it to drain. First, though, she would get him into bed so he could rest. As she opened her mouth to tell him what she planned, he spoke.

"Ricardo has a wife and two children in Santiago. His two older children are dead."

"I'm sorry."

He looked up at her then, and the sadness in his eyes was liquid. "So am I."

She looked away first, swallowing past the lump in her throat, then knelt on the floor beside him and began unlacing his boots. When the discomfort had lessened, she began talking, her tone matter-of-fact. "I'm going to put you to bed, then clean and bandage that wound. The dressing will have to be changed twice a day for a few days, and you'll have to restrict your use of that arm."

One heavy black boot hit the floor, then the other. She peeled off his socks and, holding them by the thin cuffs with two fingers, dropped them onto the floor, too. Noticing her action, Andrés smiled wryly. "I could use a bath."

"I know."

"And you could use some clothes." The tank top she wore was ribbed and clung to her like a second skin. Nothing was hidden, not the flat expanse of her rib cage or the narrowness of her waist, and definitely not the sweet curve of her breasts, small and rounded, her nipples making indistinct soft peaks under the yellow fabric. As he watched, they hardened and swelled until he ached to touch them, to taste them.

Brenna felt the flush that heated her face but tried to ignore it. "Get me out of bed in the middle of the night to work, and this is what you get. Besides, I don't have enough clean clothes to change into something else just because it suits you. Stand up, would you?"

He obeyed, rising slowly from the chair and steadying himself on the table. His gaze settled on some point on the ceiling as her hands unfastened his narrow belt, then began unbuttoning his trousers. The buttons were thick, their fit tight, and it took her several moments to loosen them. "Are you deliberately tormenting me?" he asked, his voice thick, too, his jaw set in a hard line.

"In the hospital, when we need to undress an injured patient, we use scissors. But since you have so few uniforms, I thought you'd like to keep this one reasonably intact," she said defensively. With her fumbling, she'd felt the growing hardness between his thighs, and it left her flustered. Lust was one thing—she'd dealt with it before. But lust from a man who derided everything about her, from a man who'd made her his prisoner, lust from *Andrés*—she didn't begin to know how to deal with that.

She got to her feet and busied herself with the supplies on the desk. "Maybe you'd better finish undressing and get in bed," she said, embarrassment in both her voice and the gaze that refused to meet his.

"Maybe I'd better." He walked to the cot and carefully removed the rest of his clothes, easing the coarse fabric over his aroused flesh. Lying down, he pulled the sheet to his waist, arranging it over his hips as camouflage. He'd never gone to such trouble to be treated by Hector, he thought with a moment's amusement, but then he'd never found himself in the same situation with Hector. "All right."

She pulled the chairs over from the desk, placing the oil lamp on one and seating herself on the other. "As soon as Vicente brings the water, I'll get started. Is this the only place you're hurt?"

"I have a few other aches you could take care of." As soon as he'd said the words, he saw a curtain fall over her face, shuttering her feelings from view. She thought he'd meant the arousal she'd caused with such a casual touch, and she was offended. "I wasn't talking about that," he said quietly. He'd meant the iciness around his heart, the emptiness where his soul should be. "Brenna . . ."

He raised his hand to reach for her, and she panicked. She didn't want him touching her, not now, not gently, not when she was vulnerable from two days of waiting and worrying over him. Desperately she moved out of reach, and he let her, his hand falling back to the bed.

Feeling foolish, she tried to settle comfortably in the chair. "Your friend Vicente thinks my father was involved in Esai's capture."

Andrés didn't look at her. "Did he say that?"

"Not exactly."

"What did he say?"

"That I should save my questions for you."

"Do you want to ask me?" Even as he asked, he hoped she wouldn't. He would have to tell her half-truths, because he couldn't tell her the entire story. He couldn't tell her how he *knew* that Tom Mathis was the brains behind the trap. He couldn't tell her the bait they had used to lure him in.

"No. I'd rather ask Dad next time I talk to him. You're his enemy. I have trouble believing what you say."

After the phone call to Tom two days ago, he wasn't sure he could risk letting her talk to her father again. She had sounded so damn sure of herself in those few minutes that she had probably done their cause more harm than good. If Tom even vaguely suspected that Brenna was safe, he would never agree to trade Esai for her, or he would set up another trap, or do something to beat his student at his own game.

"Suit yourself." He tilted his head back on the small, nearly flat pillow and closed his eyes, wincing as he resettled himself on the narrow cot.

In spite of the weariness that etched deep lines into his face and the wound that had drained his strength and energy along with his blood, he looked fierce and dangerous. But looking at him, Brenna felt no fear, only thankfulness that his wound wasn't serious, that for one more night he was safe.

She let him rest until Vicente came in with a bucket of water in one hand, a canteen in the other. He'd also brought, tucked beneath one arm, a basin and several towels. "Do you need any help?" he asked quietly, his gaze on his friend.

Brenna shook her head. "Thanks." After he left, she washed her hands with the scrub, then cleaned Andrés's entire shoulder with antiseptic. He stiffened but didn't make a sound when she gently probed the wound with one fingertip, judging its depth, assuring herself that no muscles were involved.

"Do you think I'll live?"

The sardonic question made her smile faintly. "You were lucky. Between the arteries, nerves and muscles that run through here, it could have been bad, even fatal. Except for a little pain, you'll be fine."

She formed a wick from a roll of gauze and inserted it into the wound, then packed it in place with more gauze. On top of that she placed a sterile dressing. Then, after washing her hands again, she took two capsules from the bottle of antibiotics, uncapped the canteen and supported his head while he swallowed the pills and drank.

"You should stay in bed tomorrow and rest," she said. "Have your meals brought to you, and let Vicente handle anything that has to be done."

Eyes still closed, he shook his head. "Can't do that," he murmured wearily. "Things I have to do... have to go to Santiago tomorrow...."

She dipped one of the towels into clean water and wrung it out, then used the end of it to gently wipe two days' grime from his face. "There's nothing urgent. Your trip to Santiago can wait until you're rested." She paused to lay her hand against his forehead, checking for a fever, but his skin was cool and dry. Bending, she rinsed the towel and repeated the process on his chest, gently wiping down his arms, careful not to disturb him. By the time she finished, he was asleep.

Brenna dropped the towel into the bucket of water and bent over in a protective huddle, letting her eyes close, her taut hold on her emotions relax.

In six years as a nurse she had never treated anyone she knew, certainly never anyone she cared for. In its own way this had been as much of a drain on her emotional reserves as watching the stranger named Ricardo Aleman die. Andrés wasn't going to die from his wound, but that knowledge didn't lessen the impact of treating him, of knowing that an inch higher or an inch deeper and he *would* be dead.

A choked sob escaped her. For a nurse, she didn't deal well with death. She was afraid of its power to shatter, to steal life not only from its victim but from the family he left behind. She hadn't handled her mother's death well; only the renewed relationship with her father had allowed her to work through it. But if anything more happened to Andrés while she was here, who would help her through that?

"Are you all right?"

Slowly she sat up. Vicente was standing in the doorway, a questioning look on his face. "I'm fine."

"Andrés?"

"He's asleep. He'll be fine, too, if you can keep him in bed for a day or so."

"Did he mention when he'll be going to Santiago?"

"He said tomorrow, but don't count on it," she said dryly, standing up and stretching her arms over her head.

"I think I should." Somberly he explained, "He has to return Ricardo's body to his family for burial. He won't want to put it off."

"Couldn't you do it?"

"I could, but I don't think he'd let me. If they're close enough, he always visits the families himself. Besides, he also has to call Commander Mathis again. He'll probably do that at the same time."

Ignoring the reference to her father, she set the oil lamp on the desk and turned down the wick. "Where is *your* family?'' she asked conversationally, returning to the bedside to pick up the medical supplies.

After waiting a long time without an answer, she glanced at him. His expression was distant, someplace far away and, judging from the bleakness in his eyes, not much better. Perhaps his family, like Andrés's, was gone, victims of this terrible war. For that reason she didn't press him for an answer.

She made one last trip to the cot, checking the dressing, gently smoothing the sheet up to Andrés's shoulders, then walked back to the center of the room. "If he tries to go to Santiago tomorrow, will you let me know?"

"Do you think you could stop him?"

She smiled faintly at the notion. "I don't want to stop him. I want to go with him."

He watched while she finished straightening the room— pushing the boots under the desk, gathering the dirty clothes into a pile by the door, carrying soiled gauze pads to the wastebasket. The only things left out of place were the weapons. Vicente gathered those up and prepared to leave. At the door, he paused and looked back at her. "I'll let you know."

He didn't have to follow through on his promise. Andrés woke her himself; he was bathed, shaved, dressed in a clean uniform and looking none the worse for wear. It was nearly eight o'clock, according to the small travel clock on the nightstand, but she felt as if she'd had only a few hours' sleep.

"We're leaving as soon as you can get ready," he said stiffly, standing at the foot of the bed and gazing down at her.

Brenna blinked to clear her eyes and started to sit up, but stopped when the sheet began to slide and Andrés's cool gaze turned decidedly more interested. Her yellow tank top, stained with blood and dirt, lay on the floor next to the bed, and that left her wearing nothing beneath the thin sheet but a pair of tiny yellow panties.

Carefully she maneuvered herself out of the bed, wrapping the sheet around her as she stood up. "Take your jacket off. I need to see your shoulder before we go."

He stared blankly at her. It had taken both him and Vicente the better part of several pain-filled minutes to get the jacket *on*. Taking it off alone would be no easy feat. "My shoulder is all right. It's been looked at." Two sentences, two lies. The knife wound hurt like hell, and no one had seen it except him. But if he told her the truth she would be difficult and cause delays, and they would never make it to Santiago today. "Now get dressed quickly, or we'll go without you."

She pulled a set of clothing from her nearly empty duffel bag, then turned to face him. "Are you going to give me some privacy, or do you plan to stay and watch?"

He recalled the feel of her hands on him last night, tending his wound, wiping his face, and lower, touching him awkwardly, accidentally, intimately. He would like to have the same privilege of touching her, or failing that, of simply looking at her. As her captor, he knew he could take what freedoms he wanted. As a man, he knew he couldn't. "Are you offering me a choice?" he asked even as he started for the door.

He waited outside in his office, knowing that it would take some time. She was fastidious about her personal appearance, not that she cared how she looked for him or any of his men. She simply wouldn't relax her own personal standards, not even in this crude little village.

There were more of them this time, Brenna noticed when she and Andrés walked outside to the truck. In addition to the driver, José and Diego, there were two other men and, in the back of the truck with them, the shroud-wrapped body of Ricardo Aleman.

When Andrés had said that his shoulder had been looked at, Brenna had assumed he'd meant by Hector. Before they were halfway to Santiago, she knew he had lied. If Hector had seen the wound, he would have insisted, as she should have, that Andrés remain in bed for at least one full day. Every rut in the road drained a little more of the color from his face; every jolt of the truck increased his pain.

She turned sideways in the seat, wiping the sweat from his face with her palm. "Who looked at your wound this morning, Andrés?" she asked in a low, sharply accusing voice.

"I did." He sounded weak, even to himself. His shoulder felt as if it were on fire, but there was nothing he could do about it—just grit his teeth and bear it.

"Tell the driver to turn around and return to camp."

"I can't."

"Damn it, are you trying to kill yourself?"

He opened his eyes and smiled weakly. "Last night you told me that it wasn't serious. 'Except for a little pain, you'll be fine.' That's what you said."

"I also said you needed to stay in bed for a couple of days. How did you manage to hear the first and not the second?"

"We have to deliver Ricardo's body."

"Someone else could have done it."

"It's my responsibility."

She dried his face again. "Having you do it in person isn't going to make Señora Aleman's grief any easier to bear. Someone else should have volunteered, and you should have stayed home."

He closed his eyes again. "I'll be all right if you'll quit nagging at me."

In a huff, she settled back in her seat, arms folded over her chest. "Fine. Die. See if I care." For a long time, she stared straight ahead, ignoring the occasional catch of his breath, the perspiration that trickled down his face, the way he tried to cushion his injured shoulder against the jouncing of the truck. But she couldn't ignore his voice when he spoke, soft and weak and unsteady.

"Brenna."

Slowly she turned to look at him. "What?" she whispered.

He reached for her hand, lifting it, palm upward, to his mouth. He pressed a kiss in its center and tasted the salt of his own sweat. Then he slowly released her, closed his eyes and turned his head away. "Thank you."

As soon as they came to a stop in front of Sofia Aleman's house, the new widow came out, drying her hands on her apron, looking curiously at them. Andrés reached across with his left hand to open the door and slid to the ground. He stood there for a moment, breathing deeply, trying to regain the balance that his weakness had drained from him.

Brenna was sliding over to join him when he shook his head. "You need help," she pointed out.

"Not here."

"Afraid that if she sees you leaning on someone, Señora Aleman will realize that you're just a man and not a god, after all?"

"No." He pulled the dark glasses from his pocket and slid them on to protect his eyes against the bright morning sun. "Afraid Señora Aleman will realize that you're American and try to kill you with her bare hands. I couldn't offer you much protection right now."

She looked skeptical, even after glancing at the taller, heavier, apparently much stronger woman standing in front of the house.

"I told you last night that their two oldest children are dead. They were killed by a band of soldiers, supplied by Americans, trained by Americans...and led by two of your American soldiers." He closed the door, then looked at her through the window. "Wait here."

She did as he commanded. By the shifting of the truck, she could tell when the men had removed Ricardo Aleman's body. Twisting slightly in the seat, she saw them carry it inside the small house, saw the woman burst into tears and throw her arms around Andrés's neck, pressing her face against his jacket. Brenna even saw him wince when she pressed too tightly and the way that holding her drained his already depleted strength.

She turned away from the scene, away from the woman's sorrow, and bowed her head, suddenly weary. She'd seen too much, heard too much, in her week in San Angelo. She wanted to go home. She wanted to wish Andrés and Vicente and Hector well, wanted to extract a promise from God that nothing would happen to them, especially to Andrés; then she wanted to go back to Florida and forget everything about them.

She sat there for a long time, barely moving, barely noticing the midday heat or the rumbling of her stomach. Even when the men returned she didn't move until it became apparent that Andrés needed assistance. She helped him into the truck, leaned across him to slam the door, then settled his rifle between his leg and hers.

Their next stop was the church. Andrés told the priest about the dead man before he led Brenna back into the office. While he placed the phone call, she pushed him into the single chair and began unbuttoning his jacket enough so she could check his wound. The tape that secured the dressing was loose on one side, where he had peeled it up this morning. She lifted it at the same point, checked the packing and the wick, then recovered the wound and rebuttoned his jacket. By the time she finished, her father was on the phone.

Just as before, Andrés spoke in Spanish. He told Tom what he wanted and, just as he'd expected, the other man denied that he could get it.

"Damn it, Montano, your cousin is an army prisoner. I have no control over them," he said angrily. "Ask for something else—anything—and I'll get it, but a prisoner is out of the question."

"I don't want something else. I want Esai Villareal." He watched Brenna as he spoke. "We're not bargaining here, Tom. Your comrades have my cousin, and I have your daughter. If you want her back—safe, secure, alive—you have to give us Esai. It's that simple."

"I told you, I have no say at all over the prisoners. I don't even know where they're holding him."

"Find out. You brag about your power here. Use it. Tell your good friend Eugenio that you need to question one of their prisoners. Tell him whatever is necessary to get the information. Then get Esai."

"How do I know you won't hurt Brenna?" Tom demanded. "How do I know you'll return her unharmed?"

"You'll have to trust me. The same way I trusted you." He slowly stood up. "No double-crosses this time, Tom. A straight trade: Esai for Brenna. No ambushes, no traps. Or *she'll* pay. Do you understand?"

"*If* I can find your cousin and persuade the army to give him to me—that's *if*, Montano, I'm not making any promises—where and when will we make this trade?"

"I'll let you know when I've decided." He paused. "She's very stubborn, Tom, and very foolish. Her conversation with you Wednesday is proof of that. She thinks this is a game. She thinks that because she's an American, because she's your daughter, because I once slept with her, that I won't hurt her. She's wrong, Tom—you know it, and so do I. Because you know it, I've decided it would serve no purpose to prove it to her... yet. After all, a stubborn, defiant prisoner is no more trouble than a hysterical, terrified one. Don't double-cross me, Tom. Don't make me prove to her what you and I already know."

Tom sighed. "Just don't hurt her," he said softly. "Don't frighten her."

"She's here with me. Do you want to talk to her?"

"Yes, please."

Without a word, Andrés handed the phone to Brenna.

She wished for privacy, since she didn't have the benefit of speaking a language that he didn't understand. But he showed no intention of leaving her alone, so she turned her back on him and faced the stuccoed wall. "Dad?"

"Are you all right, babe? Has he hurt you? Has he done anything to you?"

He had caused her emotional pain, and he had turned her entire world upside down and inside out, but those weren't the things her father was talking about. He was thinking in more literal terms—physical pain, abuse, rape. "No, Dad, I'm all right. How are you?"

He ignored the polite question. "Do you know what's going on, honey? What they want from me?"

"Yes."

"I'm going to get this guy, but it'll take some time. I'm working as quickly as I can, but these damned Angelenos..." He muttered a curse, and she could see him in her mind shaking his head in frustration. "The only thing that concerns them is their own greed. They've always got their own angles, always looking to pad their own fortunes. There's more corruption in this government than any place I've ever been. But I'm going to get Villareal if I have to break him out. It'll just take time."

She forced an uneasy smile. "Hey, I've got plenty of that."

"Are they treating you okay, babe?"

"Dad, I'm fine. I have my own private room, I get three meals a day, I'm even allowed to go wherever I want—with guards, of course. Dad—" She knew the question she wanted to ask, but she couldn't think of any way to phrase it, to mask its ugliness. They were small words, but they carried such power. They were such an insult to the integrity, honor and sense of duty that made her father such a good soldier.

Did you set the trap that caught Esai? Had he set it for Andrés, knowing that he would be taken prisoner, *knowing* that he would be killed? Had he used his authority to set up an old friend for certain death?

She didn't want to know. He was her father, and she had to believe that he was too good a soldier, too good a man, to do what Andrés and Vicente had suggested. She *had* to!

"Brenna, I know I don't tell you this often enough . . . I had the same problem with your mother . . . but . . . I love you. I was never much of a husband, and I haven't been much of a father, but you and your mother have always been the most important part of my life."

She blinked away the tears in her eyes. She could count the number of times he'd told her he loved her on only one hand. But as much as his words touched her, they hurt, too. She'd been about to accuse him of a despicable act—the question would have been the same as an accusation in his eyes. He was a better father than she was a daughter, she thought, rubbing her nose with one hand. "I love you, too, Dad."

"Listen, you behave and do whatever Montano wants, okay? Don't forget what I told you about him. Don't make him show you just how mean he can be. I'll get you out soon, I promise."

She glanced over her shoulder at Andrés. He was staring out the window, seemingly unaware of her. "You know," she said softly when she turned back, "you could just come and get me."

"Rescue you?" Tom sounded bleak and bitter. "Believe me, babe, we've considered it. The risks are just too great. Montano would kill you before we got within five hundred yards."

"Do you really believe that?"

"Yes. I do."

She rubbed her eyes wearily, feeling suddenly ten years older. "I love you, Dad. I'll see you soon."

Just as he had done the last time, Andrés slipped the phone from her hand. "I'll call you again in a few days," he said grimly in Spanish. "Know by then where Esai is being held . . . for Brenna's sake."

He hung up the phone, then turned to look at her. "You didn't ask him."

She glanced up quickly, her expression changing from lost and sad to assured. "I didn't need to. I know my father. I know he's not guilty of what you say. I think you'd like to believe you're that important to him, but I don't think it's true. My father is a professional. He's been in the military almost as long as you've been alive. He does his job, he carries out his orders, but he doesn't allow it to become personal, and he doesn't kill old friends."

"Tom has probably managed to forget that we were ever friends."

"Why not?" she challenged. "*You* certainly have."

Derisively, he shrugged, then grimaced at the stab of pain in his shoulder. "I didn't start this little war with your father, Brenna, but I'll finish it. And if it costs your life . . ."

"I still don't believe you. You've got my father terrified that you're going to kill me, but I don't believe it."

"Why not?"

"Because I know you." Because she had once loved him, and she could never love the man he was pretending to be. Because she still cared for him.

"What would I have to do to convince you? Hit you? Starve you? Rape you?" He reached down and touched her jaw, then drew his fingertips down her throat to the first button on her blouse. "Are you foolish enough to demand proof that I can hurt you? I did it before, Brenna, and I can do it again."

"You never physically hurt me."

He smiled coolly. "You're a nurse. You know that physical wounds often heal much more quickly than emotional ones. It's been six years, and you're still not over me. You still care about me. You have this pretty little picture of the people you believed we were, and you're trying to apply it to the present, but you're wrong. I never was the man you loved. Don't bet your life on memories of a man who never existed anywhere except in your mind."

Withdrawing his hand, he took a step back. "Believe what you want, Brenna, whatever makes you happy. Keep your father on his little pedestal. Keep me on mine. But be prepared to deal with the results when we both come crashing down."

"You're a selfish man, Andrés," she whispered bitterly. "You're determined to take everything from me, aren't you? My dreams, my past, my father... even my memories."

He shrugged as if her accusation meant nothing to him. "If your father doesn't get Esai for us, you won't live to miss them."

The trip home was even worse than the morning's drive, Brenna thought. Andrés was silent, staring straight ahead, teeth gritted against the pain in his shoulder. Even with the worst of the jolts, which made Brenna's bones ache, he didn't make a sound, although she could feel the tension that made his body stiff and allowed him to keep the pain inside.

She offered him no comfort, not even the reassuring squeeze of her hand. She had little to offer, and none of the impersonal nurse-to-patient variety—only woman to man. Lover to loved one.

How had he known what she had only figured out yesterday, that somewhere deep inside, some part of her caring still lived? Was it just a cruelly lucky guess, or had he seen it in her eyes, felt it in her actions? And why had he felt compelled to taunt her with it? Tears welled in her eyes, and she impatiently wiped them away. She couldn't control her emotions any better than she could her situation. She wished she hated him with every fiber of her being. She wished just as strongly that she was safely back home in Florida. But they were futile wishes. Everything she did was futile.

When they rounded the last bend and saw the tiny village before them, Brenna gave a sigh of relief. The seat was hard, the road barely passable in places, and the truck had no shock absorbers. After six hours, she wasn't sure she could have taken much more. The parts of her body that weren't numb ached from the steady jolting. Even after the driver stopped at the end of the street, she felt a tingling all over.

The men climbed out of the truck, and she waited for Andrés to get out so she could. When he didn't move, she turned to examine him. His head was tilted to one side, and beneath the dark glasses, his eyes were closed. She tried without luck to wake him, checked his pulse, then slid out on the driver's side.

José and Diego were waiting for her. As she circled the truck to Andrés's side, they followed. "Go and get Vicente," she requested as she opened the door, knowing full well they couldn't understand her.

But one of them seemed to guess what she wanted—was it José, she wondered, or Diego?—and went into the office, returning with Vicente a moment later. "Get the men to help you take him inside," she directed, stepping back out of the way.

"Is he all right?"

Her response was a shrug. "He's suffering from too little sleep, too little food and too much pain. Put him on the bed in my room, then undress him." She watched them leave, supporting Andrés between the three of them, then turned her back on the house, her head bowed, her eyes closed.

She needed to get out of here.

A few days ago she had listed to herself all the reasons why escape was out of the question. Now she listed the one reason why it was imperative: Andrés. The longer she stayed here with him, the deeper she was going to fall in love with him. There were times—few but dear—when he was quiet, likeable, even gentle. Even when he was being cold and cruel, she kept remembering the way he used to be, what had happened, how he had changed. She kept searching for the old tenderness, the old passion, and nothing he did could quite convince her that it no longer, or never, existed.

Her father had ruled out the possibility of a rescue attempt, and he'd said it would take him time to make the arrangements for the trade, so she had to take matters into her own hands. She had to get herself out of here while there was still time. While her heart could still recover.

"We're finished with Andrés, Miss Mathis," Vicente said from behind her.

She turned to look at him and spoke quietly. "I'll get Hector."

That took him by surprise. "Don't you want to look at him?"

"No." She didn't evade his compelling gaze, even though she knew he could see everything she was feeling in her eyes.

Slowly he nodded. "All right."

Hands pushed into her pockets, she turned away, heading for the clinic. Without slowing down she called over her shoulder, "Tell José and Diego where I am." For these next few days, while she made her plans, she wanted everything to remain as usual. She'd made no attempt to slip away from the guards in the first six days; she wanted them to think she never would—until she was ready to escape.

Escape. It would mean freedom, seeing her father again, going home where she was safe. It would mean never seeing Andrés again. After the past six days, she should be pleased at the prospect.

Why then did she feel nothing but sadness?

Chapter 5

The bedroom was shadowed and quiet when Brenna tiptoed in a few hours later. The makeshift curtains had been pulled over the windows, shutting out the afternoon sun and throwing shadows across the bed and the man who lay so still in it.

For just a moment she allowed herself the pleasure of simply looking at him. His eyes were closed, the lines around his mouth relaxed. Even the haggardness caused by exhaustion couldn't diminish the masculine beauty of his face—the strong jaw, the straight nose, the high cheekbones, the sensuous mouth, overshadowed by the full, coarse mustache.

His chest was smooth, not too broad, not too muscular, warm, soft bronze. The new dressing gleamed bright and white against it. There were scars she hadn't noticed last night—one over his ribs, another low on his stomach. The wound on his shoulder would add another when it healed. Souvenirs of a war that would never be forgotten. She was sure he had others. All she had to do was look.

Resolutely she turned away, took her purse from the dresser and left the room. The office outside was empty—Vicente was at dinner with the rest of the men—so she went to the cot under the window, found a position where she could lean against the wall and settled in.

She didn't carry much in her purse, and she was sure they had searched it before returning it to her that first day. She unzipped the small flat bag and began rummaging through it. Her money was still in her wallet, along with her traveler's checks. Her passport was there, too, and her keys, a tube of lipstick, a packet of tissues, a flashlight, a pen and a small pink notebook.

She would take it all with her, she decided as she pulled out the pen and notebook. All of it, with the exception of the lipstick, would come in handy between here and home. Flipping the notebook open to a clean page, she began drawing a rough map of the road to Santiago, including every crossroad and every landmark she could remember. It wasn't very good, she admitted when she'd finished. The distance was about fifty miles, and she hadn't paid very close attention the four times she'd traveled the road.

Still, it was better than nothing. She flipped the notebook shut and returned it and the pen to her purse. Santiago wasn't the wisest choice for a destination, not when she'd been there twice, obviously the prisoner of the rebels who had accompanied her.

But it was her only choice. Andrés had told her that it was the closest town with telephone service, and she had to get to a phone. She could use the money to pay, to bribe, someone to help her, to contact her father and hide her until he could arrive.

Fifty miles. Mentally she began making a list of what she needed. Sturdy shoes for the rugged terrain. The mountain forest would chew up her sandals in no time, but in the bottom of her duffel bag was a pair of heavy leather tennis shoes that would be sufficient. Food and water. Between rest stops and sleeping, she figured she could average two miles an hour, twelve hours a day. That would put her in Santiago within three days, so she needed to steal enough food for that time. Water was no problem, either. Canteens were carelessly left lying on the porches and steps until they were needed again. She could take a couple, then refill them from the numerous streams that rushed down the mountainside.

She would also need a weapon. With a sigh, she drew her knees up and rested her chin on them. She had never used a weapon of any sort against anyone, had never shot or even held a gun, and the idea of slashing into someone else's flesh with a knife made her shudder. Still, she couldn't go wandering off into the forest without some way to protect herself.

Andrés's weapons were kept locked away in the metal cabinet across the room. After studying it for a second, she admitted that she could never pick or break the lock, and she had no idea where he kept the key. The other men never let her close enough to even think of touching their guns or knives. Besides, what good was a gun when she didn't know how to load or fire it? And a survival knife like the men carried was big and, she knew from holding her father's, too heavy and awkward for her to use efficiently. She needed something smaller, lighter, something like a paring knife or even a butcher knife. Something that was readily available to them every day at lunch and dinner.

The sound of footsteps outside the door made her jump. She shoved her purse underneath the worn green blanket that covered the cot just as Vicente entered the office with a dinner tray.

"Make yourself comfortable," he remarked with just an edge of dryness as he brought the tray to her.

"I am." Dinner tonight was thick dark beans with rice, a chunk of cornbread and a piece of fruit, and the only utensil was a spoon. She would have to go to the kitchen tomorrow and get a knife, and as long as she was there, she decided, she might as well consider taking a few cans of C rations, along with one of the miniature can openers, called a John Wayne, that she'd spotted when she was there a few days ago.

Vicente sat down at the desk and watched her eat. "You're not planning to sleep there."

He said it flatly, not questioning, as if he knew she wouldn't be so foolish. She smiled sweetly. "I'm certainly not planning to sleep in my bed. Someone's in it."

"You can't spend the night out here."

"Afraid I'll try to escape?" She laughed at the amusement in his look. "I'm afraid outdoor bathroom facilities and no electricity are about as rough as I can stand it. I don't sleep on the ground, I don't commune with nature, and I don't like bugs."

She saw that he had no difficulty believing her. Was she so obviously a city-bred woman? He would be surprised when she *did* escape, when she showed that she was strong enough and independent enough to take whatever steps were necessary for survival. They would all be surprised, even Andrés.

Casually she turned the conversation away from the topic of escape. "Where did you learn to speak English?"

He took a long time to answer, and when he did, he told her nothing. "In school. When you were forced to study a foreign language back in high school, you should have chosen Spanish."

"I did," she retorted. "But if I'd known that someday I would be held prisoner in a Spanish-speaking country, I would have paid more attention."

Picking up the fruit from her tray, she tossed it back and forth between her hands. If she kept it, he would think she was saving it for a later snack. He wouldn't know until later, she thought with a secretive smile, how right he'd been. "Where was this school where you learned to speak perfect English?"

This time he refused to answer her. He was awfully touchy about his background, and it made her idly curious. She could understand not wanting to talk about his family, especially if they were dead, but where he'd gone to school could hardly be a sensitive subject. Was he hiding something? "How long have you known Andrés?"

"A few years." Impatiently he rose from his seat and walked to the front windows. "He's the best leader our people could ask for. Without him, they would give up. They believe in him, and he's made them believe in themselves. He's given them hope. That's something they haven't had in a great many years." He started to leave, then stopped to look at Brenna again. "You can sleep where you are. Another guard will be posted outside the door. Good night."

How nice of Andrés, Brenna thought bitterly as she set her dishes onto the floor, then settled in on the cot. He gave his people hope. All he'd ever given *her* was heartache and sadness…but not anymore. She was taking her life into her own hands. From now *she*—not Andrés and not her father—would be responsible for herself.

When he woke up the next morning, Andrés was hungry, thirsty, and, in spite of the stiffness in his shoulder and arm, more rested than he'd felt in months. He lay motionless in the silence, trying to remember where he was and how he had gotten there. Where was easy enough; he'd spent enough nights in this bed, in this room, in the past six years to place it instantly. How he had gotten there was another question. The last time he'd been in this room, the bed had been occupied by Brenna, lying on her back, legs apart, arms flung wide, hair tumbled every which way over his pillow, and looking incredibly sexy and beautiful and precious.

He had awakened her, and they had climbed into the truck for the drive to Santiago. Yes, the trip to Santiago, that would explain how he'd ended up in this bed with no memory of getting there. The trip had almost accomplished what all of Romero's soldiers couldn't: it had very nearly killed him, or at least, had felt as if it might.

Where had Brenna slept last night, he fretted, and who had guarded her? She should have been here, in her bed, where he knew she was safe. He'd slept so soundly that he wouldn't have minded being on the cot.

He heard movement in the outer room; then the door swung open to admit Vicente. "Hector says you're to stay in bed all day, so I've brought your breakfast."

The bowl of thick corn mush all but erased his appetite, but Andrés knew he had to eat to get better, so he awkwardly picked up the spoon with his left hand and dipped it into the food. "Is this what everyone got for breakfast, or Manuel's idea of health food?"

"That's all yours, although ours wasn't much better." Vicente left for a moment, then returned with a chair from the office. "How do you feel?"

"All right." He paused a moment, then amended that. "Still pretty ragged. Is there anything going on I should know about?"

Vicente hesitated a long moment, then said, "We got word of a prisoner transfer scheduled to take place in a few days in the copper district." He saw the flare of hope in his friend's eyes and reluctantly doused it. "Esai isn't included. But it's a chance to free a few of our men, to make the army look bad once again. I thought I would take about forty of the men and see if we could stir up a little trouble."

Andrés nodded slowly. He wished he could go along, wished that the information that excluded Esai was incorrect, wished that he could free his cousin and end this entire mess now. But he was smart enough to realize that, until his shoulder healed, he would be of little help to anyone. Any attempt to fire his pistol or his rifle right now would be painful and inaccurate, at best. "Get some medical supplies from Hector—whatever he thinks would be most helpful."

"I'll leave Javier here to help out until you're feeling better. We'll go this afternoon." He stood up, the legs of the chair scraping across the floor.

Andrés hesitated, then, his voice soft, asked, "Where is Brenna?"

"Doing her laundry at the stream."

"What did she say about my shoulder when she changed the bandage yesterday?"

"She didn't change it—Hector did. He said it looks good, that it should be healed in another ten or twelve days. There won't be any permanent damage." Vicente paused. "Do you need anything?"

"No." Andrés settled back against the pillows and closed his eyes. "See me before you go."

So Brenna had refused to change his dressing. Because she was afraid to get that close? Because she was still angry? Or because she hated him? It was probably a little of all three. She was confused by her feelings, confused by *him*, and he could do nothing to help her. He had to continue to threaten her, to remain cold to her, not so much for the success of their plan as for her own safety. She was too beautiful, too gentle, too loving, and he needed her too much. They had no chance of a future, and if he took what he wanted in the present, she would suffer. As long as he acted like a bastard to her, she would go home hating him. Hatred and anger would be far easier for her to deal with than heartache.

"You look as though you're in pain."

Andrés didn't open his eyes at the sound of Hector's unfailingly cheerful voice. "My shoulder is fine."

"Who said anything about your shoulder?" The doctor busied himself with removing the bandage and replacing it with a fresh one. "The kind of pain you're feeling isn't the kind a doctor can treat, is it? We can put broken bodies back together, and we can take people who have died and bring them back to life, but we never have learned what to do for a broken heart."

"My heart is healthy and strong," Andrés said, deliberately misunderstanding him. "Your only job is to make my shoulder strong again."

"A job that I gave to the American. What kind of patient are you that after only two days she has refused to even change your dressing?"

"Maybe she's squeamish."

"Maybe she's afraid."

Andrés looked sharply at him, his dark eyes desolate. "She has to be afraid of me."

Hector chuckled good-naturedly. "Who's talking about you? Maybe she's afraid of the situation she finds herself in. Maybe she's afraid of herself and her past with you."

"Did she tell you that?"

"No. I watch people. I see the way she acts when you're around, and when you're not around. I watch you, too, and that gives me all the answers I need."

The doctor finished, and Andrés tentatively moved his arm. The joint was still stiff, the movement painful but bearable. "I'll be glad when she's gone," he said fiercely.

"Yes, I think in a way you will be," Hector remarked as he got to his feet. "Then you can be alone and empty again. Then you can go back to giving so much of yourself to this war and your people that nothing remains for you. Then you can quit being a man, a human being with faults and flaws and feelings, and you can be a soldier." He gave the last word a sardonic twist. "Stay in bed the rest of the day. Javier is in the office. If you need him, shout."

He had many needs, Andrés thought, settling down in the bed again, and not one of them could be filled by Javier.

Doing laundry by hand in a stream was an interesting experience, Brenna decided, rubbing her hands together to warm them. Fed by snowmelt from the higher elevations, the stream rushed through the minicanyon it had carved into the mountainside, tumbling over rocks, further eroding the sides. She'd almost lost a handful of clothes in the swift current and had succeeded in giving herself an icy bath before she was done.

After wrapping the clothes in a towel, she carried the bundle back to the village, flanked by the two guards, who had been thoroughly entertained by her efforts. There, rather than turn to Andrés, Vicente or Hector for help, she pantomimed her desire for a clothesline. One of the men found a reasonably clean cord and strung it between two trees behind her quarters, and Brenna carefully hung the clothes over it. It wasn't the local Laundromat, but at least they were clean, she thought, surveying them with satisfaction, and she had done it on her own.

She managed to avoid returning to the house and facing Andrés until late that evening. She helped Hector tend to the patients and watched Vicente and his men prepare to leave. She was standing on the steps of the clinic when they climbed into the trucks and drove away. Where were they going this time, she wondered, and who would come back, injured or dying or already dead? She doubted she would be around to find out.

She ate dinner with her guards and found that the men seemed used to her presence now. The first time she had joined them for a meal she had been the object of speculative gazes, curious stares and open hostility. After seven days they seemed to accept that, for the time being, she was a part of their village. They paid her little attention, but that suited her fine. The less attention she received, the easier it would be to slip away.

It would take another day or two to get everything together. Her plan was almost too simple to deserve the name: she would wait until the middle of the night, when the village was quiet and the two guards outside her windows were made less watchful by the silence, the darkness and the boredom. Andrés was a sound sleeper; he wouldn't rouse as she made her way through his office.

Once she was outside, it would be a simple matter to slip through the village, relying on moon shadow to hide her. For the first few miles she would follow the road so she could place as much distance as possible between herself and the camp before her absence was discovered. By dawn she would be forced into the forest that lined both sides of the road, and she would have to evade the search parties that she was certain Andrés would send after her, so she would be slowed down. Still, with luck, determination and courage, she could make it to Santiago. She *had* to make it.

The temperature dropped with the setting of the sun, but Brenna remained on the bench, toying with the small knife she'd picked up with her silverware. Most of the men had wandered off to get ready for bed or to sit in quiet groups of two or three and smoke their cigarettes, but José and Diego remained faithfully with her, waiting for her to return to her quarters so they could turn the evening watch over to their replacements. She couldn't take the knife now. Maybe tomorrow, she thought with a sigh, dropping the knife and picking up the fruit instead.

After taking her laundry off the rope line, she bade good-night to her guards and went inside. The front room was dark, but she could make out two forms at the desk—Andrés and one of his men. Stiffly, feeling his gaze in spite of the darkness, she made her way into the bedroom, closing the door with a shove of her foot.

She was going to great lengths to avoid him, Andrés thought, his mind drifting from his conversation with Javier. Well, wasn't that what he wanted? Wasn't that why he'd treated her the way he had for the past week? So why wasn't he satisfied?

Maybe he should move her into other quarters. There was a small room in Hector's clinic, used for storage now but big enough to hold a cot and a small table. There was room for her in Vicente's quarters, too—Esai's room had lain undisturbed since his capture—but with a grim frown, Andrés crossed both off the list of possibilities. He didn't want her in other quarters, didn't want her sharing a house with Hector and his patients, or with Vicente, or with anyone else but him. Simply moving her, he admitted, wouldn't solve his problem. Nothing would.

"You knew her before, didn't you?" Javier asked.

Andrés's smile was troubled and weary. "Yes, a long time ago. Back when the world was normal and sane."

"It'll be that way again."

"Will it? I used to think so. I thought the war would last a year, two years, maybe even three, and then things would get better. Now I wonder if it will ever end."

"If it had ended after a year or two or three, you would have gone back to her."

"Yes. If she'd been willing to have me."

"And when it ends now?"

Andrés tilted his head back and stared up at the shadowy ceiling. "I stood a chance before...a small one, maybe, but still a chance. Now..." He shook his head. "If we win the war, I'll stay here in the village, take up farming again. If we lose, I'll be executed as an enemy of the government."

Javier struck a match on the underside of the table, then lit his cigarette. "She's a compassionate woman. She's kind and gentle with the wounded. If she spoke our language, she would be friendly with everyone. Maybe she'll surprise you. Maybe she'll understand."

"I'm sure she will." Andrés rubbed absently at the tape that secured the bandage to his skin. "But all the understanding in the world means nothing without forgiveness." And that was the one thing in the world Brenna would never offer him. Compassion, kindness, gentleness, friendliness—as Javier had said, she offered those to everyone, including him. But she would never forgive him for threatening her, or for leaving her all those years ago, and he would never forgive himself.

"I'm tired," he said, rising slowly from his seat. "Take care of things in the morning. I think I'll rest while I can."

Javier murmured agreement and left the office, closing the screen door quietly behind him.

Andrés walked to the cot, his hands at his waist to undo the buttons of his trousers. After a moment's hesitation, he went to the bedroom door, twisting the knob and pushing it open.

Brenna was bending over the bed, folding her clothes, smoothing the wrinkles from them the best that she could. She heard the door's faint squeak, and the muscles tensing in her neck and jaw warned her of Andrés's presence. Only another day or two, she reminded herself. Then she would be on her way to Santiago and safety.

His bare feet made no sound as he crossed the room to the nightstand. Striking a match, he lifted the globe off the lamp and held the flame to the black wick. It flared to life, giving off a thick black smoke that quickly disappeared. He replaced the globe, adjusted the wick, then moved to the opposite side of the bed. There he leaned on the windowsill, facing Brenna, watching her work.

"I know I told you to conserve fuel, but that doesn't mean you have to work in the dark."

"There's enough moonlight to see what I'm doing."

She continued to fold clothes without looking at him, stacking them neatly—shorts, shirts, delicate bras and tiny panties. Her hair looked more golden than brown in the lamplight, and her skin gleamed warm and soft. He longed to reach out to her but instead folded his arms over his chest, forcing his hands flat against his ribs. "You kept busy today."

"I had things to do."

"What things?"

"Tending the patients."

"What about *this* patient? Couldn't you spare a little of your time and compassion for me?"

Finished with her task, Brenna straightened and, like him, folded her arms over her chest. The sarcasm in his voice was faint, almost an afterthought, but sharp enough to set her nerves on edge. "If it's company you want, get it from your men. If it's compassion...well, I'm fresh out of that. You'll have to get that from your men, too."

His smile came quickly and faded slowly. "You're a hard woman."

"And you're a cold bastard."

She picked up the stacks of clothing and carried them to the dresser, dumping them carelessly into the top drawer. So she had finally unpacked, Andrés thought, noticing that the duffel bag and her purse were missing from the spot they'd occupied for a week. She was finally starting to accept that her father wasn't going to ride in on a white horse and rescue her. In his army training Andrés had learned the stages hostages go through in coping with their captivity: denial that they could be taken prisoner, that their lives could be in danger; delusion that the situation was only temporary, that they would soon be rescued; followed by acceptance and busywork, doing something, anything, to keep their minds off the danger. Brenna was right on track.

She pushed the drawer shut with a bang, then faced him again. "Do you want something?"

Moving away from the windows, he walked toward her, stopping only a foot away. "Don't ask leading questions, Brenna, unless you're prepared to hear the answers," he warned her softly.

She flushed with equal measures of anger and discomfort. "Get out of my room," she ordered, her voice low in the charged air. "And in the future, don't come in without an invitation."

"It's my room, my quarters, my village, my country. I don't have to wait for an invitation. I'm in control here. I go where I please."

She hated it when he taunted her, because it was a constant reminder of the man he was... and the man he swore he had never been. "I hope you go to hell!"

His mocking look was gone before the last word left her mouth. His face could have been carved in granite for all the emotion it revealed, and his eyes were hard, dark ice. "After the last six years," he said deliberately, "hell would be a picnic."

The words stunned her with their force. She stood there, still feeling the depth of the anger and sorrow they contained, long after the door closed behind him. Then, feeling as if her strength had drained away, she blew out the lamp, sank down onto the bed and cried—for Andrés and all that he had lost, but mostly for herself and all that *she* had lost. Her love, her dreams, even her memories. He'd left her nothing to cherish.

He'd left her nothing at all.

Monday was another long, empty day for Andrés. Brenna was still avoiding him, spending the entire day with Hector and his patients, eating her meals with José and Diego, staying away from their quarters—and from *him*, Andrés admitted glumly—until the sun had gone down and the night's chill had settled over the village. When she did come inside, she didn't look at or speak to him but continued past him as if he didn't exist.

Maybe he didn't, for her at least. Hostages had to call upon whatever coping mechanisms their minds could supply for survival. Nursing the patients provided her with a sense of normalcy, familiar tasks that matched her routine at home, and shutting out Andrés provided her with some sense of power, of control over a life that was largely out of her control. By ignoring him, she didn't have to deal with the memories of a past love, didn't have to handle the present bitterness and hatred. By ignoring him, she could cope.

And she made things easier for him. He didn't need to be looking at her or thinking about her or talking to her. He had an army, ragged and ill equipped as it was, to run. Once Vicente returned with the prisoners, they would step up their raids against the government troops—raids that he had to plan. He had to work out the details of the prisoner exchange—had to find a safe location where no ambush could be set up, where no double-cross could succeed. He had to set a date and a time, had to choose the men who would accompany him and Brenna, the men who would see Esai safely back to camp. He had to contact his informants in Santa Lucia, had to step up the surveillance on Tom and his men to be sure that nothing went wrong. He couldn't do any of those things with Brenna around, making him feel and want, worry and love.

Yes, she was doing him a favor by ignoring him, he knew that with his head. He sighed wearily as he prepared for bed. It was his heart that needed convincing.

It was time.

Brenna stood motionless beside the bed, mentally going over her plan. She was dressed in tennis shoes, thick socks, khaki trousers and a long-sleeved white shirt. She took a moment to wish for more concealing clothing—when the moon came out from behind the clouds, her white shirt would be as visible as a beacon—but she hadn't packed for an escape attempt. All her shirts were light colored.

There were a half-dozen pieces of fruit in her duffel bag, along with her purse. Her first stop would be the kitchen, for food and a knife; then she would sneak a few canteens from the nearest porch. She could fill them at the stream where she'd washed her clothing, before setting off down the road. There were plenty of other streams between here and Santiago where they could be refilled.

She breathed in deeply, then out. The exhalation sounded loud in her ears. On tiptoe she walked to the window and searched for her guard. He was sitting underneath the tree, an indistinct blur in the shadow, his head bent low. On the other side of the house the other guard was sitting, too, his arms crossed over his chest, holding his rifle close. She couldn't tell if he was asleep or awake. But it didn't matter. It was time to go.

She picked up the duffel bag, letting it dangle from its long nylon strap. The only thing she needed right away, to find the needed supplies in the kitchen, was the tiny penlight she had kept in her purse; it was safe in her pocket.

Her hands were clammy, and her breathing seemed labored. After eight days of waiting like a helpless woman for some brave man to save her, she was taking matters into her own hands and leaving the room that suddenly seemed so secure, wandering off into mountain forests for a fifty-mile hike to possible safety. Or possible death, if she got lost, or fell down one of the steep canyons, or met up with some wild animal or, worse, a man.

Still on tiptoe, she went to the door and opened it. The creak of the hinges sounded painfully loud to her, but rationally she knew it was just the normal, soft little creak. She stepped through the door, her gaze shifting immediately to the cot where Andrés lay.

She would never see him again. The thought was as sharp as a blade, and she squeezed her eyes shut on it. She had gone through this six years ago, and it had almost destroyed her. This time the leaving was her choice, but it was still painful. There were still memories, sweet and tender, of what they'd once shared...of what she'd *thought* they'd shared. There was still that part of her heart that wanted to believe it had been real, that he had cared for her, that she had meant *something* to him, even though he'd made it achingly clear that none of it was true.

"Can't you sleep?"

She started and quickly moved the bag behind her back, hoping he couldn't see it in the darkness. "I—I was going—" She swallowed hard to calm her voice. "I was going outside to sit on the porch. It's a pretty night."

"Sit here...talk to me instead." He shifted on the cot, propping his left arm under his head. He wasn't completely awake, his eyes still heavy with sleep, his voice soft and husky.

Brenna searched for a reason to refuse, then admitted that she didn't want to. She was leaving soon, and she would never see him again; what could a few minutes' conversation hurt?

Bending her knees slightly, she settled the duffel bag onto the floor just inside the bedroom door, then walked casually to the chair next to the desk. After carrying it across the room to his bedside, she sat down, her hands folded tightly in her lap. "What do you want to talk about?"

Her tone was guarded, her posture stiff and erect, distancing. Andrés smiled faintly. "Do you think for a few minutes you could forget that you're my prisoner?"

"Forget? When you've spent eight days reminding me?"

"You have a smart mouth, you know that?" With a grimace, he sat up, bracing his back against the rough wall, drawing the sheet to his waist. The moonlight streaming through the open window touched the dressing on his shoulder, drawing Brenna's gaze.

"Does it still hurt?" she asked grudgingly.

He glanced down at the bandage. "Some. Hector says it's showing good granulation—his way of saying that it's healing."

"It will take another two weeks or so to heal completely. Then you'll be able to go out and kill some more soldiers."

"I wish I'd never have to kill anyone again."

She bit her lip. She hadn't meant to sound so sarcastic. She knew he didn't enjoy killing. No matter what other changes the war had brought about, he still had a strong sense of honor. He would never choose to hurt anyone, but he might be forced into it. "How long are you willing to fight? How long will your people continue to die for what you believe in?"

"What we all believe in, Brenna. These people don't follow me, they follow their dreams. They've never experienced the kind of freedom you take for granted. They want to know what it's like to speak out against the government without disappearing in the middle of the night, never to be seen again. They want to be able to cast their votes at election time and know that the majority rules, that the election is valid, that the ballot boxes aren't stuffed by the very people they're voting against. They want to support their families, to give them a home, food to eat, hope for the future." His voice dropped lower, becoming more impassioned. "They want to live without fear."

"Nobody lives free of fear," she scoffed in a vain attempt to harden herself against him.

"You do. Until you came here, you had never known one moment's fear for your life. If you get married, you'll know that your husband will come home to you every night, that he won't suddenly disappear because he made the wrong person angry or because he was bold and foolish enough to speak out against injustice. If you have children, you'll know that the chances are very good that they'll live to die of old age, not malnutrition, not simple childhood diseases that other countries have long ago cured, and not murder. You can go anywhere, do anything, say anything, and your government and constitution protect you. If you don't like a law, you change it. If you don't like your government, you replace it. You have freedoms that most Angelenos don't even dare dream about."

"You've been fighting for six years. Are you any closer to winning now than you were when you started?"

"I don't know."

"How many thousands have died?"

He shook his head, not caring whether she saw in the dim light or not. Figures were impossible to come by, just generalizations. Many. Too many.

"How many more will have to die before you give up?"

He was silent for a long time. "I won't give up until we have won ... or I am dead."

"And you *will* die." Brenna leaned forward in the hard wooden chair. "If you continue to fight, your luck's going to run out, and you'll die. If you lose the war, the army will kill you."

"Or maybe my luck will hold. Maybe we'll win the war and I'll die an old man, surrounded by my grandchildren." He shrugged cynically. "I have no say in what happens to me. I don't control my life any more than you control yours."

She shook her head mournfully. "You made your choice, Andrés. You could have stayed in Florida—with or without me—and finished your training, but you chose to come here and fight."

"Remaining would have given me only a brief reprieve. The government ended the training program less than six months later and ordered all the troops home." He didn't comment on the fact that, if he had stayed, he could have married Brenna. He could have joined the American military at a lower rank but a much higher salary and lived a life of luxury compared to what he'd known at home. He could have avoided the war altogether, living happily, safely, while his family and friends and countrymen were being butchered. He could have had Brenna, but he would have lost everything else—his self-respect, his courage, his honor. Sometimes he thought it wouldn't have been a bad trade-off. Most of the time, though, he knew he couldn't have lived with himself, and although she would have denied it then, neither could Brenna. She would have hated him, and he would have hated himself.

"What have you done in the last six years?" he asked, raising one sheet-draped knee and resting his arm on it. "You finished college and got a job."

"Yes. I graduated a month after you left."

"Do you work in pediatrics?"

She stared down at her hands. That had been her plan, back when she was foolishly young and in love—to work on the pediatric ward, caring for other people's children, until she had her own. They were all going to be adorable, with their father's dark hair and darker eyes. "No," she responded. "I work on the surgery floor."

He didn't ask what had changed her mind, because he was afraid he knew the answer. How many ways had he changed her? How many ways had he hurt her? "I wish things had been different," he murmured, more to himself than her.

"So do I. I wish I'd never heard of San Angelo, and I wish I'd never heard of you." But even as she said it, she knew it wasn't true. In spite of the pain he'd caused her, he had also enriched her life. He had taught her what it meant to love.

Andrés leaned forward, touching his hand to hers. "I never wanted to hurt you, Brenna," he whispered. God, he had *loved* her, had dreamed for six years of nothing but her.

She shrugged, refusing to let the low shiver of emotion in his voice touch her. "Looking back, it's pretty clear what you did and didn't want." He'd wanted a woman for companionship and sex, and he'd wanted to please her father. What he hadn't wanted was permanence, love. What he hadn't wanted was *her*. "But it doesn't matter anymore. What happened in the past can't be changed, but it can be learned from. It taught me to judge more carefully. It taught me not to make the same mistakes twice."

And she thought that loving him was the biggest mistake she'd ever made. Andrés could read that in the careless tone of her voice, in the slack feel of her hand beneath his. She was telling him that she would never make that mistake

again, just reinforcing what he already knew, but it hurt.
God help him, it hurt.

"Maybe you've learned too well," he said, emptying all
emotion from his expression. "You're nearly thirty years
old. Most of your friends are married now, aren't they? And
some of them are starting their families. But you're still
alone."

She shifted uncomfortably on the chair. "Maybe I prefer
it that way."

"You prefer the idea of growing old alone and childless
over the idea of trusting and loving and sharing your life
with a man?"

Restlessly she pulled away from him and paced across the
room. "I'll get married someday, and I'll have children. I'm
just waiting."

"For what? Until you give up the idea of love and can
settle for someone you tolerate instead?"

She leaned against his desk, one ankle crossed over the
other, arms folded defensively over her chest. "What are
you getting at, Andrés? You think I'm still in love with you?
Is your ego so overwhelming that you think I could still love
you after everything you've done to me?" She shook her
head, the golden brown strands of her hair catching and re-
flecting the moonlight. "Well, you're wrong," she lied.
"What I felt for you ended a long time ago. I haven't stayed
single because of you. I'm not still mourning for lost love.
I'm waiting for the right man, and I haven't met him yet.
And if I never meet him, I'll have my children anyway.
There's no shortage of men willing to father a child, then
walking away from their responsibilities."

"And you would be happy that way—just you and your
fatherless baby?"

Gathering courage, she returned to the chair. "Yes, I
could be."

He studied her for a long time in the dim light, then shook
his head. "I don't believe you."

"Well, you know what, Andrés? What you believe doesn't matter. It has no bearing on my life."

He leaned forward and this time curled his fingers around her hand. "You wouldn't be happy like that. You need someone to love—a man. You need a man to love you."

She concentrated on keeping her hand limp, on concealing the tension that streaked through her every time he touched her. "I have my father, and someday I'll have my children. That's more than a lot of people have. That's more than you have."

"But I want more." Unexpectedly he tugged on her hand, pulling her out of the chair and, off balance, onto the cot. He braced her with his hands on her shoulders, holding her only inches from his chest. "I want a hell of a lot more," he murmured, his breath warm and moist against her mouth.

She knew he was going to kiss her, but she was too stunned, too startled—too hungry, her conscience whispered—to stop him. Instead she remained motionless, caught in a web of longing.

He slid his left hand into her hair, twisting it until thick strands of soft hair trapped him as surely as she'd trapped his heart so long ago. Then he kissed her.

He tasted sweet and hot as his tongue boldly pushed its way into her mouth, stroking, thrusting, arousing, making her needy. She whimpered softly deep in her throat, and he immediately gentled his touch, but that wasn't what she wanted. She wanted more, anything, everything. She wanted to fill the emptiness inside herself, wanted to satisfy the yearning that sent shivers of pain through her. She wanted Andrés.

He guided her still closer, until her breasts were flattened against his chest, until her belly rubbed his, until her hips cradled the heated fullness of his desire. He was dying—his heart pounding, his blood rushing, his lungs crying out for air—but he didn't care. There were worse ways to die than with the only woman he had ever loved.

Slowly he freed his mouth, raising her face with the tender pressure of his hand. For a long moment, eyes only inches apart, they stared at each other, his hunger and her need clearly visible. He could seduce her, or she could seduce him, and they could spend the rest of the night loving. But it wouldn't change anything. Come tomorrow she would still be his prisoner, determined to hate him, and he would still be her captor, unable to let himself love her.

His sigh, weary, sad, accepting, broke the spell. Brenna scrambled to her feet and, her eyes wide, her breathing ragged, stared down at him. He waited for her curses, for her heartless command that he never touch her again, but they didn't come. With a cry—of anger, frustration, sorrow?—she rushed into her room, closing the door securely behind her.

Slowly he slid down on the bed, pulling the sheet to his shoulders, covering his eyes with one arm. One kiss. It wasn't much, but it would have to be enough.

Incredible, isn't it? Deal yourself in right now and get 6 fabulous gifts ABSOLUTELY FREE.

1. 4 BRAND NEW SILHOUETTE INTIMATE MOMENTS® NOVELS—FREE!

Sit back and enjoy the excitement, romance and thrills of four fantastic novels. You'll receive them as part of this winning streak!

2. A LOVELY GOLD-PLATED CHAIN—

FREE! You'll love your elegant 20k gold electro-plated chain! The necklace is finely crafted with 160 double-soldered links and it's electroplate finished in genuine 20k gold. And it's yours free as added thanks for giving our Reader Service a try!

3. AN EXCITING MYSTERY BONUS—FREE!

And still your luck holds! You'll also receive a special mystery bonus. You'll be thrilled with this surprise gift. It is useful as well as practical.

PLUS

THERE'S MORE. THE DECK IS STACKED IN YOUR FAVOR. HERE ARE THREE MORE WINNING POINTS. YOU'LL ALSO RECEIVE:

4. FREE HOME DELIVERY

Imagine how you'll enjoy having the chance to preview the romantic adventures of our Silhouette heroines in the convenience of your own home! Here's how it works. Every month we'll deliver 4 new Silhouette Intimate Moments® novels right to your door. There's no obligation to buy, and if you decide to keep them, they'll be yours for only $2.74 * each—that's a saving of 21¢ per book! And there's no charge for postage and handling — there are no hidden extras!

5. A MONTHLY NEWSLETTER—FREE!

It's our special *"Silhouette" Newsletter* your privileged look at upcoming books and profiles of our most popular authors.

6. MORE GIFTS FROM TIME TO TIME—FREE!

It's easy to see why you have the winning hand. In addition to all the other special deals available only to our home subscribers, when you join the Silhouette Reader Service™, you can look forward to additional free gifts throughout the year.

SO DEAL YOURSELF IN – YOU CAN'T HELP BUT WIN!

You'll Fall In Love
With This Sweetheart Deal
From Silhouette!

SILHOUETTE READER SERVICE™
FREE OFFER CARD

PLACE
YOUR
WINNING
CARD
HERE!

4 FREE BOOKS • FREE GOLD-PLATED CHAIN •
FREE MYSTERY BONUS • FREE HOME DELIVERY •
INSIDER'S NEWSLETTER • MORE SURPRISE GIFTS

*YES! Deal me in. Please send me four free Silhouette Intimate Moments®
novels, the gold-plated chain and my free mystery bonus as explained on
the opposite page. If I'm not fully satisfied I can cancel at any time but if I
choose to continue in the Reader Service I'll pay the low members-only price
each month.*

240 CIS YAD6
(U-SIL-IM-06/90)

First Name		Last Name	
PLEASE PRINT			
Address			Apt.
City	State	Zip Code	

Offer limited to one per household and not valid to current Silhouette Intimate Moments® subscribers.
Orders subject to approval.

SILHOUETTE® NO RISK GUARANTEE

- There is no obligation to buy – the free books and gifts remain yours to keep.
- You'll receive books before they're available in stores.
- You may end your subscription at any time—by sending us a note or a shipping statement marked "cancel" or by returning any shipment to us at our cost.

Remember! To win this hand, all you have to do is place your sticker inside and DETACH AND MAIL THE CARD BELOW. You'll get four free books, a free gold-plated chain and a mystery bonus.

**BUT DON'T DELAY!
MAIL US YOUR LUCKY CARD TODAY!**

Chapter 6

According to the clock on the nightstand it was two o'clock. Huddled in a tight ball on the floor, Brenna listened hard to the village and heard only the eerie silence of sleep, of vulnerability. At this hour the men slept their deepest, storing up strength and courage for the new day that would face them in a few hours. If she didn't go now she would have to wait until tomorrow night, would have to spend another long day in the village, reliving Andrés's kiss, aching deep inside for more.

Slowly she got to her feet. The bright flash of white in the mirror made her wish once more for a dark shirt, something with long sleeves that would hide her in the night and keep her warm against the chill. Something like the jackets in Andrés's drawer.

Easing the drawer out, she counted the folded jackets. There was one more in the camouflage material than in the solid green. She took the top one, sliding her arms into the too-long sleeves, folding back the extra fabric, fastening up the buttons. It covered her from chin to thigh, hiding her shirt and a good portion of her trousers. She felt like a child playing dress-up in Daddy's uniform, but this was no game. Her heart and her sanity, not to mention her life, were at stake.

Opening the door between their rooms just a few inches, she peered through the gap until she made out Andrés's form in the bed. He had rolled onto his stomach, his arm cushioning his head, his pillow supporting and protecting his wounded shoulder. His breathing was slow, steady, deep. Slinging the duffel bag over her shoulder, she slipped through the door, leaving it open, and crossed the room, easing out the screen door.

She stood in the shadows of the porch until clouds passed over the moon, then moved down the steps and across to the nearest building on the right. Safe in the darkness, she could see one of her guards, arms still wrapped tightly around his gun. Listening to her heart pounding in her ears, she slipped around the building, moving cautiously toward the kitchen. There she gathered cans of food, bypassing their regular stores of meat, fruit and vegetables and taking instead the seldom-used C rations—small dark green cans containing such dishes as beans and wieners, beef and potatoes, spaghetti and meatballs. Not too tasty, according to her father, but filling and reasonably nutritious. With the aid of her penlight she located a small cardboard box of can openers and took one, then, as a precaution, pocketed a half dozen more. A lot of good the canned food would do her if she lost her only opener. She also took two knives for protection, sliding one inside her duffel and tucking the other into one of the jacket's roomy pockets, and a spoon to eat with.

Her bag was getting heavy, she thought as she added a few more pieces of fruit. She would have a backache within an hour, but she needed every ounce. At least it would get lighter with each meal. Now all she needed was a couple of canteens, and she would be on her way.

Checking cautiously for signs of her guards, she left the kitchen, laid her pack on the ground and circled to the front of the building. There, hanging from their straps on a nail in the corner post of the porch, were nearly a dozen canteens. She took two, holding them in one hand, judging their weight, their capacity. Water weighed seven and a half pounds a gallon, she recalled, which meant the lightweight canteens, filled to the brim, would add only a few more pounds to her burden. Reaching up on tiptoe, she took one more, then stealthily made her way back to her duffel.

Although she knew there were guards in the village at night, she had no idea how many or where they were stationed. Since she needed to find the stream anyway, she headed directly into the woods, feeling her way with her hands and feet and using what little light the moon occasionally offered.

She heard the rushing water long before she saw it. Carefully she knelt on a rock at the edge and leaned over, dipping each canteen underneath the surface to fill it. After tightening the lids, she put two into her duffel and hung the third by its strap over her shoulder.

Now she had to find the road.

She stumbled through the forest, careful to keep the sounds of the swift-flowing creek on her right. If she didn't get turned around in the darkness, the stream would lead her to the bend in the road, out of sight of the camp, and then she would be truly on her way.

She was already feeling the weight of her supplies when she reached the road. It led away, a narrow ribbon of sandy brown against the dark green of the forest. With a surge of adrenaline rushing through her, Brenna moved to one side of the road, where the dirt was hard packed but not rutted, and broke into a trot.

She was free—not out of danger, she admitted, but *free*—and she'd done it on her own. She was euphoric, feeling as if she could run all the way to Santiago, as if now that she'd taken this first big step, nothing could go wrong for her.

But the emotional high didn't last long, and the adrenaline rush faded even quicker. She wasn't in shape for this. Her breathing was rough, quick uneven gasps of air entering her lungs that couldn't expand, couldn't fill. The altitude, she realized, grinding out a savage curse. In all her smug little plans, she hadn't considered the difference in altitude between San Angelo—the entire country lay between four and six thousand feet—and Orlando, barely a hundred feet above sea level. She'd expended so little physical energy in the village that she hadn't really experienced the effects of altitude.

Now she was feeling them full force. Her steps slowed until her pace was no more than a rapid walk. Her lungs hurt, her back ached, and her legs felt as if they were weighted with lead. She forced herself to breathe deeply, to place one foot in front of the other over and over, to ignore her body's protests and pleas for rest. She would rest at sunrise, she promised herself.

At sunrise.

Andrés lay in bed, the pillow folded in half beneath his head, his fingers loosely twined and resting on his belly. The door across the room stood open a few inches, which meant that Brenna was already up and had gone to breakfast. Under normal circumstances she wouldn't have been able to slip by him so easily, but there was nothing normal about these circumstances.

He had slept fitfully last night, disturbed by dreams of her, of loving her the way he was meant to. They had been sweet and tormenting at the same time, reminding him of the way they used to be and taunting him that they could never love like that again. Hadn't she said that what she'd felt for him had ended long ago, that she wouldn't make the same mistake again?

He couldn't call anything about their past a mistake, though. Dating her, becoming her lover, loving her—it all had come so naturally to him. His mother had told them all when they were young that love would come to them in its own time and fashion. Moisés had found it with a neighbor's daughter, Martín and Maria with friends from a nearby village. Long after his younger brother and sister were married and raising children, Andrés had remained single, fond of several women but loving none.

Until Brenna. He never would have chosen to fall in love with an American. His home and country were too important to him. How could he ask any woman to give up the very things that he himself would never give up? And he never would have chosen a career woman. No, if he'd had a say in the matter, he would have fallen in love with a local girl, as Moisés and Martín had done, a woman who was satisfied to be his wife and the mother of his children, to keep his house and cook his meals and share his bed.

But he hadn't been given a choice. Love had come in its own time, as his mother had promised, and its own fashion. Then it had ended.

Made restless by his dreams and melancholy by his memories, he forced himself out of the bed. After pulling on the trousers he'd discarded the night before, he went into the bedroom and dressed, glancing only briefly, wistfully, at the unmade bed where Brenna had slept.

There was no sign of her outside when he joined the small group of men who hadn't accompanied Vicente. Considering how eager she had been to avoid him yesterday, he thought dryly, he would be lucky to catch even a glimpse of her today, after last night's kiss.

When the meal was over he held an informal meeting with Javier and Benedicto, discussing the details of the exchange. They would choose a safe place, one that could be guarded easily, one they could leave as easily as they arrived. There he would see Esai for the first time since his capture nearly two weeks ago. There he would say goodbye to Brenna for the last time.

Her name echoed in his thoughts; then he realized that Hector was speaking to him from the clinic steps. "Where is Brenna? She should have been here nearly an hour ago. I need her help with one of the patients."

Andrés looked blankly at him. "She's not with you?"

"Have these last few days off affected your brain?" Hector asked with a good-natured grimace. "If she were with me, I wouldn't be asking where she is."

Swiftly Andrés got to his feet, heading toward his quarters. "She was already gone when I woke up this morning. I just assumed that she was with you. José! Diego!"

Both men jumped up and hurried to the front of the house.

"Where's Brenna?"

They exchanged puzzled glances. "In her room," Diego answered. "Rico said she hadn't come out yet when I relieved him this morning."

"No, she's not." Andrés took the steps two at a time, followed by both guards and, behind them, Hector. He shoved open the bedroom door and jerked open the two dresser drawers he'd emptied for her. The first held her clothes, still in careless piles. The second was empty. Her purse, with its passport and money, and the duffel bag were missing.

He felt his heart thud painfully in his chest, spreading tremors of fear so strong that he could taste it. "My God, she's gone," he whispered.

No one willingly approached him for the next hour. Each bit of bad news added another layer of ice to his already-frozen shell. Both men on the night watch had admitted to dozing off. Another man had discovered several canteens—he wasn't sure how many—missing from the post where he always hung them. Manuel's kitchen had been raided, an unknown quantity of food taken. A few scuffed places were found in the hard dirt at the bend of the road that might or might not be recent, might or might not be footprints.

"At least she went prepared," Hector commented glumly.

Andrés didn't spare a glance for him. "She's going to Santiago."

"That's foolish. It's fifty miles, a three-hour drive. It would take her at least..." Hector considered the varying factors. "Seven days, maybe longer. She can't last that long out there."

Andrés covered his eyes with one hand, squeezing them shut. God, if anything happened to her...! He wouldn't have to wait for Tom Mathis to kill him. His own guilt and grief would do the job for him. "We've got to find her, Hector."

"Maybe she'll come back."

"No. We can't wait around for that possibility. We have to find her." He issued a sharp command to Javier, who was waiting nearby. "Call the men together. I want to talk to them."

Brenna sat on a fallen tree trunk, staring ahead but seeing nothing, hearing nothing but her own labored breathing and the rapid, unsteady beat of her heart. Under the sun's glare she had removed Andrés's jacket and now wore it tied by the sleeves around her shoulders, using the fabric to cushion the pack and canteen. She wore no watch and had left her travel clock on the nightstand, but she estimated from the sun's position that it must be late afternoon.

She'd been gone about fifteen hours, and she had probably traveled less than fifteen miles. She had foolishly estimated two miles an hour, twenty-four miles a day, a twenty-five hour journey. At this rate it would take her at least four days, and she didn't have that much food or water.

Where were all those streams she'd seen from the truck? she wondered numbly. She had already emptied one canteen and half of another to replenish the fluid that she'd sweated out since sunrise. Until she found another water source, she would have to conserve what she had, which could lead quickly and dangerously to dehydration. And *that*, she knew, would kill her.

She was tempted to climb up the steep hill to the road, to find a shady spot and stretch out for a nap. Sooner or later Andrés's men would find her—she had already seen three truckloads of men pass, had already hidden successfully from two search parties. But she resisted the notion. That would mean giving up. It would mean that she wasn't as smart or brave or courageous as she thought. It would mean going back and waiting for her father to save her while Andrés destroyed her.

It would also mean living, she pointed out practically. If she didn't find more water soon, she would die.

But not yet. She knew the water was there, somewhere ahead of her. What if she gave up, only to discover that the stream was just on the other side of this slope?

Slowly she pushed herself to her feet. Her joints protested her brain's command to move, but reluctantly obeyed. She'd started out this morning with long walks broken by short rests. By noon her rest periods had almost equaled the periods of movement. If she didn't give in to her body's exhaustion soon and find a place to spend the night, she would be sitting ten minutes for every five minutes of walking.

She had been a fool. She repeated that to herself as she climbed over a fallen tree, ducked under another, skirted a boulder and slid in the loose soil. She had thought walking through this forest would be like a walk in the park, only with more trees. She hadn't counted on stands of trees so densely packed that they were impenetrable. She hadn't considered the delicate task of climbing down into and up out of the deep, rocky canyons where fast-flowing streams had literally carved out the mountainside before drying up or diverting into new easier beds. She hadn't known about the rock slides that seemed to have come from nowhere, tearing down trees, uprooting shrubs and leaving wide swaths of loose stone that shifted underfoot, threatening her with a sprained ankle or worse.

At least she hadn't run into any animals, she thought, with barely enough energy to be grateful, and the only men she had seen were Andrés's, their faces familiar, even if their names weren't.

Leaning forward, she continued up the hill, circling a large shrub that was taller than she was and whose thorns grabbed at her clothes, skin and hair. She ignored her hunger and especially her thirst and pushed on. She had to make it to the other side, to the valley at the bottom. There she would find a place to spend the night. By the time the sun set and darkness fell, she would be grateful for the jacket she'd stolen, would forget the discomfort of the sun's heat that drenched her in sweat. She would rest her aching body on the hard ground and sleep, not because she was comfortable but because she was exhausted. And tomorrow she would start again, feeling even more miserable than ever.

She had planned to rest, but her feet kept moving. The valley below was narrow, less than a quarter of a mile across, she estimated, and covered with heavy vegetation. She could find a place down there to stop. She had to.

She found her shelter, a shallow ditch bordered on one side by a fallen tree, when she literally stumbled over it. She took off the pack and canteen and dropped them to the ground, then sank beside them. Closing her eyes, she leaned against the tree. In a moment, she told herself, she would see about dinner, water, fixing a bed of some sort.

In a moment...

Andrés stood beside the jeep, staring into the darkness, straining to see, hear or feel *something* that would lead him to Brenna. Every man they could spare had been out all day, combing the area, slowly moving farther away from the village, but the fact that they'd found nothing didn't mean a thing. The forest was so dense that any one of them could have walked within ten feet of her and not seen her.

"Are you ready to go back?"

He gave no sign of hearing Javier's question. A nighttime search was futile. Even if they had flashlights and lanterns powerful enough to light the woods, it would be too dangerous. They would become targets for anyone who happened to be nearby.

Just as Brenna was a target. He closed his eyes but couldn't shut out his anguish. She was out there in the night, alone, probably frightened, and in danger, and it was all his fault. If he hadn't threatened her and tried to scare her, if he had never even considered kidnapping her...

"Andrés?"

Javier had come closer, but Andrés still ignored him. He knew his aide wanted to return to camp, for they were at risk out here alone on the road. The trucks carrying the men had already gone back after the night's darkness had called a halt to the search, but Andrés hadn't been able to leave. How could he go back to the safety of the village when he knew that Brenna was out here?

"We have to go."

Summoning what little inner strength he had left, Andrés turned and climbed into the jeep, bracing himself as Javier swung wide to make a U-turn. As tired as he was, he knew he wouldn't sleep tonight. He would be out here again at dawn tomorrow, and then, he promised himself, he wouldn't leave until she was found.

She had to go back.

Brenna leaned against the nearest tree, spreading her fingers wide over the rough bark. She had finished the second canteen of water this morning and was beginning to feel the effects of dehydration—nausea, dizziness, light-headedness. There would be other symptoms soon—vomiting, weakness, confusion, lethargy. If she found one of those damn streams, she would be all right. If she didn't . . .

She had to go back. So what if it meant admitting failure? Wasn't being alive and Andrés's prisoner better than being dead and free? If she could only make it back to the village. Right now she wasn't even sure which direction to go. She'd gotten confused in the tangled woods and had somehow traveled away from the road. When the sun began its afternoon descent it would give her a clue, but right now it was straight overhead, hot and useless.

She sank to the ground, resting her head on her drawn-up knees. Andrés was going to be really angry with her for this. His men had wasted an entire day looking for her, and now she was going to come dragging back, another patient for his overworked doctor to care for. He wouldn't understand that she'd had to escape, that she'd had to stop herself from falling in love with him again. And he wouldn't care, either.

If she made it safely back to the village she would quit running, quit pretending, quit lying to herself and everyone else, she promised as she closed her eyes to slow the dizzy images whirling in her brain. She would make Andrés understand, would make him forgive her.

She smiled drowsily. She would make him love her.

She was in that hazy place halfway between sleep and wakefulness when slowly she lifted her head and looked around, a curious expression on her face. She smelled the smoke of a fire, and it wasn't far away. The aroma of the food being cooked—fish, she thought, wrinkling her nose— was enough to make her queasy stomach threaten, but she stood up and followed the scent. Fish meant water, and a cooking fire meant men, Andrés's men, she assured herself as she doggedly made her way through the trees.

She stumbled unexpectedly into the clearing and came to an abrupt halt. Little details about the camp registered in her mind—like the crude shelter off to one side, and the smoldering fire in the center, and the burned fish that hung over the edges of a battered tin plate—but she saw the important details from a distance, from someplace safe and unreachable inside herself. Things like the stream not twenty yards away. Like the gun that was pointed at her. Like the man holding the gun. The man wearing the uniform of the Angeleno army. The man who was most definitely not one of Andrés's men.

She stared at him, and he stared back, his expression almost comical. Of all the things he'd expected to see coming through the forest, she would bet that an American woman wasn't even on the list. But she was here, and if she tried to run away, he would catch her before she'd gone ten feet. She was too weak and dizzy, and he looked like a strong, fast man.

He spoke to her, the words sounding far-off and slurred, yet threatening. She didn't understand any of them, but she understood the look in his eyes as he realized that she was obviously alone and just as obviously in no condition to escape. He moved toward her, and she backed away, stumbling over her own feet.

Fear worked its way through the confusion that clouded her mind, making her tremble as she tried to evade him. He just laughed and cut her off, wrapping his fingers around her wrist, pulling her to him. He was grimy and unshaven, and stank from long days without bathing. Brenna pressed her free hand to her mouth, not to stifle her shriek of pain but to control the roiling of her stomach.

The man raised one filthy hand to her hair, stroking the light brown strands. "Pretty," he murmured in a harsh voice, his breath a heated stench in her face.

"No." Her whisper was barely audible, her efforts to free herself barely noticeable. His hand was huge, and his fingers easily encircled her wrist, squeezing so tightly that her own fingers were growing numb.

His clumsy caresses moved from her hair to her throat, then her breast, and Brenna panicked. After nearly thirty-six hours of being absolutely as quiet as she could, she opened her mouth and screamed.

It was the most terrifying sound he'd ever heard. Andrés and the men assigned to his search team grew still, trying to pinpoint the direction; then another scream verified it for them. As one, they broke into a run, crashing through the woods, moving too quickly to worry about stealth. There was one last cry, a small one that vibrated with pain, then nothing else.

Andrés's lungs were constricted, his heart beating too rapidly. Although he tried not to think, the questions kept coming: What had caused Brenna to scream? Had she hurt herself, or was someone hurting her? Why was she silent now? She had to hear them—they were making enough noise. If she needed help, why didn't she call out to them? Was she unable to speak, unconscious or . . .

As she had done, they burst into the clearing unexpectedly. One moment they were fighting their way through thick stands of trees and thicker undergrowth; the next they were in the camp. The man looked at them—seven soldiers, with seven rifles pointed at him—and tightened his hold on Brenna's wrist.

She was all right. Andrés offered a silent prayer of thanks, then shouldered his rifle and moved a few steps closer. "Let her go," he commanded, the Spanish words rough with tightly controlled fury.

The man stubbornly shook his head. "I found her first," he boasted. "If you want her, you wait your turn."

This time Andrés shook *his* head. "She's *my* woman. If you hurt her . . ." He proceeded, in quiet, graphic words, to explain exactly what he would do.

Brenna swayed unsteadily on her feet. The pain in her wrist was excruciating, but it couldn't lift the haze that dulled her mind. She knew Andrés and his men were there, could hear his words, although they made no sense. He would take care of things, she thought, lethargy taking over. There was no need for her to be afraid, no need to worry.

Her knees buckled, and she sagged, as if in slow motion, to the ground. She felt the man yank at her wrist, caught off balance by the sudden dead weight; then she felt nothing. Thankfully, peacefully nothing.

Something cool and damp was touching Brenna's face when she regained consciousness. Had she fainted? she wondered. Had some soldier captured her and had Andrés rescued her, or had she imagined the entire episode? Dehydration could cause mental confusion, she knew, and she was certainly confused.

She opened her eyes and saw bright sunlight filtered through a wet green cloth. Someone was wasting precious water to wash her face when she desperately needed it to drink. She could smell it on the cloth, could smell it all around her, intensifying her craving until she couldn't stand it. She struggled to sit up, and strong hands grasped her shoulders, not to push her down again but to help her up.

"Do you want a drink?"

The voice was Andrés's, and it was the harshest, coldest, most unforgiving sound she'd ever heard. She hesitantly raised her gaze to his face. His expression perfectly matched his voice. She had known he would be angry, she thought, but not this angry. She hadn't thought he would hate her. How could she make him understand if he hated her? How could she make him care?

He offered her a canteen, and she reached for it with trembling hands. He helped her steady it as she lifted it to her mouth, and he controlled the flow, pulling it back before she'd taken more than a few sips. The water was tepid and had a strong mineral taste, but she thought it was the sweetest she had ever drunk.

While he waited to see if her stomach would tolerate the water, Andrés reached for her left hand to examine her wrist. It was puffy, and darkening bruises ringed it. The swelling would disappear, and the bruises would fade, but he would never forget the way he'd felt when he'd seen that bastard holding her—fear that she'd been hurt, outrage that the man had dared to touch or threaten her, sickening guilt that it was all his fault. When she had fainted, his heart had nearly stopped beating. Now he could admit that it was the best thing that could have happened under the circumstances. It had caught the soldier off guard and had allowed Andrés's men to move in and disarm him.

He had scooped her up and carried her here to the stream bank, out of sight of the camp, holding her tightly, whispering to her all the things he'd longed to tell her in words he knew she couldn't understand. He had bathed her face and waited for her to regain consciousness and look at him, her gentle brown eyes full of hatred and revulsion for what he'd put her through.

"I'm not going to throw up," Brenna said uncomfortably, extending her hand for the canteen. Again he held it for her while she drank. She knew she had to take it easy and slowly replenish the fluid volume she'd lost in the past day and a half, but she thought longingly of drinking water by the gallon. After drinking a few ounces she wiped the back of her hand across her mouth. "I can't believe I was this close to water."

She opened her arms wide to indicate the distance, and Andrés pushed her hands together until scant inches separated her fingertips. "And you were this close to dying."

The unveiled fury in his voice made her look away. This place he'd brought her to was beautiful. A sudden cliff upstream created a waterfall, which in turn created a small, calm pool, while the creek continued its angry flow down the mountain. It was beautiful . . . too beautiful for such darkly vicious emotions.

Leaning forward, she dipped her hand into the pool. The icy water soothed the throbbing in her wrist, but quickly left her fingers numb. When she lifted it out, Andrés handed her the cloth he'd used to wash her face. She wiped away the excess water, then rested her arm across her lap to dry. "How did you find me?"

"You mean besides the screams?" He tried to control the nasty edge of his voice, tried to focus all his emotions inward. "You were careless this morning. You left the cans from your breakfast sitting on top of a fallen log. Hector warned us that the longer you went without adequate fluids, the more confused you would become and the more difficult it would be for you to evade us."

"I knew there was water," she said in a small voice.

"The streams go underground for a few feet, a few yards, half a mile. You have to know where to find them."

He watched her drink a little more, then turn her attention to her hair, combing out the tangles with her fingers. She hadn't yet looked at him, eye to eye. Because she couldn't bear to? Because she hated him so much?

Her cheeks and nose were tinged a faint pink from exposure to the sun, and there were shadows of fatigue beneath her eyes. Her shirt, with the sleeves rolled to her elbows, was damp with perspiration and clung to the soft curves of her breasts, and her khaki trousers were damp, too. But she was beautiful. If she'd been made-up and dressed up in her fanciest clothes, she couldn't have been any more beautiful than she was right now.

He had almost lost her today. Because of him, she had almost died, and nothing in the world could ever change that fact.

Brenna watched him lower his head and press the heels of his hands to his eyes. She wanted to reach out and touch him, to offer him apologies for what she'd done, promises that it would never happen again. She was reaching for him when he suddenly looked up, and his dark eyes locked with hers.

"Why?" The single word was torn from him, a deep-throated growl. He had to know what he had done to make her run away like this. "I haven't hurt you. I've treated you well—given you your own room, fed you, kept you safe. Do you hate me that much, Brenna? Are you so desperate to get away from me that you would rather *die*?"

"I wish I did hate you," she whispered. "I wish you didn't hate me."

He paid no attention to her words. "Those warnings I gave you weren't meant to frighten you but to discourage you. I wanted you to understand the danger so you wouldn't risk it. And you did it anyway. Like a fool, you waltzed right into it!" With a tautly controlled gesture, he pointed in the direction of the makeshift camp. "That man was going to rape you. If he thought you were good, and if you weren't too much trouble, he might have kept you for a while, until he'd taken all the pleasure your body could provide. Then he would have killed you. Do you understand, Brenna?" His hand clenched into a fist. "You would be dead!"

The fact that she knew he was right didn't make his anger any easier to bear. Defensively she shrugged. "You made the same threats yourself."

He stared at her in dismay. "You think that being his prisoner would be no different from being mine? Do you think he would treat you one-hundredth as well as I have? Do you think he would politely hand you over to your father when he comes?"

"That's why you're angry, isn't it?" she challenged. "If that man had killed me, you'd have nothing to bargain with. You would have nothing to hold over my father's head, and you'd never see your dear cousin Esai again. I interfered with your plan. I almost ruined it, and you can't stand that, can you?"

That she could believe that, could think so little of him, drained his anger. For two days he had lived with terror, had felt it squeeze the last bit of warmth from his heart, had endured its sinking, twisting, clawing sickness in his belly, and *she* believed that he was upset because she had almost ruined his plan.

He opened his mouth to speak, closed it again, then swore savagely. Brenna seemed to shrink under his blistering curse. "I—I was going to come back," she whispered, a plaintive offer meant to appease him.

Slowly he raised his hand, cupping his callused palm to her cheek. As his thumb rubbed gently back and forth, absorbing the heat from her sunburned skin, he leaned forward until his face was level with hers, until his eyes locked with hers. "Maybe you were," he agreed softly; then his voice turned brutally hard. "But you wouldn't have made it. You would have died first."

His soft, certain promise made her flinch as if he'd struck her, but he didn't notice. He refilled the canteen from the stream, capped it and slung it over his shoulder. When he spoke again, it was in his normal, granite-hard voice. "We've got to get back to the village. Hector will want to look at you." He rose easily to his feet, then helped her up. She clung to his hands, fighting to still the trembling in her legs; then he lifted her into his arms.

She didn't protest, didn't struggle to get away. She rested her head against his shoulder, closed her eyes and gave in to exhaustion.

She'd made it only thirteen miles from the village, Brenna found to her dismay on the ride back. What took them less than an hour in the jeep had been a thirty-six-hour ordeal for her on foot.

And what had she accomplished? she wondered as she wearily undressed in the safety of her room. She was dehydrated and aching in every single part of her body. She had

almost gotten herself killed. She had made certain that if
Andrés hadn't already thoroughly despised her, he did now.
And she had gained further proof that he cared nothing for
her. His concern hadn't been for her life, but for his plan
and his cousin.

That hurt the worst. No woman should ever have to love
someone who saw her only as an object, a commodity to
trade for other, more valuable things. No woman should
ever have to love a man who had already broken her heart
once.

Stifling a sob, she dropped her dirty clothes in a pile near
the dresser and pulled a clean T-shirt from the drawer. She
would have loved to take a bath and wash her hair, but
Hector had been insistent that she get straight into bed. With
plenty of rest and fluids she would be feeling as good as new
in no time, he'd promised cheerfully. A lot he knew, she
thought with a scowl as she climbed into bed. The only kind
of rest that was going to make her feel better was the Rip van
Winkle kind. By the time she woke up from a twenty-year
nap, she would have forgotten what—or who—was causing
this ache around her heart.

Just as she rolled onto her side, the door opened. Hoping it was Hector or José or Diego or possibly even Vicente,
was futile, because none of them sent shivers down her spine
just by walking into a room. She squeezed her eyes shut,
hoping he would believe she was asleep, hoping, too, that
the tears that had threatened only moments earlier wouldn't
start now.

Andrés knew she was awake. There were lines of tension
across her forehead that weren't there when she slept. He set
the canteens he carried on the nightstand, then stood beside the bed and stared down at her for a moment. He had
almost lost her today, and once she was safe he had pushed
her away. At a time when she'd needed comforting he had
yelled at her, had given her accusations and insults. At a
time when she'd needed gentleness he'd offered her fury.

She didn't know his fury was self-directed, didn't know that his burden of guilt was so heavy it was crushing him. All she knew was that she had needed someone and he had failed her. Again. He had always failed her.

He crouched beside the bed and smoothed the sheet over her shoulder. "There's water here if you get thirsty," he said quietly. "If you need—" He broke off suddenly. He'd almost said "me." She had needed him plenty of times, but he had never been there. "If you need anything I'll be in the office."

Brenna kept her eyes shut, her emotions too raw and vulnerable to face him now. After a moment she heard him stand up, walk across the room and head out the door. She turned onto her stomach and buried her face in the pillow, fighting the tears, but they came anyway. Fortunately for her—and for Andrés, listening in the office—sleep followed soon behind them.

Chapter 7

Vicente returned Thursday afternoon, accompanied by thirty-six of the thirty-nine men who had left with him four days earlier, along with seven other men. Prisoners.

Andrés stood on the porch, his hands braced on the railing, and watched as the men were helped or carried out of the truck. He didn't know any of them, or maybe he did and simply couldn't recognize them like this. They were emaciated, unshaven, filthy, their uniforms in tatters. They had been beaten and denied medical care for their injuries; they had been starved and mistreated. Hector would do what he could for them, and if they were lucky and God was with them, they would survive—possibly crippled and forever scarred, but alive. Maybe one day they would be strong enough to fight for their country again.

When the prisoners had all been taken into Hector's clinic, Vicente came to Andrés to report. He climbed the steps and followed his leader inside, gratefully accepting the chair Andrés offered. In a low emotionless voice he related the events of the past four days, gave the names of the three men who had died and of the seven men they had rescued.

Andrés kept his questions to a minimum. He knew his lieutenant needed food and rest; detailed reports could wait. "Get something to eat and go to bed."

Vicente hesitated. "I questioned some of the prisoners on the way back. They'd heard rumors that you had been captured." He paused only an instant. "Apparently for the first day or two after Esai was taken, the government believed they had you."

It was the first news he'd had of his cousin since his capture, and it wasn't good. The army didn't know Esai Villareal from a hundred thousand other Angelenos, but they had damn good reasons for hating Andrés Montano. The mistake in identity could only have made Esai's treatment worse. "Did they know where he was being held?"

Vicente shook his head. "They said that for a few days the guards taunted them with the fact that you had been captured. Then they said nothing."

As Andrés nodded grimly, the door between the two rooms opened, and Brenna came in. Without looking at her, he asked sharply, "What are you doing out of bed?"

She didn't look at him, either, but instead at Vicente. The combination of grime, sweat and filth didn't bother her—until she'd finally managed a bath and shampoo this morning, she had undoubtedly smelled pretty rank herself—but the grimness of his expression, the exhaustion that lined his face, and the heavy growth of beard, did touch her. He looked like a completely different person from the impossibly polite, handsome man she'd met at the airport nearly two weeks ago. "I heard Vicente's voice and figured that Hector could use a little help."

She sounded frail and uncertain. Andrés dared to look at her, letting his gaze skim quickly over her without meeting her eyes. Except for a brief trip out this morning for water to bathe, she had kept to her room, where she had slept practically the entire twenty-four hours since her return. He suspected it was as much from her desire to avoid him as from physical exhaustion.

He started to send her back to her room, but she was right. Hector could only do so much, and he'd just been handed seven new patients. Pushing his chair back so hard that it scraped the floor, he walked to the door, shoved it open and stepped outside. "José, Diego!"

Brenna winced at the harshness of his voice. When she saw Vicente watching her, puzzled, she smiled weakly. "I'm on restriction. I'm not allowed outside alone anymore." With another faint, sad smile, she joined Andrés on the porch until her guards came.

"What happened?" Vicente asked when Andrés returned to the desk.

"She escaped."

"When?"

"The day after you left. She took food, canteens, one of my jackets and a couple of knives and disappeared into the forest. By the time we found her she was lost, dehydrated and had been caught by a deserter from the National Army." Andrés closed his eyes briefly. More than twenty-four hours later, he still felt the fear of what that bastard would have done to her. It still sickened him.

"She's got more courage than I expected," Vicente said admiringly as he got to his feet and walked to the door. He glanced back at his friend. "She deserves a lot more than your anger. If you feel guilty, take it out on yourself, not her."

Andrés stared after Vicente long after he was gone. He knew his friend was right. He couldn't continue yelling at Brenna or it would destroy him. But if he stopped, if he let her know how frightened he had been, how furious he was with himself, how terrified he'd been that something horrible would happen to her...

It would mean opening up to her, letting loose everything he'd kept buried inside for so long, giving up the rigid control of his emotions that allowed him to function day to day. It would mean falling even more in love with her and, too soon to contemplate, losing even more than he already stood to lose.

He couldn't do it.

Forcing his mind back to business wasn't easy, but he managed. That was another way he held on to his sanity. For six years the war had been his life; it had ruled his every thought, his every action. Until now. Until he had foolishly brought Brenna here. He had stupidly believed he could see her, talk to her and live with her without hurting her, without betraying himself and his love for her.

Now he relied on the strict, emotionless discipline that six years of war had perfected. Some of the prisoners had heard about Esai's capture. Although he doubted that he would learn anything more, he would talk to each of them, would question them thoroughly. Maybe they would remember something else, anything, even the most insignificant comment by a guard.

The clinic was crowded with patients and helpers. Andrés stood in the doorway, watching for a moment. Hector was giving instructions to two of Andrés's men, while Brenna was kneeling beside one cot, gently washing away dirt and dried blood caked around the prisoner's wounds. She spoke occasionally, aware that he couldn't understand her but also aware, Andrés knew, of the soothing value of a calm, friendly voice.

Brenna worked until her back and knees and hands ached, until she was numb inside. She treated wounds—old and new, serious and minor, healing and infected—all deliberately, brutally inflicted. Their guards had used whatever was at hand—knives, guns, cigarettes, fists—and their punishment had been planned to cause as much pain as possible without causing death.

She listened to the conversation around her, particularly to Andrés's. He spoke quietly and at length with each prisoner, each time bringing up the name of Esai Villareal. He was looking for news of his cousin, and from what she could gather, some of the prisoners were giving it. How terrible it must be for him to see the way these men had been treated and know that his cousin was receiving the same, or possibly even worse, treatment. For Andrés's sake she hoped Esai was safe, that he had fared better than these seven men. She hoped that her father had found him by now and was looking after him, keeping him safe for the exchange.

After dinner Hector dismissed her, ordering her back to her quarters and bed. She didn't protest but wearily obeyed him. Once there, she paused on the porch, where Andrés sat in shadow. "Did you learn anything about your cousin?"

He didn't look in her direction, didn't seem to move even to breathe. "Do you think if I did I would tell *you*?"

She was used to the sting in his words now. It didn't even make her flinch. "I hope he's safe."

"Do you?" He sounded skeptical. "Were you concerned about his safety when you sneaked off in the middle of the night? Did you even consider the effects of your escape on his safety? If you'd gotten away, if you had made it to Santiago and found a way to reach your father, you would have killed Esai. The army would immediately have executed him so he could no longer be of use as a bargaining tool."

"I do hope he's all right, for his sake and yours," she said quietly, "but no, I didn't consider him when I planned my escape. I was trying to save myself, no one else."

When she would have gone inside, he spoke again. *"All right?"* he echoed quietly. "You saw what they did to those men. Some of them will be permanently crippled. Maybe in the States, with your skilled doctors and your well-equipped hospitals, they could be helped, but down here we can offer them nothing. But even worse than the physical damage is the emotional, the spiritual pain. Those men will never be the same again. They'll never be able to forget the horror of what they've endured."

He fell silent for a long time, but she sensed that he wasn't through. There was more he wanted to say. Patiently she waited.

"Esai is a farmer. His degrees and titles are fancier, more important sounding, but in his heart he's a farmer. He teaches people what crops to grow, how to enrich their soil, how to avoid depleting the minerals and nutrients in their fields. He brings them new variations of old crops, specially developed to grow in high altitude or heavy rainfall. He introduces new technology and shows them how to market their crops so that they can quit subsistence farming and actually make a profit.

"He uses his head, of course, but he relies on his hands, his arms, his feet, his legs, his back. What good is a farmer who can't till the fields or plant the seeds or harvest the crops?" He raised one arm in the direction of the clinic. "One of those men has no fingers. Another can't use his arm. Another has one leg that's now three inches shorter than the other. All of them are sick, and they will remain that way for a long, long time. Some of them will never get better. None of them will ever be 'all right' again."

"And you're afraid Esai will be like them. Scarred, broken, handicapped." Her voice was low, her expression troubled. She knew Esai probably *would* be like these patients, and Andrés would add one more guilt to his burden. One more sorrow. "The Esai you've described to me is a strong, courageous man. He'll survive this. He'll adjust. Maybe he'll have to work from an office and send some strong young man out to do the things he can no longer do. Maybe he'll no longer be able to work at all. Maybe he'll have to rely on the kind heart and gentle love of his cousin for support. It may not be easy, Andrés, but with your help and the help of his friends here, he'll do it. He'll have to, because if he doesn't . . .'' She let the last word trail off, taking a breath to control the quaver that had crept into her voice. ''If he doesn't, Andrés, he might as well be dead.''

Andrés listened to the soft swish of the screen door, then the quiet click of the bedroom door as she closed it. *Kind heart and gentle love.* Odd words for her to use. She had relied on his kind heart and gentle love for herself, only to find that, for her, neither one existed.

Soon he *would* be kind to her, *would* show her how much he loved her: when he let her go. Tomorrow he would call a meeting of his advisors, and the arrangements for the prisoner exchange would be finalized. A day or two after that he would contact Tom Mathis, and a few days after *that* Brenna would be returned to her father. She would go back to Florida, to her safe, comfortable life there, with Andrés's promise that he would never bother her again.

It wouldn't be an easy promise to make, but he would make it, and he would live with it.

God help him, he would die with it.

Andrés returned from his meeting late Friday evening and found José and Diego sitting on the bottom step of his quarters. At the top sat Brenna, huddled against the chill air, leaning against the railing, her eyes closed. She'd spent another long day helping in the clinic, and it showed in her face even in the moonlight. She was pushing herself too hard, using all her inner resources to care for the patients when she herself wasn't yet recovered from her escape attempt. If she didn't rest she would end up back in bed, as much in need of a nurse as the prisoners were.

He spoke quietly to the guards, dismissing them after making certain the night watch was in place. Then he sat on the step in front of Brenna, turning to face her. ''Why did you spend the day helping Hector? Any fool can see you're not up to that yet.''

She opened her eyes and looked at him. "Do you have to try to be so unpleasant, or does it come naturally to you?"

Her question caught him off guard. While he searched for a response, she continued.

"You've been on my back for two days now, and I'm tired of it. I'm sorry I tried to escape. I'm sorry you had to spend so much of your precious time looking for me. I'm sorry your cousin was captured, and I'm sorry I nearly screwed up your plan, and I'm sorry about your war, and I'm sorry that I even exist! Now leave me alone!" She jumped to her feet and rushed inside, hoping to get away from him, but he was right behind her, catching her arm as she reached the bedroom door.

"Brenna—"

She snatched her arm free, then wiped futilely at the tears in her eyes. "There's nothing else you can say to hurt me— nothing else you can do! I've had so much pain in the last two weeks that I don't even feel it anymore! So please... leave me alone."

He reached for her again, this time grasping her shoulders and pulling her close. Before she could protest—before she could decide if she even wanted to—he was kissing her. His mouth was hard, demanding, taking away her breath, her tears, her sorrow. She whimpered once, a helpless, hopeless sound, then gave in to the taste of him.

He needed her. That was the only coherent thought Andrés could manage. Whether it was right or wrong, whether she allowed it just for the moment or forever. It wasn't a desire that he could keep saying no to, or a hunger that could be satisfied with something else, but a need that ran through his veins with his blood.

Without words he urged her to touch him, and she slid her arms around him, holding him tight, pressing herself closer. She wanted to crawl inside him, to be a part of him that he could never walk away from, could never forget or live without. Desperately she returned his kiss, matching his passion with her own, exploring his mouth with her tongue while her hands clung to him for support.

He was sweet and harsh, life-giving and threatening. With no more than his mouth and his hands he spread heat through her, surging, burning, consuming. It had always been like this, she remembered. Desperate, feverish, frightening and oh, so satisfying.

Andrés broke the kiss and dragged in a deep breath that scorched his lungs. Resting his forehead against hers, he whispered in a rough-edged voice, "Tell me to go away, Brenna, before it's too late."

Tell him to go? How could she, when she needed him so badly? Even though he swore they had no future, even though she knew she would pay for this decision with more heartache, at least she would have this night. At least she could love him one more time. She pressed a kiss to his jaw, then nipped his ear. "I don't want you to go away. I want you to stay. Tonight. All night."

A groan escaped him when she moved, rubbing back and forth against him. "For your own good—"

Her response was a low-throated chuckle. "What about *your* own good? Do you want me, Andrés?"

She knew he did, he realized. She'd felt the proof swelling against her belly, and it had given her the courage to offer him this gift. Sliding his hands into her hair, he held her gently while he kissed her. "You know I do," he whispered. "I've never stopped wanting you. You're in my blood, in my head, in my heart. No matter what I say, no matter how I act, I'll want you until I die."

This time his kiss bordered on violence. Six years of emptiness, six years of loneliness and sorrow and need, were about to end, and he trembled with hunger. Some small part of his mind knew that this was wrong—she was weary and sad and emotionally raw tonight, and he was taking advantage of it—but he needed her too desperately to refuse. Tomorrow he would pay with more guilt, more anger, but tonight, just for tonight, he would quit being an honorable man, and he would love her.

The buttons on her blouse were small, evenly spaced and slid open with ease at the touch of his fingers. He felt her tremble as he slipped his hands inside, pushing the pink fabric from her shoulders. He guided it down her arms, free of her hands, then dropped it to the floor, a pale splash of color in the moonlight. Her bra came off easily, too; then for a moment, Andrés stood motionless, his hands almost but not quite touching her.

"I remember the very first time I saw you," he murmured. "Your father's car wasn't running, and you came to the base in your little red sports car to pick him up."

Brenna shuddered as finally he eliminated the distance and laid his hands, big and warm and callused, over her breasts. He was a man of such extremes, she thought, closing her eyes to savor his slow, sensual caresses. He could be harsh and forbidding, dangerous and threatening. He could terrify men twice his size, and yet he could touch her this gently, this lovingly.

Her nipples responded to his touch, growing harder, swelling against his palms. He hungered for a taste of her—the dark, heated flavor of her mouth, the sweetly innocent savor of her breasts, the mysterious, sensual tang of her femininity. "You were everything I associated with America," he said, continuing his memory in a voice heavy with longing, taut with restraint. "Golden hair, long legs, sexy, joyful—even the little red sports car. I thought you were the most..." He cupped her breast in one palm, pushing it up so he could touch his lips to her nipple. The kiss was brief, painful, sweet. "The most beautiful woman I had ever seen."

And he had fallen in love with her right then. Tom had called him over and introduced him, she had offered her hand, and he had been struck with shyness, with awe, with longing, with an almost anguished desire. As if he had known even then that he would love her and lose her. As he knew it now.

He closed his mind to that thought and lifted her into his arms. It was a few steps to the bed, where he placed her, for the second time in a few days, on top of the sheets. This time, though, he didn't turn and walk away. This time he knelt on the floor beside her and lowered his mouth once more to her breast while he stroked her silken skin with both hands. He suckled her nipple, pulling it deep into his mouth, while his right hand struggled with the fastening of her shorts. The button popped free, the zipper slid down, and he began the caresses again, over her belly, inside the fabric, down to the fragile barrier of her panties.

Brenna was trembling. She raised one hand to his head, tangling her fingers in his hair, torn between pushing him away so she could kiss his mouth and pulling him closer still to increase the torment he was creating. "Let me touch you, too," she pleaded. Then he bit tantalizingly at her nipple, and she arched her back, forgetting what she'd been saying, forgetting everything except this exquisite pleasure.

"I want you to want me, Brenna," he whispered, his voice as thick and heavy as his desire. "I want you to need me the way I need you. When I look at you and know I can't have you, I feel as if I'll die. When you touch me, even just your hand on mine, it starts a fever that burns out of control. Someday it will destroy me."

He slid his fingers underneath the elastic band of her panties, through soft, fair curls, to touch the dampness of her desire. He stroked inside her, and she stiffened, groaning, quivering beneath his hand. "Want me, Brenna," he pleaded, barely audible over her ragged breathing. "Need me. Just for tonight."

She tried to tell him yes, not for tonight but for always, but her voice refused to work, her lungs refused to fill, her brain refused to think. With strength born of desperation she pushed him away and rapidly, her fingers fumbling clumsily, unbuttoned his shirt, then his trousers. While he removed his clothes, she struggled out of hers, then reached longingly for him. "I want you now, Andrés," she murmured. "Now, inside me now."

He joined her on the bed, the squeak of the springs barely registering. He moved between her legs, sheathing himself inside her with one long, deep, smooth thrust. For a moment he remained motionless, feeling the tiny little tremors around his hardness deep inside her; then he lowered himself to cover her body with his, until they were nose to nose, icy dark gaze locked with soft brown. *"Siempre te amaré,"* he said fiercely, knowing she couldn't understand the words, knowing his secret was safe. Then he covered her mouth with his.

He moved inside her, making her writhe, feeding her need until she cried out helplessly, and then he satisfied her, bringing her release, emptying himself into her, his groans mingled with hers. And there he remained, his desire temporarily sated, his need momentarily abated, his rigid flesh softening in her warmth, and he whispered again, his voice drowsy and gentle, *"Siempre te amaré."*

I will always love you.

When he awoke the next morning Brenna was already awake, lying on her side, head propped on one hand, watching him. He searched her face for regret and didn't find it, but he was too uneasy to feel relief. She looked so solemn, so heartbreakingly serious.

She was undoubtedly angry with him for seducing her, he thought bleakly. She had realized what he had known last night, that she was vulnerable and he was taking advantage of her, and she wasn't going to forgive him. He smiled, a faint, halfhearted failure, and spoke softly. "I guess this is where you say it won't happen again."

Slowly she shook her head. "I figured that would be *your* line. In which case I was going to respond with this." She leaned over, her breasts rubbing his chest, and covered his mouth with hers while her hand made its way sensuously down his body to the coarse black hair between his thighs and the rapidly growing hardness it encircled.

Andrés closed his eyes with a prayer of thankfulness. He hadn't lost her yet. The reprieve was too brief, would end too soon, but he would treasure it. He would once more find his peace inside her, would once more offer her all his love. Then he would once more be alone.

Brenna shifted beneath the sheet, pulling it around her shoulders as she moved astride him. With a smile of pure, sweet bliss, she slid over him, taking him inside her, into that heated, welcoming place. She played with him, bringing him to the edge, pulling him back, teasing him, torturing him; then with all the skill that he'd taught her, with all the love that she'd nurtured, she gave him relief, once more taking his seed deep inside her.

Then, before she could relax, before she could complete the smug smile that had begun, Andrés slid his hand between them. He moistened his fingers inside her with his own fluid, then stroked slowly, steadily, unmercifully over that small sensitive nub of flesh that made her quiver. She gasped for him to stop, but she couldn't move away, couldn't do anything but feel. Her head fell forward, her hair a soft tangle around her face, her lips parted.

"Andrés..."

He wet his fingers again, then continued rubbing her. He watched as she gasped, as the satiny skin of her belly rippled, as her muscles deep inside clenched convulsively around his hardness. He exerted more pressure, making her groan, making her head roll back and her eyes flutter shut.

Trembling, needy, she grasped his hand with both of hers and moved against it, pressing his fingers tight, rubbing herself against them once, twice, then shuddering violently, her cry helpless. She collapsed against him, her face pressed against his chest, and he held her, stroking her until the shivers passed, whispering soft Spanish words to her, brushing softer kisses over her.

When she was still, when their breathing had returned to normal, Andrés moved her onto the mattress, beside him, and tenderly brushed a strand of hair from her damp forehead. "You are so beautiful."

She sensed his sorrow, sensed the rejection that was coming and tried to shield herself from it. Even as he spoke again, she was pulling away.

"But it *can't* happen again." He watched her slide out of his arms, feeling the loss all the way to his toes. She pulled the sheet with her and sat up on the opposite side of the bed, her back to him, her shoulders rounded. "Brenna, you don't understand—"

"Sure I do," she interrupted. "There aren't too many women in these mountains. That makes it kind of hard to pick one up, doesn't it? It means a long time without getting laid. Even feeling the way they do about Americans, I doubt there's a man in this village who would have turned me away last night, except maybe Vicente. He seems a little more discriminating than the others."

He gritted his teeth together as he sat up. "Damn it, Brenna—"

"It's okay. We both got what we wanted." She stood up, gathering the sheet around her for protection, and faced him. She was smiling, but her eyes were suspiciously bright, and her lower lip was trembling the way it always did just before she started to cry. "You'd better get out of here before someone comes looking for you and finds out . . ."

Swearing in a low voice, Andrés got up and pulled on the briefs and trousers he had discarded so quickly last night. He reached for the shirt, then threw it back to the floor with a vicious curse and stalked around the bed to her, grasping handfuls of the sheet and dragging her close. "I didn't 'get laid' last night," he said in a dangerously low voice, his face so close to hers that she couldn't look away. "I *made love* to you. And you can be damn sure there's not another man out there who would dare touch you, because they know I would kill them. As for someone finding out—'' He spared a glance for the bed, then looked back at her with a crooked smile. ''As creaky as those springs are, I imagine someone already has.''

Feeling the sting of tears, Brenna covered her face with her hands. ''Don't make fun of me,'' she whispered plaintively.

''I thought you couldn't feel any more pain.'' He was whispering, too, his voice as gentle as his hands when he pulled hers from her face.

''I lied. It does hurt, Andrés. I thought maybe it wouldn't, because I was already so accustomed to being used by you that being used by you in bed couldn't be any more painful than being used to free your cousin. I thought . . . I thought maybe it would make a difference in the way you treat me, that maybe you would quit acting as if you hate me.'' But those were lies, too. She hadn't thought of anything at all except how badly she wanted him. How desperately she needed him. How hopelessly she loved him.

Sadly he shook his head, then raised his hand gently to stroke her hair. ''I don't hate you, Brenna,'' he said quietly. ''But we can't have an affair. It's wrong.''

''Why?''

''As soon as your father has Esai in his custody, we'll make the exchange as planned, and you'll go back to Florida.'' Once back there, she would settle into the daily routine of her life, would deal with her kidnapping, her escape attempt and her close brush with death. Now she would also have to deal with last night. She might someday understand, but, as he'd known all along, she would never forgive him. ''We have no future, Brenna,'' he said softly, almost apologetically.

Because he didn't *want* a future with her, she acknowledged. That was nothing new. He'd seen no future for them six years ago, either. Well, she could accept that.

But one night wasn't enough. She had thought it would be, but now she knew it wasn't. She was greedy. She wanted everything he could give her—if not love, then sex. An affair. Memories.

Looking him directly in the eye, she asked, "Then how about the next few days?"

He felt as if his world were tilting. "What?"

"How long will it be until you trade me off? Three days? Four? A week?" She shrugged carelessly, and the sheet slipped to reveal the rosy-colored nipple of one breast. "What can a week-long affair hurt? People have them all the time."

Andrés backed away, unbalanced by her suggestion. If she hated him, surely she wouldn't be interested in even a short-term affair with him...would she? But she *had* to hate him, had to despise him for what he'd done. "*You* don't have affairs, Brenna. You have relationships. You fall in love."

She smiled, hiding the ache in her heart. "Is that the problem? You're afraid I'll fall in love with you and make demands on you? Try to come back here after you send me back to Dad? Try to hang around and make life miserable for you?"

No, he thought, already miserable. He was afraid that she *wouldn't*.

"No demands, Andrés. Just what we had last night. No more fighting, and just a little loving." Just something to remember in the years to come.

He walked away, back to his side of the bed, picking up his jacket from the floor and straightening it. He put it on and buttoned it, then bent to pick up his boots. At the door he stopped and looked at her for a long time. "No," he said flatly. "I'm sorry, Brenna."

As soon as the door closed behind him, she sagged against the wall for support. She had offered him the perfect affair—no strings, no demands, no love, nothing but good sex—and he had still turned her down. How he must hate her, in spite of his claim to the contrary!

But she could live with that, she told herself, eyes squeezed shut on the pain. If last night and this morning were all she could have, she would accept them graciously and not mourn what could have been. He was probably doing her a favor by turning her down, she reasoned. An affair would be meaningless to him, but it would lead to certain heartache for her. She didn't need that. She could get over needing him.

But it just might take a long, long time.

"How would you like to be in charge for a while?"

Brenna looked up from feeding one of the newly released prisoners the thin broth that constituted his lunch to see Hector smiling brightly at her. "In charge of what?"

"My clinic. My patients."

"For how long?" she asked warily. She was a good nurse, but she knew her limitations. Although all the patients were stable, anything could go wrong at any time. She didn't want the responsibility.

"A day, maybe two. I got word from the next village that Raúl's wife is in labor—she's having twins. It's her first pregnancy, and she's frightened, so I need to go. But I need someone in charge here, preferably someone who knows something about medicine."

She considered it for a moment, then gestured to José and Diego. Instead of waiting outside as they had done in the past, they had orders now to keep her in sight at all times. "I'm still in the doghouse for running away. I'm not sure how they'd feel about giving me more responsibility right now."

Hector laughed merrily. "Andrés isn't angry with you for escaping—he's angry with *himself* for pushing you to it. And if I want you to take over my patients and you're willing, he has no choice but to approve. You're the only one here with any training."

"And the only one who can't talk to or understand them."

"You come up with more objections...." He gave an exasperated shake of his head. "Are you willing or not?"

After a moment she nodded. "If it's all right with Andrés."

"I'll tell him now."

She turned back to her patient, a young man named Paco with long black hair and lifeless brown eyes. He was in his early twenties, but his eyes looked decades older. The things they had seen... She gave a shudder. The Angeleno government denied mistreating or torturing its prisoners; the United States and even her father backed them up. Lies. They were all telling lies. How would they explain Paco's mangled hand, the cigarette burns that marked his body, the long wide scars on his back from a belt? How about Fernando's shortened leg, caused by an untreated fracture? Or Esteban's injuries, or any of the others? When she got back to the States, she was going to tell....

Tell what? Who would believe her? She would be one person speaking out against the San Angelo and American governments, challenging her own father. One person—a woman, it would come out, who had once been in love with the leader of the rebel forces. A woman who *still* loved him. She would accomplish nothing...but she would try.

The sound of footsteps interrupted her thoughts. Standing up, she faced Andrés, Hector and Vicente. She hadn't seen Andrés all day, and now she found it hard to see the hardness that was back in his face. Only his eyes had changed, seeming to have softened, but maybe she was imagining it.

"Hector says you're going to take over his job while he delivers Dorotea's babies."

"Do you object to that?" she asked calmly, sliding her hands into her shorts pockets.

"You're not a doctor."

"Thank you for reminding me of that." She heard Hector's chuckle, saw Vicente's mouth quirk in a smile and reminded herself not to amuse them at Andrés's expense. "When he's gone, I'm the closest you've got. Of course, if you don't trust me with the men..."

Andrés ignored the leading remark. She knew he trusted her. "How will you communicate with them?"

She glanced around the room at the patients. There were five in here and four in the next room, most of them listening with interest to the conversation they couldn't understand. Then she looked back at Andrés. "Maybe Vicente could stay with me."

His eyes grew dark. "You want me to assign my best man to sick bay as an interpreter?"

She recalled his comment early this morning—*there's not another man out there who would dare touch you, because they know I would kill them*—and she smiled slowly. He sounded jealous. It had been so long since any man had been jealous over her, and she liked it. "If he's your best, why not?"

Slowly he began walking toward her, and she uneasily backed away. When several yards separated them from Hector and Vicente, he spoke in a bare whisper. "Don't push me, Brenna. Don't play games with me in front of my men."

She leaned forward and responded in an equally soft tone. "Does that mean I can play with you when we're not in front of your men?"

Frustration etched small lines at the corners of his mouth. "Damn it—"

"*You* stay with me."

For a long moment they stared at each other, the echo of her words hovering between them. She was asking him to spend time with her—not in bed, not making love, just simply together. He could handle that, he thought hesitantly.

"Is it a deal?" She thought he was going to turn her down, and she was already looking for a gracious way to handle his rejection when he spoke.

"All right." Before he could see her response, he was turning away, going back to Hector and Vicente, speaking to them in Spanish. When he was done, Vicente left and Hector began gathering supplies. Quickly he discussed each patient's care with Brenna; then he left with Raúl and another soldier—Dorotea's brother, Andrés told Brenna.

"I guess I'm spoiled," she said as she began sweeping the floor. "But I can't imagine giving birth like that, with no hospital staff, no sterile facilities, no anesthesia."

"We have hospitals with sterile facilities and American-trained doctors and nurses. But they're only for the rich. A poor woman like Dorotea would be allowed to die on the steps, along with her babies, before they would take her inside for treatment. It's that way for most of our women." He stared off into the distance, his eyes dark and grim. If he ever married, his wife would probably give birth as Dorotea would—on a soiled mattress, if she was lucky, or on a woven mat in a dirt-floored, tin-roofed shack—and she would probably see one or more of her babies die before reaching the age of two. Brenna, on the other hand, would go to her hospital, where she would lie in a clean bed in a sterile room, attended by an obstetrician, a pediatrician, an anesthesiologist and a team of nurses. Her baby would be born with a minimum of trouble, receive the very best medical care and live a long, full life.

Her baby. It pained him to think of her one day giving birth to another man's baby. If life had been different her children would be *his*. But it hadn't been different. And it never would be.

"Why don't they use birth control?"

His smile was tinged with bitterness. "San Angelo is about ninety-five percent Catholic, and the church prohibits its use. For those who are willing to use it anyway, where would they get it? Even you, a rich, educated, privileged American, can't get it here." He saw her eyes widen with realization, and the bitterness in his smile increased. "I'm a poor Angeleno rebel. I can't get my hands on something like that. That's just one more reason why you and I can't have an affair. With your luck, you'd get that baby you talked about sooner than you expected."

Would he hate that? she wondered, turning her attention back to her sweeping. Would it disturb him to know that, thousands of miles away, she was raising his child? She had talked about finding a man to father her baby, one who would then walk away and leave the responsibility to her. She hadn't known that man might be Andrés.

But he wouldn't walk away—maybe from her, but not from his baby. If he knew that she'd had his child, the minute the war ended he would be on his way to Florida. He would demand the responsibility. He would probably even take her in the bargain.

Catching his gaze on her, she smiled sweetly. "With *your* luck, Andrés, I've already got it."

"You'd better pray you don't," he said, forcing all the harshness he could into his voice. "Your father would never accept my illegitimate child into his family. He would make life miserable for you."

"Would you?"

He looked away, then warily back at her. "Would I what?"

"Accept a child of mine into your family."

With all his heart, he thought bleakly. "I've seen enough children killed that I treasure all of them." He beckoned her

to follow him through the rooms to the tiny back stoop.
There he pointed to the back of the church. Neatly spaced
beneath the branches of a massive tree were three rows of
white crosses, twelve in all.

"Those mark the graves of the children of this village.
After my family was killed, other families still lived here—
Javier's, Benedicto's, Manuel's, Reynaldo's, Rico's, about
a dozen in all. My men and I were gone most of the time, so
the women cultivated the fields, planting and harvesting the
crops that fed their families. While they worked, Father
Hidalgo watched the children. One day the army came back.
Father Hidalgo gathered the children in the church in the
hopes that the soldiers wouldn't violate its sanctuary,
but . . ." He sighed, his breath stirring a strand of her hair.
"They killed the children right there in the church, but left
the priest unharmed so that he could deliver a message to
me. They had chosen this village because it was *my* village.
They had killed these children because they lived in the same
place *I* lived."

Brenna swallowed past the lump that had formed in her
throat. "That's why the church is no longer used."

"It was a sacred place, and they desecrated it. The parents could no longer bring themselves to enter. We buried
the children, and Father Hidalgo moved on to Santiago.
Then I did what I should have done months earlier: I made
the village an armed camp. We moved the remaining families out—the mothers and grandmothers, the elderly grand-
fathers. We sent them to other villages where they would be
safe. It didn't guarantee that the army would stop raiding us,
but it did ensure that everyone here was capable of defending himself. There would be no more slaughter."

He blamed himself for it. Brenna knew that from his low,
passionate tone as surely as if he'd said the words. She ached
for him, for the sense of duty that made him accept responsibility for everything, whether it was his or not. It

strengthened him, but it also tormented him. One day it would destroy him.

"When the war is over," he continued softly, "if I live, I will accept and love any child—not just mine, not just yours, but any child. Until then, I cannot. A child with my blood would be targeted for death here. So would a child with my love."

She turned to face him, laying her hand on his chest. "When will it end, Andrés?" she whispered. "When will you find peace?"

"Maybe soon. Maybe never. The first year or two, I used to pray that one day I would wake up and the world would be a different place—no fighting, no hunger, no suffering, no dying. Then I started praying that it would end and I would be alive. Now ... I just pray for it to end."

He sounded as if he'd lost hope ... or faith. But Brenna knew that wasn't true. He might be tired physically, mentally and especially spiritually, but he hadn't given up. "But you still believe in what you're doing. You still believe in your people and their right to be free. You still believe that Romero has to be stopped."

"Yes," he said quietly.

"What will you do when it's over?"

Looking down, he touched her hand lightly with one fingertip. "I try not to think about it. Dreams have a way of being snatched away from us."

"Only if we let them. You can grab your dreams and hold them so tight that no one can ever take them from you."

His smile was weary and sweet and infinitely sad. "My dreams are already lost." He'd lost them the day he'd given a photograph of her to Vicente and told him to pick her up at the airport. "You'd better get back to your patients. I need to do a few things. I'll be back soon. If you need help, send José to my office for Vicente." He lifted her hand from his chest, hesitated, then raised it to his mouth for a kiss.

"You're a good woman, Brenna. You deserve better than I've given you."

She watched him step off the porch and start away, then called, "What if I don't want better, Andrés?"

Briefly he glanced over his shoulder. "You'll get it anyway."

She leaned back against the house, watching until he was gone. Maybe she would, she mused. Maybe she would get exactly what she wanted.

Chapter 8

"Want to go for a walk?"

Andrés watched Brenna stretch her arms, then roll her head from side to side, easing taut muscles. She had put in a long day at the clinic, preceded by a long night with him. Surely she was tired, but if she wanted to take a quiet walk, who was he to turn her down? "Where do you want to go?"

"Toward the stream?" The path from the edge of town, the one she had avoided the night of her escape, was clear, and the moon was full. "Do you suppose José and Diego could stay behind this time?"

He considered it for a moment, then agreed. As he'd done once before, he borrowed a rifle from one of the men before dismissing them for the night. He slung it over his shoulder as naturally as she would her purse, Brenna thought with a slight smile.

They walked side by side, their feet scuffing over hard-packed dirt and tough grass. For the first hundred yards Brenna kept her hands together, her fingers laced lightly. Then, with an unself-conscious ease that Andrés envied, she reached across and tucked her hand securely into his bigger palm. "It's really beautiful out here," she remarked in a hushed voice.

"You think so? Even after what happened to you?"

She smiled. "That was *my* fault—not the mountains' or the forest's. Not yours."

"You can't escape if you're not held prisoner."

Her laughter was soft and airy, like the tinkle of distant bells. "I wasn't running from you. I was trying to escape what I feel for you." Quickly, before he could respond, she continued. "But you blamed yourself, didn't you? If I'd died, you would have carried that burden. If that man had raped me, you would have taken that guilt, too." She gave a shake of her head. "It isn't easy being Andrés Montano, is it? You have to be so responsible, so dedicated to duty, so honor bound. When is the last time you were selfish, the last time you took something you wanted, something just for you, without thinking of anyone but yourself?"

There was no hesitation in his answer. "Last night."

She shook her head. "You didn't take anything last night that wasn't freely given, and you were as considerate of me as any man could have been."

"But it was wrong, and it was selfish."

"Why? Because for a few hours you were not a soldier, not a leader, not a national hero, but just a man?" She smiled gently. "You're entitled to that, Andrés. You're entitled to feel and to want and to need."

He stopped in shadow and pulled her around to face him. "But not you. If I want a woman, I should find one of our own, an Angelena, one who lives with the war and horror and hardship, as I do. I'm not entitled to want or to need *you*. You're an American. You're my prisoner. In another week you'll be back in Florida, where you belong, where you'll find an American husband and raise American kids."

"Is it that easy for you? You tell yourself that it's wrong to want an affair with me, and poof!—the desire is gone?"

"Is it that easy for *you*?" he challenged. "To have an affair that will last only days? To give yourself to a man who can't offer you anything?"

"Can't, Andrés? Or won't?"

He stared at her a long time, then dropped her hand and walked away. She caught up with him at the bank of the stream. "Tell me that you don't want to make love with me," she demanded. "Forget about the future, about the past, about the war and being my captor. Tell me that you don't want me."

With an oath he dropped the rifle to the ground, dragged her into his arms, hard against his body, and tangled his hands in her hair. "Do you want me to hurt you, to be cruel to you? Would that convince you?"

"No," she whispered. "If you weren't gentle with me, if you didn't look at me as if I mattered, if you didn't respond each time we touched...then I would be convinced."

He slid his hands inch by inch through her hair and down her spine to her hips, where he drew her intimately against him. She felt his hardness, strong and powerful, searing her belly through their clothes. "I respond to you as I would respond to any woman," he growled in her ear. "It's a purely biological response, Brenna. Didn't you learn anything in nursing school?"

"Maybe it is, maybe it isn't. Maybe any woman would do. But either way, I'm the only woman you've got."

He squeezed his eyes shut on the image of her moonlit face and prayed for the courage to walk away from her. "God, Brenna, why are you doing this?" he groaned. "I'm trying to protect you, and you make it so hard."

"To protect me from what?"

"From me. From yourself. From the situation."

"I don't want to be protected. I'm a woman, Andrés, not some brainless child. Let me make my own decisions. Let me accept responsibility for my own actions."

"And what if you get pregnant? Are you prepared to accept responsibility for that, too?"

"Yes." She wanted a baby sometime. She would gladly have Andrés's baby anytime.

He groaned again, this time from deep inside. "It's wrong, Brenna," he murmured, his lips brushing her temple. "It's wrong of me to touch you, to want you like this."

She tilted her head back, seeking his lips with hers. "For tonight, quit being Andrés Montano the great leader and let me love Andrés Montano the man."

His eyes closed, he searched for strength but found none. The bonds of duty, obligation, honor—they were gone, too. All that was left was desire. Longing. Fever. Hunger. Love.

When he kissed her, Brenna knew she'd broken through his defenses, and she felt the prick of guilt. Was it wrong of her to seduce him when he so obviously didn't want to be seduced? Maybe...but she needed him so much, and time was running out. As he kept reminding her, soon the exchange would take place, and she would return to Florida. She had to gather whatever memories she could, had to give whatever love he would take.

His kiss was slow, deep, his tongue probing. He shifted, pulling her closer, as if he couldn't touch her enough, as if they could merge into one form, one being. His hands moved sensuously along her spine, massaging, caressing, now tickling.

Brenna strained against him, her mouth giving, her body yielding. Blood surged through her, heated, burning, its sound mingling in her head with the rush of the stream. This feeling of pleasure, of power, of weakness and love, was worth all the pain, all the heartache, the world could hold.

Laying her hands on his chest, she felt the rapid beat of his heart. She maneuvered them underneath the fabric, over his belly and chest to his nipples, flat, round, hard. There was no hair on his chest, no coarseness to distract from the sensual texture of silken skin and corded muscle.

Andrés's groan was strained, vibrating deep in his chest. Forcefully he ended the kiss, then brushed his mouth over hers, gently biting her lip, bathing the spot with his tongue. "We have to go back."

She protested wordlessly, too dazed to find the power of speech.

"It's dangerous to stay out very long after dark, and the ground is hard and your skin is cold," he said, rubbing his hands over her bare arms to prove it. "We'll go back to our quarters."

She liked the sound of that, Brenna thought dreamily. *Our* quarters.

Andrés bent to pick up the rifle, then put his arm around her, hugging her to his side—for warmth, he told himself. But to provide warmth for her... or take it for himself?

As they neared the end of the trail, the sounds of activity in the camp became audible. Brenna felt Andrés growing tense beside her, as if he sensed disaster, and she quickened her pace to match his. By the time they reached the road, they were practically running; then they stopped short.

Trucks and jeeps were parked in the road, engines running, and half-awake men were rushing out of their quarters, struggling with uniforms, weapons and supplies. Andrés pulled away from Brenna and raced ahead, yelling questions, shouting orders.

When she caught up with him, he was talking to Vicente and several others, his expression hard and grim. There was no sign of the man who had kissed her only moments ago, of the man who had needed her as much as he needed air or water. She waited impatiently, frightened by the commotion, frightened for Andrés.

He glanced at her, seeing the fear and the effort she was making to hide it. He longed to offer her reassurance, but this wasn't the time or the place. "The village where Raúl's wife lives was attacked tonight," he said tersely.

"Hector? The babies?"

He shrugged. "Vicente is going to take you someplace safe—"

"But what about the patients? Hector put me in charge. I can't leave them."

"*I* put you in charge, and I'm ordering you to go with Vicente."

"Let me go with you. Hector will need help, and I can give it. Let me—"

His glare was ice-cold, his eyes hard. The transformation back into the heartless, pitiless, unfeeling soldier was so complete that it stunned Brenna into silence. "You'll follow orders. One of the men will stay with the patients. Wait in that jeep."

She stared numbly at him. That was it? No goodbye, no hope, no promises that he would return?

"Damn it, Brenna, go!"

When she didn't move, Vicente took her arm and guided her to the jeep. With a glance over her shoulder at Andrés, she climbed into the back seat, wedged between a stack of bedrolls and Vicente. The engine sputtered to life, and they drove away, followed by another jeep carrying four more people.

She didn't look back. Andrés watched until they were out of sight, wishing she would give him one last glance, wishing he could go with her, sorry he couldn't have handled things differently.

Instead of following the road out of the village, their driver turned onto a narrow, long-abandoned track that led straight up the mountain. He drove without headlights, as did the vehicle behind them, steadily climbing in the bright moonlight.

Brenna sat with her back straight, head bowed, angry, hurt, frightened, bewildered. As the elevation increased, she grew colder, but she didn't notice until Vicente unfastened the ties that held one sleeping bag in a tight roll and spread it over her. Immediately she began shivering, and she huddled deeper into its warmth.

Their journey took about an hour, their destination a gaping black hole carved out of the mountainside. The jeeps stopped in front, and the men jumped out, unloading supplies. Vicente gestured for Brenna to get out, too; as soon as she did, the driver left, followed by the second one. "What is this?" she asked, although she didn't much care. Nothing this far from Andrés interested her.

"It's an abandoned mine." Vicente watched as the men checked the interior with powerful flashlights. Certain it was safe, they carried the supplies inside, then disappeared into the surrounding mountainside. With a courtly sweep of his arm, he invited her inside.

"I don't suppose we get any light." Brenna stubbed her toe on something, felt her way around it and finally located the side wall. Wrapping the sleeping bag around her shoulders, she slid to the cool stone floor.

"No. Sorry."

Her eyes gradually adjusted to the darkness. She saw the remaining bedrolls, a couple of gallon jugs of water and a carton of C rations. Beside Vicente, directly across from her, were several M-16s, a couple of pistols and boxes of ammunition. "You believe in being well armed, don't you?"

He didn't respond to her sarcasm. "It's saved my life many times. Tonight it might be responsible for saving yours."

"Why do you say that? What's going on?"

He was staring out the entrance a few yards away—keeping watch, she supposed. For a long time he remained silent; then he glanced at her. "The soldiers who attacked the village were searching for someone. Several of the villagers heard them mention '*la americana*.' The American."

Fear tightened around her heart. "Do..." She swallowed hard and forced the question out. "Do you think my father has broken his agreement with Andrés and sent troops to find me?''

Vicente shrugged.

"What will Andrés and the others do?''

"Some of them will help the villagers clean up—treat the wounded, bury the dead. The others will try to pick up the trail. The soldiers won't be able to move too quickly through the forest, so there's a good chance that Andrés will find them. Most of the men in this camp are native to this region. They know these hills the way you know your backyard.''

Treat the wounded, bury the dead. The phrase echoed in her mind. Had those people been killed because of her? Because her father had lied to Andrés—had lied to *her*—and sent soldiers after her anyway? She prayed that she was wrong, that she was jumping to conclusions. The army routinely attacked villages; this time didn't have to be her fault.

Vicente stood up and walked outside the mine, checking to make sure the guards were in place. When he returned, moving quietly and surely in the darkness, he laid down his rifle and turned to the sleeping bags. Wordlessly he spread out two, one on top of the other, then placed the last one on the opposite side, where he'd been sitting. "It gets cold up here. Keep one bag on the bottom, one on top, and sleep in the middle one. You'll be more comfortable.''

She shook her head. "You can have one more.''

His smile was barely visible in the darkness. "I dressed for the occasion. You didn't.''

Murmuring thanks, she moved to sit on the bags, keeping the third one wrapped around her. "You'd rather be down there with them, wouldn't you?''

"I've been in a lot of fights with the army. There will be a lot more.'' After a long silence he suggested, "There will probably be plenty of work for you when it's safe to return. Get some sleep.''

For a little while she ignored him; then, cold, tired and sick with worry, she crawled into the second sleeping bag, using the third for cover as he'd told her. She was starting to drift off when she heard a soft scuffle and Vicente appeared at her side. In his hand was a .45 caliber pistol.

"Have you ever fired a gun, Miss Mathis?"

"No."

He released the safety, pulled the slide back and reset the small lever. "There's a round in the chamber, six in the clip. All you have to do is move the safety like this—" he showed her "—and it's ready to fire. It has a kick, so you should probably hold it with both hands. Just make sure you don't shoot me or one of our guards."

When he held the gun out, she simply stared at him. "You're giving it to me?"

His gaze was impassive. "We're not holding you prisoner up here, Miss Mathis. We're trying to protect you."

"But . . . a gun . . ."

"If I get killed, you'll have to protect yourself."

She accepted the gun, wrapping her fingers around the grip. "Andrés—"

"Told me to give it to you." He returned to the other side of the narrow shaft and settled onto the floor again. "Good night, Miss Mathis."

She stared at the unfamiliar weight in her hand for a long time, then slipped it between the bottom two bags, close enough to reach, far enough away to feel safe. Andrés trusted her, she thought, wonder sending a faint shiver of warmth through her. In spite of her escape attempt, he trusted her enough to give her this weapon.

She fell asleep repeating a silent prayer for his safety.

It was early the next afternoon when a messenger arrived, ordering them back to the village. Vicente spoke to him, then told Brenna that Andrés was safe, that Hector, too, was unharmed and that Dorotea's babies, a boy and a

girl, were fine. As soon as they arrived in the village she
went to the office, ignoring the men gathered around the
desk, walking up to Andrés. "Was it Dad?"

He didn't look at her, simply shook his head.

"Were they looking for me?"

"Yes."

"But—"

"It was the soldier."

Then he did look at her, and she saw that he was exhausted. He needed rest, peace and gentleness, comfort and
love, or this war was going to kill him. He couldn't go on
much longer bearing all the burdens of San Angelo by himself. "What soldier?"

"The one who attacked you in the forest. I didn't order
him killed, because I knew it would upset you. Instead the
men took him beyond Santiago and let him go. Apparently
he met up with a unit of soldiers from the base at Dom-
ingo, and he told them all about the pretty American woman
he'd nearly captured. As long as they were raiding, they
thought they would look for you, too—liven up their nights
a bit. Have a little fun." He looked at her, through her. "I
should have killed him myself. If I had, those people..."

Tears welling in her eyes, Brenna clamped her hands over
her ears in frustration. "Who put you in charge? Who made
you God in this miserable little war? You're not responsible for everything that happens here! The only ones responsible for the deaths of those people are the men who killed
them... and me." Her voice dropped to a whisper, and she
began trembling in spite of the day's heat. "Oh, God...I'm
sorry."

She whirled away and rushed into the bedroom, slamming the door behind her. Andrés stood there a moment,
stunned by her outburst, then turned back to the men.

"Go to her."

Vicente's command was given in English so the others wouldn't understand. Andrés answered the same way. "She'll have to wait."

"She can't wait. Go to her now. Talk to her."

"And tell her what? That if she hadn't tried to escape she never would have met that soldier, he never would have told the others about her, and they never would have come looking for her?"

"Do you blame her?" Vicente demanded.

"Of course not."

"Then tell her that. Tell her the real reason those villagers were killed. Because this is a war, and people die in war, and it's not her fault, or yours. That soldier had nothing to do with it, just as you didn't, just as she didn't. The army would have raided that village anyway, and they would have killed those people anyway."

The two men stared at each other for a long time, until Andrés suddenly turned and went into the bedroom. Closing the door behind him, he stood feeling momentarily helpless, indecisive. Then he walked to the bed where Brenna lay crying, sat down, leaned back against the iron headboard and lifted her into his arms. She didn't fight him, but she didn't snuggle close to him as he'd expected, either.

Her tears were the only sound. He didn't offer her false comfort, didn't tell her that everything was all right when it wasn't. He simply held her, his arms tight around her, and stroked whatever part of her was within reach. When the sobs finally ended and the last tears had fallen, he cupped one hand beneath her chin and lifted her face to his. "Don't blame yourself, Brenna. Don't fall into the trap, the way I have, of thinking that you're somehow responsible for everything. It will give you a load of guilt that will break you."

She wrapped her fingers around his wrist, unaware that her grip was tight enough to hurt. "In my head I know it

wasn't my fault, but in my heart . . . it hurts to think that
maybe somehow I could have prevented those deaths."

"But you couldn't have. The army raids the villages. It's
a harsh, simple fact of war. They won't often attack us directly—they do it through our families and friends. They kill
our women, our children, our elderly, because they're weak,
defenseless and unarmed." He shifted her more comfortably on his lap, held her more intimately. "That village was
only fifteen miles from here. The soldiers knew that this was
our camp. They knew that the American was probably with
us. But they didn't come here looking for you, did they?
Because you weren't their primary goal. Killing was. Pleasure came second."

She slid her fingertips through the space between two
buttons on his jacket, pressing them against the warm expanse of his chest. "Then you couldn't have stopped them,
either. Even if you'd ordered that man killed, the soldiers
still would have come."

"Yes." But the acknowledgment came from his head, not
his heart. Like her, he hurt to think that maybe he could
have prevented more needless deaths. "I think Vicente has
the best grip on this. It's a war, he said, and people die in
war. It's sad and unfortunate, but it happens, and blaming
ourselves won't help. It doesn't stop the killing, it won't give
life to the dead, and it will eventually destroy us."

It was a lesson he himself needed desperately to learn, she
thought quietly. He lived with such guilt that she was surprised he could still function. "I was afraid last night," she
whispered.

Eyes closed, Andrés brushed his cheek over her hair.
"When you're safe back in Florida, you'll forget what it's
like to fear."

"No . . . not as long as you're here. I was afraid for you,
not me." She rested her head on his shoulder and rubbed her
hand over his unshaven jaw. His skin was beard-prickly, his
lips soft, his mustache sensuous. She loved touching him,

looking at him. She loved *him*. "All in all, I definitely would have preferred making love with you all night."

He licked the tip of her finger with his tongue, then nipped it. "Sweetheart, if I could find the time and the energy..."

"You find the time and *I'll* find the energy," she promised, then slid off his lap. "Go to work. I've distracted you long enough."

"Do you think you'll be any less of a distraction just because I can't see you?" he asked with a lazy smile. He pressed a kiss to her mouth, then stood up. "Why don't you rest?"

"I'm all right. I'll help Hector."

He considered giving her an order to stay here, where he knew she was close, where he knew she was safe, then decided against it. He nodded acceptance of her choice and left the room.

The night was dark, the moon hidden behind a bank of clouds, the air heavy and still. Rain was coming. It would mean a quiet night for the village.

Andrés leaned one shoulder against the rough post that supported the roof. Brenna was still in sick bay, tireless in her dedication to help. Hector would send her home soon, and Andrés would welcome her. He would dismiss her guards for the night, take her to bed and make love to her as sweetly, as tenderly, as he could.

He had struggled with his desire for her, with the futility of loving her, for so long. He had tried to do the right thing, the honorable thing, in keeping his distance, but today he'd given up the fight. There was nothing wrong, nothing dishonorable, in loving her. She knew that whatever they shared was temporary, that it would end the day she was returned to her father. She knew there was no future for them, had asked for nothing more than a brief affair with no strings attached. Let me make my own decisions, she'd told him last night. Let me accept responsibility for my own actions. She wanted an affair and was willing to accept her share of responsibility for having it.

Willing to take the decision out of his hands. To make him see that he couldn't control everything everyone did. That he could decide whether *he* wanted an affair, but had no right deciding whether *she* should have one.

The lack of absolute control was a new situation for him. For six years he had given orders, had directed and commanded everyone he came in contact with. He had chosen when they would fight, how they would attack and, in too many cases too painful to remember, where they would die. He'd had power over the most insignificant details of his men's lives, and because they'd trusted him, because they'd believed in him, they had allowed it.

But Brenna had changed that. He could no longer turn her away with feeble protests that it was wrong, or for her own good. It wasn't his decision to make. All he had to choose was whether he wanted to be with her. Whether he wanted to make love with her. Whether he wanted to face the emotional risks of having an affair with her. And he had to let her make those same choices for herself.

He smiled crookedly. The reasoning sounded good in his head, but he couldn't help but wonder if he was only making excuses—searching for a way to give in to what he wanted, what he *needed*, without having to deal with the guilt of taking what he shouldn't have.

No more soul-searching, he thought with a deep breath as Brenna came out of the clinic. For the next few days he was going to be Brenna's lover. He was going to show her how much he loved her. He was going to be happy.

Then he was going to let her go.

She wore shorts, pale blue cotton that made her legs seem to go on forever, and a T-shirt, white with flamingos painted in soft hazy shades of lavender, blue, softest pink. She walked between José and Diego, comfortable, as if with friends, leaving them at the foot of the stairs.

He dismissed the guards and told them to release the others, assigned to the night watch, too. It was going to rain tonight, and Brenna wasn't going anywhere. There was no need for anyone to get wet for nothing. Then he followed her inside the house, through the office, into the bedroom.

Brenna knew he was behind her, knew that tonight there would be no cajoling, no seduction, no guilt. Tonight he had chosen to stay with her. She walked to the nightstand and picked up the box of matches there. With a twist, the glass globe came off the lamp. With a strike, the match flared into flame, and the flame consumed the burned tip of the wick. She replaced the globe, adjusted the flame, then slowly turned to face Andrés.

"It surprises me at times how quickly I've gotten used to having no light after sunset," she said, her voice curiously teasing, erotically husky. "But there are still times when I need the light. When I need to see."

Andrés was still standing by the door, "Do you want me to go?"

She shook her head.

Slowly he raised his hands to his waist, unfastening his wide belt. The holstered pistol made a soft clunking sound when he laid it, belt and all, on the dresser. Still watching her, he unbuttoned his jacket, one round thick button at a time, and dropped it to the floor. He leaned back against the door and removed the heavy black combat boots with the ease of a man who'd worn them for years. When his socks dropped, too, he stopped and simply watched her.

"Oh, please," she said in a shaky, amused voice. "Don't stop now."

He unbuttoned the trousers, removed them and his briefs, and started toward her. He was beautiful, Brenna thought. His body was lean, rippling muscles, flat planes, velvet-soft skin. There were scars, on his shoulder, his ribs, his belly, one long and angry and nasty-looking down his thigh, but they didn't detract from his beauty.

And he was aroused. Fully. Completely. Without so much as a kiss, a stroke, a whispered promise.

She remained where she was, waiting for him to come to her, feeling the tingle of anticipation dance along her spine. He would touch her, would start the burning with his fingers, with his lips, with his eyes.

He stopped in front of her, reached out and traced one long, narrow finger over a feathery flamingo on her shirt. The bird's head curved over her breast, its body spreading along her belly, its long, slim legs disappearing inside the waistband of her shorts. Her nipples hardened, forming stiff peaks underneath the soft cotton shirt, making him hunger for their taste.

His eyes moved over her breasts to her throat, along her jaw to her face, finally meeting her eyes, bringing his own special brand of heat with them. Brenna couldn't look away, couldn't speak, couldn't move, could only stand and endure. Enjoy.

Her lips were parted, her breathing uneven. As he rubbed one blunt fingertip back and forth over the cotton that covered her nipple, she gasped, dragging in badly needed oxygen. With one kiss, he knew, he could rob all the air from her lungs, could have her weak, trembling, clinging to him for support. And he *would* do it, but not yet.

Boldly he slid his hand away from her breast, over her belly, positioning it intimately between her legs. There was such heat there, he marveled, such need, and it was for *him*. He moved his fingers tentatively, pressing, teasing, and a tiny whimper escaped her, but still she never looked away.

"Take your shirt off," he whispered in a rough stranger's voice, his fingers still rubbing. "Let me see your breasts."

It was a simple act—crossing her arms over her chest, grasping her shirt with both hands, untucking it from her shorts and pulling it over her head in one fluid movement—but everything about it was erotic, from his first glimpse of her breasts, small, full and naked, to the faint blush on her face as she pulled the shirt off, to the sensual tumble of her hair falling free. It made him swell even more, made the thick, heated length of him moist with desire. "You're a beautiful woman, Brenna."

She knew it wasn't true, knew other men found her passably attractive, maybe even pretty, but only Andrés had ever called her beautiful. But she *felt* beautiful with him—beautiful and well loved.

"For six years I've dreamed of you," he murmured. "Of touching you this way. Of holding you in my arms. Of making love to you, filling you . . . Sometimes I wanted you so badly that I thought I would lose my sanity, but most of the time, I knew that you *were* my sanity." He pulled his hand back and moved closer to her, sharing his warmth with her, cradling his hardness against her, and he kissed her, a gentle, slow offering of his mouth, his tongue, his hunger.

She was shivering, aching, overwhelmed by a tearful desperation. She needed him *now*. If he didn't touch her again between her legs, with his fingers or his mouth, if he didn't fill his place within her soon, she was going to shatter into a million fragments that could never be rejoined. Her muscles were trembling, her nerves tingling, her desire simmering.

She wrenched her mouth free of his and whispered against his lips, "Please, Andrés . . ."

As he kissed her again, his tongue stroking deep into the moist warmth of her mouth, he slid his hands down her spine until they encountered soft blue cotton. Hooking his fingers inside the waistband, he continued pushing, taking the shorts with him, a few inches later catching the narrow elastic of her panties. Brenna helped, stepping out of them, kicking them away.

He lifted her against him, supporting her with powerful muscles while, with one hand, he guided himself through her soft fair curls and inside the tight, fiery place that was her, that was his. She braced her hands on his chest, wrapping her legs around his narrow hips.

"Can we do this?" she whispered, wriggling, settling, the muscles in her belly coaxing him deeper.

He laughed softly, bit at her lip, stole her breath. "We *are* doing it."

It was different. It was restricting—she was afraid to move, half-afraid Andrés would drop her—but it was... sensuous. Erotic. And—she gasped as his body grew taut, as he gave one final thrust, then filled her with his hot, liquid release, as the heated sensation pushed her over the edge into her own release—and it was satisfying. Oh, yes. It was definitely satisfying.

"Andrés?" Brenna's whisper was tentative. If he was asleep, she didn't want to wake him, but if he was awake, there was something she wanted to ask.

Beneath her hand, his chest rose and fell in slow, steady breaths. He was probably asleep, she thought. They had made love a second time tonight, this time more conventionally, with him lying so perfectly over her on the bed. He had already been tired, so it was no wonder he'd fallen asleep almost immediately afterward.

But he wasn't asleep. He picked up her hand and guided it to his mouth for a kiss, then held it, fingers twined tightly together, on his chest. "What?" he asked through a yawn.

For a long moment she listened to the rain on the tin roof. It was soothing; it made her feel safe and secure... or was Andrés, lying beside her, responsible for that feeling?

She knew he was wide-awake, waiting for her question, but now she was afraid to ask it. What if it spoiled this special intimacy they now shared? What if he thought she was making demands, one thing she had promised not to do? What if he pushed her away?

And what if he didn't? logic countered.

"What do you want to know?" He turned onto his side to face her, but even this close, he couldn't make out her features. The lamp had been extinguished, and there was no moon to light the room.

She asked it quickly, blurting it out. "Could I stay here?"

The tension spread through him so fiercely that even where their bodies weren't touching, she could feel it. She wished she could call back the question, wished she could disappear inside herself, but she couldn't.

Rolling onto his back, Andrés stared into the darkness, breathing deeply, struggling for control. Her question appalled him at the same time that it filled him with a savage hope. It was a hope he couldn't afford. How could she believe he would ever let her remain in a place with such danger, where every day she would face the risk of death? And how could he handle the ridiculous idea that she cared enough to face that risk, that maybe she even loved him enough to try?

When he was calm enough to speak he asked sharply, "Here? In this bed? In this village? In this country?"

"Yes."

"Instead of going with your father? Instead of returning to Florida?"

"Yes." This time her answer was softer, a faint whisper.

"Why?"

Because he was here. Because she loved him. Because she didn't think she could endure her safe, routine life in Florida without him any longer. "I—I can help."

"You think we need help from an American?" He heard the derision he placed on the last word and winced, but didn't stop. "You want to help us? Then go back to your country and tell your people what's going on here. Tell your congressmen about the death you've seen, about the misery and the suffering and the need. Tell your newspapers about the prisoners we freed, about the torture and mistreatment and abuse they suffered at the hands of the government. Tell your fellow Americans that their tax dollars are bringing death and destruction to innocent people.'' He let the silence linger for a long time, then finished in a low, dark voice. ''But don't offer your help here. We don't need it.''

''You mean *you* don't *want* it. You don't want *me*.'' She kept the self-pity and pain from her voice. She had known all along that all he would give her was a few nights in his bed, a few nights to satisfy a long-unfed hunger. She wasn't even sure where the idea of staying had come from. It must have been born in the warm afterglow of their loving. Of *her* loving, she corrected, and his...

She didn't know how to describe his role in what had taken place here tonight and two nights ago. He had given to her as if she mattered, had taken from her as if he cared. He had been gentle and loving and passionate, and she had let herself hope that it meant something, that no matter how he denied it, in some tiny private place he loved her. But he would be gentle and loving with *any* woman in his bed. It was the way he was. It meant nothing.

''No,'' Andrés agreed quietly. ''I don't want you living here.'' He wanted to offer more: after the war is over, after life has returned to normal again... But how could he? The war might end tomorrow, or it might last thirty years. He might not live to see its end, or he might be executed as an enemy of the government to celebrate its end. She might hate him, might never forgive him, might be madly in love with another man by then. The future was too uncertain. Too bleak. He couldn't offer her—or himself—false hope. He couldn't offer anything.

''It was a stupid idea,'' she said with a fragile shrug. ''I don't even know why I suggested it. I really wouldn't like living here. Roughing it is all right for a while when you know that it's going to end soon, but I'd get fed up with it pretty quickly if I knew it would always be this way—no plumbing, no electricity, no heat, no air-conditioning. I guess I've gotten spoiled by all the modern conveniences we take for—"

Andrés covered her mouth with his, swallowing her last word. When he released her, he gathered her against him. "Lie in my arms so I can feel you even in my sleep. Let me hold you, and for the few days that remain, let me make love to you."

She didn't move away, the way she should have, the way he deserved. He held her close, his arms gently imprisoning her, one hand cupped tenderly over her breast.

For the few days that remain. He squeezed his eyes shut, focusing the anguish inward. That wasn't enough. God help him, a lifetime would never be enough. But a few days were all they had.

Chapter 9

Come on, get up. We've got things to do."

Brenna rolled onto her stomach, hiding her face in the pillow that smelled tantalizingly of Andrés. "I'm tired," she mumbled. "Sleepy."

Andrés dropped down onto the mattress beside her, brushing her hair back from one ear so he could tease it with his tongue. "Maybe you should go to bed earlier."

Rolling over again, she wrapped her arms around his neck. "Doesn't matter what time I go to bed. *Someone* keeps me awake."

"Maybe he should start sleeping in his own bed."

Eyes still closed, she tightened her embrace. "Never. Who needs sleep, anyway?" Then slowly she realized that those were clothes beneath her arms, that the cheek she was brushing her lips over was clean shaven and smelled faintly of soap. "Why do you have clothes on?"

"We've got to go to Santiago today." He watched as she slowly opened her eyes, untangled her hands and slid away from him. She sat up in bed, holding the sheet under her arms, combed her fingers through her hair and rubbed her eyes. In a matter of seconds she'd gone from drowsy lover to wary captive.

"Why do I have to go?"

"Because your father will want to talk to you."

"What do you expect me to tell him?"

He sighed softly as he traced feathery patterns over the back of her hand. "I don't expect anything, Brenna. He'll want to know if you're all right. He'll want to know if we're mistreating you."

"What am I supposed to tell him?"

"The truth."

"The truth?" She cocked her head to one side. "Don't you think that might be counterproductive?"

He simply looked at her.

"You've been threatening to kill me, and you've convinced him that you'll do it. What is he going to think when he finds out that instead of mistreating me, you've been making love to me?"

Andrés considered that for a long moment, then stood up and went to the dresser. He pulled open the top drawer and began tossing items of clothing onto the dresser—black shorts, a black-and-white striped shirt, red panties, a bra. Gathering them together, he threw them onto the bed. "It's going to scare the hell out of him," he muttered darkly. "It's going to make him more anxious than ever to get you out of here. It's going to make him think that I can use you just as effectively as he can."

"What do you mean?"

"Get dressed. We have to go."

Brenna rose to her knees on the mattress. "What are you talking about, Andrés? My father doesn't use me. He never has."

"I'll be back in five minutes. Be ready."

"Andrés—" When the door had shut, she threw his pillow at it. Angrily she got up and began putting on the clothes he'd chosen for her. Still tucking her shirt in, she barreled into the office, not caring that she was interrupting his conversation with Vicente. "What are you accusing my father of?"

He scowled at her. "Nothing."

"You said you could use me as effectively as he could. Is that what last night was about?"

Andrés's scowl deepened. Vicente leaned back in his chair, carefully avoiding looking at either one but clearly listening to the conversation.

"Is it?" she insisted. "Is that why you came to me last night?"

After glancing at his lieutenant, Andrés approached her, backing her away until she had reached the front door. There he leaned over her, nose to nose, and whispered in a heated voice, "I came to you because I wanted you. Don't *ever* accuse me of using you that way."

She opened her mouth to speak, then saw the look in his eyes and thought better of it. With an offended sniff she pushed open the screen door and went outside, waiting at the bottom of the steps.

"Too bad she can't stay," Vicente remarked casually. "She certainly livens things up around here."

Andrés shifted and glared at him.

The other man quickly changed the subject. "Are you going to tell her about her father?"

"No."

"Why not?"

"Why? What would it accomplish?"

"She trusts the bastard with her life, and to him she's just a pawn, something to be used or forgotten, whatever suits him."

Andrés listened to the anger in Vicente's voice as much as the words. His friend sounded bitter, too bitter to be talking about a woman he hardly knew and a man he'd never met. "She does trust him," he agreed. "More than that, she loves him. She thinks he's the bravest, strongest, most honorable man she's ever known. Why disillusion her?''

"Because she's wrong."

Andrés shook his head. "She'll be gone from here in a few days, but she has to spend the rest of her life as his daughter. Let her believe in him."

"She's not going to quit asking," Vicente warned.

"No. But I've lied to her before." He looked out the door to where she was standing, her back stiff, and sighed wearily. "I can do it again." He picked up his rifle and started toward the door. "I'm taking some extra men, in case there are any patrols in the area. The army can't be too happy about losing those twenty-one soldiers."

"Take care."

Andrés sighed again as he walked out the door. All his life he'd taken care. He'd been mature, responsible, reliable, even as a child. Why, then, was his life in such a mess?

The church was empty when they arrived, its doors locked. "Father Hidalgo must be at the village," Andrés said as he fished the key from his pocket. "They'll be burying the dead as quickly as possible."

"Don't any of your villages have names?" Brenna asked, fidgeting under the hot sun. She was still in a bad mood from the morning's little talk. All the way to Santiago, she had puzzled over Andrés's remark about her father but hadn't found an explanation. Somehow she would force one from him. She didn't know how—but somehow.

"Only the larger ones." Andrés swung the door open and gestured for Brenna to enter. "My village was always referred to by the Montano name, because we had the most fields, the most prosperous farm, the largest house. Only the bigger ones have official names."

"That must make it difficult to find your way around," she said dryly, automatically heading toward the office.

"Well, the army is working hard to make it easier. In six years they've wiped out dozens of our villages." He turned on the dim light on the priest's desk and reached for the phone, dialing the number from memory. As soon as there was an answer on the other end, he offered the receiver to Brenna without a word.

Sinking into the single chair, she took the phone, her hand trembling. "Hello."

"Brenna, is that you?"

She took a deep breath. "Hi, Dad."

"Honey, where are you? Are you all right? I've been hearing rumors...."

"What kind of rumors?"

"About an American woman in the mountains out west who was almost taken prisoner by a corporal who had deserted his post a few weeks ago. The description sounded a lot like you, but I knew it couldn't—"

"I escaped. But I got found again. I guess I should have paid more attention when you took that navy survival course, right?" Her attempt at humor fell flat, and her voice began quavering. "Dad, have you found his cousin?"

"Yes. I persuaded the president to turn him over to me."

She didn't like the sound of that. "You aren't planning anything, are you? You're not going to double-cross Andrés, are you?"

Tom was silent for a moment, then reluctantly admitted, "No. But if you weren't involved, if it could be done without endangering you, I would set up the biggest ambush that bastard has ever seen."

There was such anger in his voice. It made her ache to hear it, to know that the best example of love she'd ever seen could turn into this. "Why do you hate him?" she whispered.

"He made a fool of you, of me, of the entire U.S. Navy. You should hate him, too, Brenna. After what he's done, you *have* to hate him."

Closing his eyes, she shook her head. "I don't have any hatred left inside me, Dad. Just sorrow."

"Has he hurt you?"

She could feel Andrés close behind her. When she looked, she saw him gripping the back of the chair with both hands. "No. He keeps his distance," she lied. "He doesn't have much interest in me."

"He never did," Tom said bitterly, not realizing—or not caring? she wondered—that his words were hurtful. "But don't worry, babe. As soon as you're safe at home, he'll pay for what he's done to you. I promise you that."

"Dad, I don't want—"

"Let me talk to him, okay?"

She silently held out the phone to Andrés. He hesitated for a moment, then unclenched one hand to take it. This time he spoke in English. This time he wanted her to know what he was telling her father. "Do you have any questions about how I'm treating your daughter?"

"She told me that she escaped," Tom said smugly.

"Yes, and almost died in the process. What else did she tell you? That I keep my distance from her?" His eyes, dark, sad, resolute, locked with hers. "She lied. She's trying to protect you from the truth. The next time you talk to her, ask her where she slept last night, and the nights before that. Ask her who she slept with."

"You son of a bitch." The insult was whispered, furious, deadly. "Isn't it enough that you've kidnapped her, that you've held her prisoner, that you've threatened her and frightened her for two weeks? Couldn't you let her keep anything?"

"Sorry," Andrés said callously. "Good women are hard to come by out here. Listen closely. Make sure you get this right." Still watching Brenna, he gave Tom directions to the meeting place he'd chosen with his advisors. It was a valley roughly equidistant from the camp and Santa Lucia, high in the mountains, remote and difficult to reach. Because of the nearby peaks and treacherous air currents overhead, it was inaccessible by air, and only one road crossed it, a road controlled for miles on each side by the rebels. It was as safe as they could get.

She couldn't stand any more, Brenna thought numbly. Without sparing a glance for Andrés, she walked out of the office, closing the door quietly behind her, and found a seat on one of the pews.

Andrés named a date and time, then added one more warning. "Don't bring any Angelenos with you—only your Americans. If we see any government soldiers, I'll disappear with Brenna so deep into these mountains that you'll never find us, and my men will take Esai from you anyway."

"How do I know you won't try anyway?" Tom demanded.

"Because I don't want her. She's fine for a little fun, but I don't want to keep her." He ended the call, turned off the light and left the office. In the sanctuary, he sat down on the pew a few feet from Brenna. "Such lies in the house of God," he murmured with a weary sigh.

She stared at the rows of burning candles. "Tell me, Andrés, did you make love with me so you could tell him about it, or did that idea come later?"

He drew one finger down her bare arm, making her shiver. "I told him to scare him. He knows you once loved me. If he thinks I'm getting close to you again, it will terrify him."

"Why?"

"Because he hates me."

"Why?"

Andrés turned sideways on the bench to face her. "Tom Mathis is a very proud man. He doesn't trust many people. He likes even fewer and can count those he loves on one hand. He needs to be in control. He needs power over the people around him. He needs to be *right*. Tom Mathis never makes a mistake. He never makes a wrong decision, a wrong choice."

Those were things she already knew.

"He trusted me from the very beginning. He liked me." Andrés was silent for a moment. "I think, in his way, he even loved me."

She knew that, too. There had been a lot of times when she'd thought her father had loved Andrés more than his own daughter. He had always wanted a son, someone to train and to teach, to follow in his footsteps. Andrés had been ideal. "But you betrayed him by coming back here. By disappearing with that shipment of weapons and diverting them to the rebels. By using the very training he taught you against your government, your own army, and, through their alliance, against our government."

He nodded. "But there was more to it than that. I didn't marry you, the way he wanted me to. I didn't become a true-blue American like him. Worse than that, *I* made the choices, the decisions in my life. I took the power and the control that meant so much to him, and I used them to do what I had to do. He was wrong about me. He'd made a serious error in judgment. It hurt him personally and professionally. He wants to punish me for it."

They sat in silence for a long time before she spoke again. "You never answered my question. Did you make love to me so you could tell Dad?"

He grasped her chin, forcing her to look at him. "I told you this morning: don't accuse me of using you that way."

"You also told me this morning that you could use me as effectively as he could. Was this what you meant?"

For a long time he stared at her, studying her face as if to memorize it. Then he gently released her, sat back on the bench and faced the front. "I've been using you for a long time, Brenna, for a variety of reasons—to get Esai freed, of course, but for so many other things. To get through the nights. To remember better times. To remember what it's like to feel peace and love and comfort. To give myself hope. To remind myself that there are good people in this world, people who don't have to punish and dominate and destroy to be happy.'' He watched as one candle melted to a small pool of liquid wax in its glass holder, flickered, then went out, sending up a puff of black smoke and a brief singed odor.

"I wish it hadn't been necessary to tell your father about last night, but I need to keep him off balance. As long as he's afraid for you, he'll follow orders. The moment he begins to believe that you're safe, we're lost...and Esai is dead. Even if it weren't true, even if I hadn't touched you once, I still would have told him the same thing. It's one more way of frightening him, one more thing for him to worry about—not just your physical safety, but now also your emotional well-being, and even the possibility of a child."

Unconsciously she touched her stomach. That was something she would hope for, would pray for every night until she knew. "That would be quite a souvenir. Most people bring home straw hats, T-shirts, useless little knickknacks, from their vacations."

Again he turned to her, reached out to touch her, this time clasping her hands in his. "If you are pregnant... will you have the baby? Will you keep him and love him in spite of his father?"

Brenna pulled her hands free and stood up, walking to the end of the pew. There she stopped and faced him once more. "In spite of his father?" she echoed and shook her head. "*Because* of his father. I love you, Andrés. For whatever it's worth. For whatever it matters." Then she turned again and walked out of the building, leaving him alone in the dim light.

He bowed his head, covering his face with his hands. Later, when he was stronger, he would remind himself of all the reasons not to trust in her declaration of love, but for now, for just these few quiet moments, he let himself believe, let himself feel the warmth and the peace and the joyful gratitude because he'd heard those words from her one more time.

It would be over soon. One more day. Tuesday evening they would leave for the valley, traveling under the cover of darkness, and Wednesday he would exchange Brenna for Esai. He would trade the most important person in his life for the second most important. He would say goodbye to her and watch her walk away, knowing that he would never see her again.

Never. The word was a threat, a bleak promise that drained all life from him.

But she'd said she loved him.

He gave a shake of his head to chase away the false hope, countering it with grim reality. Because of their past relationship she was vulnerable to him. Because of their current situation she was dependent on him—for shelter, for food, for protection, for her very life. Studies had shown that hostages often became sympathetic toward, even friendly with, their captors because they desperately wanted to live. Because their need to survive was stronger than their need to hate.

That need to survive allowed Brenna to believe she loved him, and he had no doubt that she *did* believe it. Today. Here and now. But next week, next month, when she was safe at home and her journey to San Angelo had faded into a distant nightmare, she would know what he already knew: her feelings of love had been only a means of coping. For a time her feelings toward him would be ambivalent—anger, hatred and fear mixing with concern for him—but eventually she would put him out of her mind. Permanently.

Feeling old and weary and defeated, Andrés got to his feet and left the church. Outside, Brenna was waiting with the nine guards who had accompanied them. They stood silently while he locked the door; then they moved together to the old pickup and the jeep parked behind it.

As soon as they reached the village Brenna started toward the clinic, but Andrés stopped her with his light touch. "Take a walk with me."

She knew she could turn him down, walk away, and he would let her go, just as he was willing to let her go once Esai was free. With a taut smile she nodded. Hands stuffed into her pockets, she walked at his side, but not close enough to accidentally bump into him.

She wasn't sorry that she'd told him she loved him. Even though he'd offered no response, even though once he'd come out of the church he'd acted as if nothing out of the ordinary had happened inside, she wasn't sorry. She hadn't expected a reciprocal declaration. Whatever Andrés felt for her, or had felt in the past she had finally made peace with, she wouldn't delude herself into thinking it was love. He had sweet words to offer, and sweeter loving, but she wouldn't tell herself he loved her. It was enough that she loved him.

They walked past the church, lonely and empty, with its twelve little crosses in back. When the war was over and the families returned to the village, she hoped they would use the church again for their weddings, their christenings, their worship and, yes, their funerals. She hoped they would let their new lives, their new love, heal the tragic memories of loss.

"A long time ago when you showed me the pictures of your family, your village and your country," she said softly, glancing sideways at Andrés, "I wanted to come here. I wanted to meet your parents and your brothers and Maria. I wanted to see where you'd grown up, where you'd gone to school, where you'd lived in Santa Lucia. Did you know that?"

"Yes."

"But I never asked. I was afraid you would think I was pushing you, trying to force you into some sort of commitment." The memory made her smile. "Men seem to react strangely to that. Asking to meet their parents on the other side of town is enough to frighten a great many of them off. Asking to go to another country to meet them . . ." With a laugh, she shook her head.

"They would have welcomed you."

Lacing her fingers behind her back, she turned, looking at the village as she walked backward beside him. "The house where Hector has his clinic—that was your family's home, wasn't it?"

"Yes. How did you know?"

"Hector told me once that it had been owned by the most influential family in the village, but they had died, so the remaining relatives had allowed him to use it. Today you said that your family had the most prosperous farm and the largest house."

"You pay attention to meaningless details that should slip by."

With a spin she turned to face forward again as they reached the path that led to the stream. In silent agreement they turned onto it. "I do. And I'm usually pretty good at figuring things out. So why don't you tell me how my father's using me?"

Andrés said nothing, just continued his leisurely pace along the broad path.

"Does it have anything to do with Esai's capture?"

He still said nothing.

"I think it does. I think Dad was responsible for Esai's capture, wasn't he?"

Finally Andrés stopped walking and looked down into her face. Her expression was calm, her gaze steady. There was a hint of determination in her soft brown eyes, a thread of dismay, a shadow of pain. She thought she knew the worst, he realized, and she was prepared to accept it. But she was wrong. She didn't know the worst.

She touched his arm. "Tell me, Andrés. I know he hates you." Remembering the loathing in her father's voice, she winced. "He'd like to see you dead, wouldn't he?"

Stubbornly he refused to answer.

Muttering a curse, Brenna dropped her hand and walked away, then came back. "He set a trap for you, and your cousin was captured instead. I know that, because you said he engineered Esai's capture, and Vicente said he was taken in your place."

"Vicente and I talk too much," he said, his expression settling into a familiar scowl.

"Too much, not enough." She shrugged carelessly. "How was I a part of it?"

"Drop it, Brenna," he warned.

"I can't. As long as I'm here, I'll keep asking you, and I'll ask Vicente, and when I leave here, I'll ask my father, until *somebody* tells me the truth."

"Do you love your father, Brenna?"

"Of course I do."

"Do you respect him?"

"Yes."

"Then let it go. What happened doesn't matter anymore. As long as I get Esai back, as long as you're safely returned to Tom, nothing else matters."

She walked to a boulder at the edge of the path and sat down on it, bracing her feet on the sloping sides. It was warm from the sun's rays. "It matters to me. You people are playing games with me. I'd just like to know how." Clasping her hands around her knees, she leaned back, arching her spine, then straightened. "Nothing you could tell me would make me stop loving my father. Maybe it would affect my respect for him, but I'd rather be disillusioned and know the truth than be uncertain and know nothing. Please, Andrés..."

Slowly he walked to the boulder, reaching out to stroke his hand over her hair. What he was about to do would give her more reason than ever to hate him, in spite of her bold words about disillusionment and truth. If she believed him, she could hate him for tarnishing her image of her father. If she didn't believe him, she would hate him for making up such a tale.

"Three weeks ago I got a message from your father. It was the first contact I'd had with him since he came here. He asked to meet me at a little cantina in Bernadino. I discussed it with my advisors, who were in agreement that it was a trap. I should ignore it, they said. But Tom's message said it was urgent. I felt I had to go. When we got to Bernadino, Esai insisted on going into the cantina first, to check it out."

"Was my father there?"

He shook his head. "According to our contacts he was two hundred miles away in his office in Santa Lucia. But there were soldiers there, with orders to pick me up. When Esai sounded the alarm, there was a battle, and he was captured. The trap had been set for me, but because he was concerned for my safety, because he entered the cantina in my place, Esai was taken prisoner."

Brenna rested her chin on her knees. "You're sure the message was from my father."

"Positive."

"Why? Anyone could have used his name. Anyone could have made you believe it was from him."

He crouched beside the rock so he could look up into her face. "Perhaps. But no one else could have known to send that message to me."

She gazed away from him, her eyes shifting restlessly from tree to shrub to trail and back again. She had claimed that hearing this wouldn't touch her love for her father, that even if it affected her respect for him, she wanted to know. Now she half wished she had dropped the subject, as Andrés had warned. Perhaps, in this case, he did know what was best for her.

But she'd come too far, heard too much, to drop it. She looked up at him, touched her fingers to his hand and asked the hardest question. "What did the message say?"

"'I need to tell you about Brenna.'" It had been that simple: *I need to tell you about Brenna.* Not "I'd like to talk to you about Brenna," but *I need to tell you.* Seven words that hinted at urgency, at a secret, at importance. The thoughts that had raced through his head—that she was hurt, ill, dying, even that she'd had his child six years ago and needed him now. He had been sick with fear. Nothing could have kept him from that meeting.

"Oh, God." Brenna slid to the ground and paced back and forth, anxiety turning itself into restless energy. "But how did he know that you would come?"

Rising to his feet, he shrugged. "Your father knew me better than anyone else in this country. He knew my strengths, and he knew my weaknesses."

"He used me...to set a trap for you...so you could be killed." She rubbed her hands over her eyes before facing him with a weary smile. "I didn't know he could hate like that."

"Or love like that." He opened his arms, and she went to him, laying her head against his chest. "He loves you as much as any man could love a child. I think he could have dealt with all my other betrayals if I hadn't hurt you. When you see him, talk to him, Brenna. Try to convince him to give up his post here. Living down here, fighting in our war—it's just feeding his hatred. Get him to go back to Florida, so he can spend time with his daughter. So someday he can spend time with his granddaughters."

They stood there for a long time, holding each other. It was sweet and warm and comforting, the sort of thing Brenna had dreamed of through long years alone. It gave her the strength to return to another painful subject. "I meant what I said in the church, Andrés. I love you."

He tilted her head back and pressed a kiss to her lips. "I know you meant it." She believed it was true as surely and strongly as he believed it wasn't. But he wouldn't insult her by telling her that. He would be selfish, as she had once urged him to be, and take these few days of happiness and love for himself. When she got back to Florida she would discover the truth, and she would deal with it better than he would.

"I have work to do—"

"As usual," she interrupted.

"I'll be gone for a couple of hours. Be waiting for me. Please?"

When she nodded, he kissed her, very gently, very possessively; then they returned to the village. He left almost immediately, accompanied by a dozen heavily armed men. Brenna watched him go, then went into the clinic, greeting Hector with a slightly sad smile.

The exchange was going to take place very soon, she knew. Andrés wouldn't have given her father the location until it was almost time. Even after last night, she had foolish hopes that he would change his mind, would ask her to stay, would ask her to spend the rest of her life with him. Whether he loved her or not, whether the war ended or not, she would have said yes. She would give up everything—her job, her home, her father, her country—if only he would ask.

But he wouldn't. She knew that, too. Even though he enjoyed making love with her, even though he knew she loved him, even though he needed her, he would never ask her to stay. He wouldn't subject her to the dangers or the hardships on more than a temporary basis. And he wouldn't offer her any promises or hopes for a future. Even that, as little as it was, would have been enough. If he said, "I'll come for you when the war ends," she would wait—a month, a year, ten years, however long it took.

But he didn't want her to wait. He didn't want her here. And he didn't love her.

Her sigh was so sad that both nearby patients turned concerned gazes her way. She forced a smile for them as she went about the task of sweeping the floor.

She swept a small pile of dust out the door, then sat down across from Hector. "If I want to get in touch with you after I go home, Hector, how can I do it?"

His smile was merry. "That's a good question. Mail service in San Angelo is sporadic. Mail service for the freedom fighters is nonexistent."

"Say I needed to send you . . . a package."

"A package?" His eyes lit up. "As in medical supplies?"

She nodded.

"I'll give you the address of a church across the border in Ecuador. The priest there is a friend of Father Hidalgo's and is sympathetic to our cause. He'll get it to us." As he scribbled the information on a scrap of paper, he asked, "Are you anxious to be going away from us?"

Honesty formed her answer. "No. I offered to stay, only . . . I can't be of any help here. But I can at home."

"You've been a great deal of help here," he told her softly. "To me, to my patients, especially to Andrés. He needs a woman like you."

She smiled sadly. "His need for me has almost ended. Now he needs to win this war, so he no longer has to be a brave, honorable soldier and can be just a man."

"He's a good man."

"Yes, he is."

"And you love him."

"Yes, I do."

"When this is over . . . if he comes for you . . ."

"I'll be waiting."

After dinner she pantomimed her need to José for a bucket of water from the church well. While Diego escorted her back to the house, the other guard ran her errand. Closed up in the lamp-lit bedroom, she stripped off her clothes, bathed and washed her hair. She dressed in the yellow ribbed tank top and matching panties, combed her hair with her fingers and climbed into bed, stuffing the pillows behind her back, pulling the sheet to her waist.

In the still night she heard the trucks return, heard Andrés and Vicente and several others talking in the outer room. Tilting her head back, closing her eyes, she waited, knowing he would come to her when he could.

Andrés ended his meeting as quickly as possible. The valley was secure, he told the men. Their troops had been in place for the past several days, watching the road, patrolling the surrounding forest. No government troops could penetrate their perimeter. There could be no trap, no ambush.

It would be a major operation. Only a small contingent would be left behind to guard the village; everyone else—even Manuel, the cook, and Hector, to tend to Esai—would go along. Nothing could go wrong. Esai had to remain alive, and the American—he winced at his impersonal reference to the woman he loved—had to remain unharmed.

When there were no questions, he dismissed the men. Manuel had sent over his dinner, and Raúl had brought him water to wash away the day's grime. He ate a little, then removed his uniform and bathed, dressing again in the clean trousers he'd left on his cot. Unable to delay any longer, he walked to the closed door and twisted the knob.

She was beautiful. The lamp cast its soft golden glow over her face, her shoulders, her hair. Once again she wore the flimsy top that clung tightly to her breasts and her flat belly and revealed the peaks of her nipples, swelling under his gaze. Although her eyes were closed, she was aware of him. He saw it in the curve of her lips, in the simple gesture of one hand lifted from her lap and offered to him.

"Is your work done for the night?" she asked, listening to the soft, almost imperceptible sounds of his steps as he came to her.

"I think maybe it's just starting."

She smiled again. "Let me rephrase that. Are you mine for the night?"

For this night and every night, he silently promised her. It was so much more satisfying than the answer he gave aloud. "Yes."

He sat down on the mattress beside her, and she raised her head, opened her eyes. She clasped his hand in hers and rested it on his thigh. She studied his face for a moment— the exhaustion that was permanently etched around his eyes, the hard line of his jaw, the sad set of his mouth. "It's almost over, isn't it?" she whispered.

Lowering his head, he focused on their hands. Hers was slim, so small, so delicate, and yet so strong. Capable. Like her. "The exchange is set for Wednesday. We leave tomorrow evening. It's a long journey."

So this was to be their last night alone together. She felt the stab in her heart, half wishing he hadn't told her, wisely grateful that he had. She would make the most of this night, of these last few intimate hours with him. She would create the most beautiful memories a woman could ask for, memories to treasure for the rest of her life.

And maybe something more, she pleaded in a silent prayer. If she couldn't have Andrés, she asked God to please let her have his child. Let her have someone to love.

Her hands were gentle on his skin, starting with the healing wound on his shoulder, brushing downward, across his chest, over his ribs, skirting the flat circles of his nipples and moving to his belly. Andrés closed his eyes as she fumbled, as she had once before, with his trouser buttons, popping each one open with a maximum of effort. When she slid one hand inside, over his bare skin, he stiffened. When her hand moved lower, her fingers wrapping tenderly around the swollen length of his manhood, he sucked in a deep breath to control his shudders.

"Tonight I want to make love to you," she whispered, leaning forward to touch her lips to his. "I want to look at you and touch you and kiss you. I want to feel the heat of your skin against mine. I want to make you so hard and so hungry that you can't bear it any longer.''

His jaw was stubbly, scraping her tender skin as she left a line of wet kisses down his throat. Carefully she released him and stood up, then pushed him onto his back. After blowing out the lamp, she joined him on the bed, lying on her side, arranging his arms at his sides, out of her way. When he reached for her, she pushed his hand back. ''Not yet. Soon.''

When she bent over him, her hair fell, soft and damp and smelling sweetly of shampoo, rubbing like silk over his chest. He started to reach for it, to tangle his hands in it and pull her to him, his prisoner not just for tonight but for always, but remembering her admonition, he clenched his hands into fists at his sides instead.

Her lips closed around his nipple in a heated, wet kiss, her tongue laving it until it was hard and peaked. Catching it between her teeth, she suckled, and he groaned, a low, helpless sound.

While her mouth continued its sweet torture, her hands began their own, stroking over his bare skin—his face, his chest, his belly, his arms—spreading fire and need so strong that he trembled. When she dipped beneath the coarse trousers once more and took him in hand, he swore, desire and frustration thick in his voice. ''I want you now,'' he commanded, but Brenna evaded his hands.

''Not yet.'' Sliding to the edge of the bed, she began removing his trousers slowly, tormentingly, an inch at a time, while with her mouth she caressed each bit of newly revealed skin. When his hardness was free, she tasted the sensitive tip, wetting it with her tongue, sensuously stroking the entire length.

He swore again. His muscles were rigid with restraint that was close to shattering, and his eyes were squeezed shut tightly, creating bright colors in his head. Desperately he reached for her, wrapping his hands in her hair, urging her with his body to relieve the need that was twisting in his belly all the way into his soul.

She ended her intimate kiss, pulled his hands away and swiftly finished undressing him; then like a sleek, powerful cat, she moved over him, settling into place over his hips. She leaned forward, her entire body in contact with his, and kissed him slowly, leisurely exploring his mouth with her tongue while the different textures that were her—the satiny length of her bare legs, the downy softness of her clothes, the wet silk of her hair, the firm, velvety pressure of her mouth—tantalized him.

Restlessly he moved against her, his hardness burning through the thin cotton of her panties. "Now, Brenna," he growled when he wrenched his mouth free of hers, "or 'soon' will be too late."

In a moment that made him grit his teeth on a groan, she slipped out of her panties and, wearing only the tiny top, moved back into place. Their hands bumped, and he pulled his back, savoring the feel of her small fingers wrapped around him, guiding him inside her. The rocking of her hips lured him deeper until his entire length was gloved in her heat.

Andrés settled his hands on her thighs, feeling the shifting and tensing of muscle underneath satin skin as she stroked him. "Take your shirt off," he whispered, forcing each word through clenched teeth, and she obeyed, tossing it onto the mattress. He watched her, his vision made hazy by the intensity of his feelings, and he loved her more than he had ever loved her before.

Deep inside, her muscles convulsively flexed around him, sending a wave of near-pain through him. He could no longer lie passively while she destroyed him with sensation. Gripping her hips, he took control, thrusting deeply with long, rapid strokes, in and out and in again, rising to meet her, making her cry out, making her explode around him;

then came his own release, pumping hot and violently into her.

Even as he gave himself up to the soul-shattering end, there was one thought, bleak and unwelcome, in his mind.

How could he live without her?

Brenna lay on her stomach, her head resting on Andrés's chest, listening to the slowly evening sound of his breath. She longed for conversation, for the sound of his voice to soothe her, for any reason to keep him awake at her side. It was their last night together, and she didn't want to waste any of it sleeping. But after loving like that, what was left to say?

She had said, "I love you," and he had hugged her so that she couldn't see his face. So she couldn't see that her love wasn't returned. She wished she could tell him that it was all right, that he didn't have to love her, that she could settle for nothing more than nights like this and be happy. She didn't need promises of love—she needed *him.*

But he didn't need her.

"What are you thinking?"

She nuzzled his chest. "Nothing."

"You're thinking something. I can feel the tension spreading through you."

Slowly she raised her head, settling her chin on his ribs. Should she lie so he wouldn't feel guilty? No, he would know she was lying. She'd never been very good at it anyway, and especially not about anything that mattered. "Wouldn't life be easier," she remarked, her voice soft and unsteady, "if people could only fall in love with people who would love them back?"

He looked stricken; then he lifted his hand to her hair. "Brenna, I'm sor—"

Quickly she broke in, forcing a smile that didn't reach her eyes. "No. You ask a silly question, you get a silly answer. Talk to me, Andrés. Tell me what it was like growing up here. Tell me about your family and your friends. Tell me about Santa Lucia and San Angelo and this village that has no name. Tell me . . ." Everything. Anything. Something.

It was a long time before he trusted his voice enough to speak, and then only because she was watching him with such an uneasy, wary look, as if she might break down any moment if he didn't distract her. If she cried he would comfort her, hold her and whisper to her—promises, assurances, words of love. And that would be a mistake. Her place, her life, her future, were in Florida. Not here. Not with him.

"Ask your questions and I'll answer them all."

She sighed softly, grateful that he wasn't going to pursue the other subject any further. If he had offered an apology for not being able to love her, she would have screamed her way into hysterics. Now she searched for an easy, uncomplicated topic and seized on the first one that crossed her mind. "Tell me about Vicente."

"Well . . . he's a good soldier. A good friend. He's saved my life a number of times."

"Where is he from?"

"I don't know. Somewhere in the east, I guess."

"How long have you known him?" She snuggled closer to him, feeling the tension slide away as the easy, meaningless conversation progressed.

"He's been with us a couple of years—about three, I think."

"And you don't know where he's from? Did he just show up one day and say, 'Hi, I'd like to join your war'?"

Andrés's laugh rumbled in his chest. "Not exactly. Someone brought him into the group—I just don't know who, offhand. I've never asked him a lot of questions, but I'm sure if I did, he would answer them. But this isn't like the army. I don't need a man's life history to decide if I can trust him. Vicente is totally trustworthy. He's a good man."

Ducking his head, he pressed a kiss to her forehead. "Why are you so interested? Trying to make me jealous?"

"Do you *get* jealous?" she asked innocently. "I thought the great Andrés Montano was above such petty human feelings."

His humor faded, and he hid his face in her hair. It muffled his voice when he spoke again. "The great Andrés Montano is a myth, created to lead the people of San Angelo into a war that is costing them dearly," he said in a low, sad voice. "Just like the Wizard of Oz was a sham, an ordinary man hiding behind a legend, so am I. I'm not great, not a leader, not a hero. Just a tired, empty man."

"*I* think you're great," she murmured, stroking his chest with her fingertips, tracing the scar over his ribs. "Your people respect you, and your enemies are terrified of you. What more could you ask for?"

"Peace. Quiet. Solitude."

"You'll have that when the war ends. Romero and his cronies will be thrown out of power, and a new, just government will take over, and you'll live a peaceful, quiet life, with your wife at your side and your children around you." Her voice quavered only slightly at the end. As much as it hurt, she knew it was true. He would find a wife, a woman he could love, a woman who could give him a dozen children to fill his heart and his empty village, and he would forget all about *her*.

But she would never forget him. Even though someday she would have another man's child, she would never love any man the way she loved Andrés.

Silently he, too, acknowledged the truth in her statement. Someday he *would* get married and start a family. He couldn't live the rest of his life alone—if he had a life when the war ended. He would find a woman, an Angelena, one who shared his love for his country, one who knew the hardships they would face and could bear them, and they would marry. Someday they would have children. And maybe someday he would even learn to care about her.

"What if they want you to run the country the way you've run their war?" she asked, forcing her thoughts away from dark-haired, dark-eyed babies in some other woman's arms. "Will you accept?"

"What do I know about running a country?" he scoffed.

"You know how to be fair. You understand justice, and you understand people. You allow even your prisoners to hold on to their dignity and some sense of self-worth. You would make a wonderful president."

Slowly he shook his head. "I'm tired, Brenna. I don't want to tell anyone what to do. I don't want to bear anyone else's problems."

Sadly she hugged him tighter. "I wish I could help you."

"You have."

"How? With a few nights of sex?"

A protest against her demeaning description of their lovemaking automatically formed on his lips, but he kept it inside. Let her call it that, he warned himself, if it helped her to deal with their relationship. "You've made me remember a time when things were better. When I was happy. When there was peace."

Brenna waited expectantly for his denial of her words—wanted to hear him once more insist in his rough voice that they had made love. When he didn't, she sighed deeply, pushing away the emotion that made her feel so tearful. Tonight wasn't the time for tears. "Maybe Vicente could be your new president. He seems to be qualified. He's intelligent, well educated, reliable, trustworthy, and he has the sophistication and polish to deal effectively with foreign government representatives." Slowly she rolled onto her back, scooting up to pillow her head on Andrés's arm. "He reminds me of a friend at home, a doctor at the hospital where I work. She shares all the same qualities, especially the polish. She acts like an ordinary person, but there's something different about her. Something special. There's something different about Vicente, too.''

This doctor was the first friend she had mentioned in her two weeks here, although he was certain she had many. She was too sweet, too warm and giving a person, to live without a large group of close friends around her. ''Will you be glad to see your friends when you get back?'' he asked cautiously, not certain what he wanted to hear in reply.

The question was so simple, so bland, so meaningless, that it made Brenna's temper flare. Why was she lying here beside him discussing old friends, Vicente, and a wife and children for Andrés, when her heart was breaking? ''No,'' she said flatly, sitting up and searching in the jumbled sheets for her clothing. When she found the shirt, she pulled it on, leaving her hair standing on end. Next she struggled into her panties, then sat cross-legged on the bed, fists clenched, arms folded over her chest. ''I don't care about seeing my friends. I don't care about getting back. I don't care about much of anything right now except you. Don't you know that? Or doesn't it matter to you?''

''Brenna—'' He sat up, too, leaning back against the headboard. ''Don't start . . . not now.'' Not when he was vulnerable. Not when he might say things that he would have to take back tomorrow, might make promises that he could never keep.

''Oh, this isn't a good time for you?'' she asked sarcastically. ''Maybe next time I should demand the discussion before the sex. That seems the best way to hold your attention.'' The unfairness of the accusation stung her but didn't slow her down. ''When *would* the time be right? Wednesday afternoon? Or better yet, how about Thursday morning, when I'm on a plane heading away from here? Do you think you might find time to talk then?''

He swung his legs to the floor, found his trousers and pulled them on.

"Go ahead," she challenged, tears filling her eyes as she watched him fasten the buttons. "Walk away. You did it before."

Furiously he turned to her. "And I warned you that I would do it again."

"The only promise you ever made me," she said, her tone ugly to match the feelings inside her. "And since you're such a man of honor, of course you'll keep it."

"You got what you wanted—an affair. A few days. No demands. So why are you complaining?"

Her bravado and anger disappeared, and her shoulders slumped. "I *love* you, Andrés."

"No, you don't." He said it harshly to convince himself as well as her. "You want to believe that because it will keep you safe."

Slowly she shook her head in disbelief. "You're wrong."

"No, I'm not wrong. Call what you're feeling 'love,' if you want, but it's not, and you'll realize that when you get back to your real life."

"What is this? You tell your people what to do, when to eat, where to go, who to fight. Do you also tell them what to feel? Do you think you have any idea at all what I feel inside? Do you think you know my heart better than I do?" Angrily she wiped away the tears that rolled down her cheeks. "Don't tell me why I made love with you, and don't tell me that what I feel for you isn't love, because you don't know. If you need to have excuses to justify being in my bed, fine, but don't make excuses for me. I prefer to deal with the truth."

"And what is the truth?" he asked in a low, emotionless voice.

"The truth is I love you, and I know that doesn't matter to you. It doesn't mean anything to anyone but me. But that's okay, because it's me I'm talking about—*my* feelings, *my* heart. I'm going back to Orlando, and I'm going to go on living my life for *me*. There will be times when I'll miss you, when I'll need you so badly, and you won't be there, but I'll deal with them. And there will be times when I'll hate you for not loving me back, but I'll deal with that, too. I'll always worry about you, and I'll always pray for your safety. But..." She paused for a long, heavy moment. "When you find that woman you choose to marry and have children with, I hope that you never have her love. Just so you can see how it feels."

Chapter 10

Andrés stared at her for a long time, his expression for once open and revealing the pain inside. Then he regained control, stiffened his spine, rebuilt the defensive wall, drew the blank curtain. "Pray for whatever you wish. Hope for whatever pleases you. There's just one problem, Brenna. When I find that woman I choose to marry and have children with... I won't love her, and I won't want her to love me."

He sounded so positive, so determined. What had love ever done to him to make him react so negatively? she wondered woefully. Was it because he had loved his family and lost them? Or had the war cost him so much that he was no longer capable of loving, of giving that much of himself?

"Then along with my love and concern, I will also pity you," she said quietly. "Because a man who can't love might as well be dead."

He came back to the bed and cupped his hand gently to her cheek. "I didn't say I *couldn't* love her. I said I *wouldn't*. I can't give something that's already been given away." Bracing one knee on the mattress, he bent and kissed first her cheek, then her lips. He saw the look in her eyes go hazy, saw her catch her breath and open her mouth, and quickly he laid one fingertip across her lips. "Don't get all soft and forgiving, Brenna. Stay angry with me. Go away hating me. It will be better for both of us in the long run."

She caught his wrist when he started to pull away. "How will it be better?"

"You're going to end up hating me anyway." Whether her love now was real, as she insisted, or simply her mind's way of dealing with the stress of her captivity, as he believed, the result would be the same. Hatred. "Get a head start on it."

"And how will it be better for you?"

He shrugged and repeated a variation of the same answer. "You're going to end up hating me anyway. I may as well start getting used to it now." He tugged gently at his wrist until she released it, then left the room.

She sank down in the bed, hugging the pillow he'd lain on to her chest. Why hadn't she kept her mouth shut? she wondered sadly. Why hadn't she spent her last night in Andrés's arms, where she longed to be, instead of arguing and driving him away?

But what difference would it have made? Spending another night with her wouldn't have changed the way he felt—or didn't feel—about her. It wouldn't have made him love her, wouldn't have made him want her. It would only have delayed the inevitable. In less than thirty-six hours he would be sending her away, out of his sight, out of his mind, out of his life. The sooner she began dealing with that the better off she'd be.

But she didn't want to deal with it, she whispered into the pillow as tears filled her eyes. She didn't want to be better off. She wanted to love Andrés, wanted him to love her. She wanted to spend the rest of her life with him.

* * *

Andrés was sitting on the low stone wall around the church when a tall, slender shadow approached. He watched Vicente swing one leg over the wall and take a seat facing him.

"You can't sleep tonight, either?" Vicente asked, his voice as soft as the night.

"No."

"Problems?"

Andrés's smile was wry. "Aren't there always?"

"Yes, but none that can't be dealt with."

"I can deal with this one. It will just take a very long time." Maybe the rest of his life.

"If you asked for my advice, I'd say hold on to her."

Sharply Andrés looked at his friend, but could see nothing of the expression he wore. "I didn't ask for your advice," he responded with a scowl.

They sat in silence for several long moments. The village was quiet, the lights out everywhere except in Hector's clinic, where a lone lamp burned. Idly Andrés wondered if one of the patients had taken a turn for the worse. He hoped not, because he desperately wanted the doctor to accompany them tomorrow night. Esai was sure to need medical care, and with Brenna gone, there would be no one else to offer it.

"Why are you so willing to ask for advice on military matters and so adamant against asking for it on personal ones?"

The anger that flamed into life with Vicente's sudden question was hidden by the soft, even tone of Andrés's voice. "My personal matters *are* personal."

"But you're the first to admit that your judgment is as fallible as the next man's professionally." Vicente excused his probing with an apologetic shrug. "So why do you always trust it personally?"

Andrés stood up and walked away, intending to disappear deep into the forest, where he knew he would be left alone. But when he reached the end of the wall, he stopped, then returned to the same place. "What can I do? Ask her to forget what I've done? To forget that I kidnapped her and threatened her and put her life in danger? To go home to Florida and wait for me there until the war is over? To wait six months or another six years or God knows how long? To spend her entire life waiting if the war never ends?"

After considering the questions for a moment, Vicente answered. "Yes. Or, better yet, you could let her stay here."

"God help me," Andrés muttered, rubbing his hands over his eyes. "Ask her to stay here? *Here?*" Opening his arms wide to include the village, he turned in a slow circle. "This is an armed military camp. It is isolated, primitive and backward, and it's under constant threat of attack from the army. And you suggest that I should let Brenna *stay* here?"

"Yes. We could use a nurse, and you could use *her*." Again Vicente shrugged. "She's been here sixteen days and no harm's come to her—and not for lack of trying on her part. And though the village *is* under threat of attack, that threat has never materialized, not since you sent the families away and turned it into an armed camp. She would be safer here than anywhere else in this country except possibly Santa Lucia."

Dismayed, hearing none of Vicente's reasoning, Andrés shook his head and demanded, "Have you ever loved a woman?"

There was a longer pause, then the same answer. "Yes."

"And when you left to join us here, did you ask her to wait for you?"

"No." Vicente stared at the ground, his tension palpable. "But if I had the chance to bring her here—even by kidnapping—and to live with her here, in this isolated, primitive, backward armed military camp, I would do it."

Andrés couldn't accept that. It was too foolish, too dangerous, too selfish...and far too close to what he wanted for himself. "You say you love this woman, yet you would put her life in danger just to have her near, just so you could see her and be with her."

Vicente looked at him then, and his gaze was cool and level. "Yes, I would. Maybe I'm not as noble and honorable as you, but then, I'm not as selfish, either. You have no regard whatsoever for Brenna's feelings or her desires. All you're thinking of is yourself. So what if you love her so much that the idea of losing her is about to kill you? If there's one thing you've learned from this war, it's how to suffer. First your brother, then your family, then the children. Now Esai and Brenna. Suffering makes you strong. It helps you to endure. But you have enough of it, Andrés. You don't need to add more."

Torn between longing and duty, love and honor, Andrés paced back and forth. "How can I ask her to risk her life by staying here? If she goes back to Florida, she'll be safe."

"Unless her plane crashes. Unless she has an accident driving from the airport to her home. Unless someone breaks into her house, or mugs her on her way home from work, or shoots her by mistake in the commission of a crime." He paused briefly. "There are no guarantees of personal safety anywhere in this world, Andrés. Yes, she could die here, but the same thing could happen to her in Florida. Besides..." He paused again, remembering words from another time in another voice. "Being safe and alone is a much more difficult life than sharing danger and hardship with someone you love."

Vicente stood up, tilting his head back to study the sky for a long time. When he finally looked at Andrés again, the moonlight showed something Andrés had never seen in his friend's face. Sorrow. Bleak loss. "Before you give her up, be sure that you know what you're losing. Because I can promise you, if she goes away you'll continue to live, you'll still function, but inside . . . you'll be dead." With that he turned and walked away, crossing the wide road, but instead of entering his quarters, he went behind them, disappearing into the shadows.

Wearily Andrés sank down again, this time sitting on a patch of tough grass inside the churchyard and leaning back against the wall, stone and mortar cutting into his bare skin. Vicente was hurting inside, there was no doubt of that. Any other time Andrés would have offered him . . . what? Reassurances that everything would be all right? Words that were so bland, so trite, as to be offensive? Sympathy because he shared his sadness? Friendship that couldn't ease his pain?

He had nothing to offer, not to Vicente, and certainly not to Brenna. She would be all right. In a few months she would have forgotten the trauma of the past two weeks. She would be back at work, seeing her friends, settling back into the comfortable routine she needed. She would put Andrés where he belonged—in the past, in the dark part of her mind reserved for memories that no longer mattered. In the beginning thinking of him might be painful, but before long that would fade. Before long the memories of him would disappear.

Before you give her up, be sure that you know what you're losing. Oh, he knew. He was losing his future. His hopes. His dreams. He was losing the only woman he had ever loved, the only one he ever *would* love. He was losing the woman who had made him a better man, a better person. He was losing the chance to live a fulfilling, happy, loving life, no matter how long—or how short—it was.

He tilted his head back against the rocks, and his eyes drifted shut. He couldn't share Vicente's sentiments. He couldn't consider asking Brenna to wait for him. What if the war never ended? What if he died? Was it fair to ask her to put her life on hold for the possibility that *someday* he might come for her, that *someday* they might be together? What if she agreed, then stopped loving him before "someday" came? What if she met another man, one who could give her all the love and tenderness and happiness she deserved right now?

And what if she didn't?

He knew how rare love was. Some people lived their entire lives without finding it. Others settled for something less, for affection and friendship instead of passion and intensity. Just as he knew in his heart that he would never love another woman, what if the same was true for Brenna? What if she never found another man to love? She would live her life alone, or she would settle for second best—for affection, for friendship or mutual respect. She deserved better. She deserved all the love one man could give, deserved to give her love the way she was aching to.

Maybe he could talk to her. Maybe he could ask whether she would wait for him. Maybe he could suggest—

Stubbornly he cut off the thought and pushed himself to his feet. It was after midnight, and he was tired. He needed to sleep. Tomorrow would be a big day, the next day even more so. He needed to rest. To stop thinking about Brenna. To stop searching for some way to keep her when he knew in his head that there was none.

Wearily he walked down the road to his quarters. The screen door squeaked when he opened it, thumped quietly when he closed it. Without bothering to remove his trousers, he lay down on the cot, pulled the thin green blanket over him, closed his eyes and soon was asleep.

The camp was busy Tuesday. Trucks and jeeps were brought out and refueled from barrels stored outside the village. Supplies were stacked on porches, waiting to be loaded: water, food, bedrolls, radios, flashlights and weapons—pistols, rifles, crates of ammunition, even hand grenades.

Brenna tried to work in the clinic, but there was little to do. Hector was busy packing medical supplies, worrying aloud about what condition Esai would be in, about how difficult the return trip to the village would be for him, if he would simply need patching up or if surgery would be required.

She listened for as long as she could, but finally she left the building, standing outside on the steps for a long time. Everyone was busy; everyone had a task to do…except her. She was the most important part of their little game plan, she and Esai, but she was being left totally out of the preparations. There was no way she could help, nothing she could do except stay out of their way.

Andrés had been gone when she got up this morning. She'd heard him come back in, had heard the soft rustling sounds he made as he settled into bed on the small cot. She had hoped that he would come back to her, would lie beside her for the rest of the night, and disappointment because he hadn't had lain heavy in her chest.

Now he was down the road, talking to a group of men gathered around the tattered map spread out on the hood of a jeep. Although the basic plans for the exchange had been in place for several days now, she guessed there were still minor details to attend to. She knew that only a small group of men would be left behind to care for the patients and to guard the camp against attack. She knew, too, that the men as a group were eager to go, eager to see Esai again, to bring him home where he belonged. She imagined that more than a few of them were just as eager as Andrés to see her go.

Resting her chin in one cupped hand, she wondered about Esai Villareal. He seemed as popular in the camp as Andrés. Hector had told her that the cousins were a great deal alike—both courageous, both intelligent, both highly respected and deeply loved by their people. Esai's release would be a cause for celebration.

For everyone except her.

She raised one hand to wipe the sweat from her forehead, then became aware of Andrés watching her. After one quick, furtive glance, she pointedly looked the other way. He'd seen her several times today but had made no effort at all to talk to her. This was probably the way he wanted it to end, she thought with a scowl—angry, distant, unfriendly. This way he wouldn't have to tell her goodbye. He wouldn't have to face her, wouldn't have to acknowledge the hurt that he'd caused her.

But this time he wasn't going to ignore her. Andrés folded the map, stuck it under his arm and started toward her, his stride long, his expression inscrutable. Before he got too close she stood up and turned to climb the stairs, intending to hide in Hector's clinic. Andrés would never cause a scene in front of the doctor and his patients.

"Brenna."

She was reaching for the handle of the screen door when he spoke her name, not sharply, as she had expected, but softly. Imploringly.

"Would you come to the office with me?"

For a long time she hesitated. She wanted to turn him down. She wasn't strong or courageous. She couldn't keep seeing him, couldn't keep being alone with him, when she knew that after tomorrow she would never see him again. But that was precisely why she had to say yes. Because she needed this little bit of time with him. Because it might be all she would ever have.

She came down the steps and walked by his side to their quarters. She didn't look at him, didn't get close enough to touch him, and once they were inside she quickly chose a seat at the table, sitting straight backed in the wooden chair.

"I realized that everyone knows our plans except you. I thought you might be interested in what's going to happen," he said, sliding into the opposite chair. He spread out the map on the tabletop and pointed to locations as he spoke. "Here's Santiago, here's our village, and here—practically on the other side of the country—is Santa Lucia. The valley we chose for our meeting is right here. It will take us about six hours to get there. We'll be leaving after dinner tonight, so we should make camp sometime after midnight."

"Why tonight? Why not tell Dad to come in the afternoon and leave after breakfast instead?"

"Because we want to be in place when the American troops arrive."

"You don't trust my father."

He sighed heavily. "I don't think he'll double-cross us . . . this time. But you can be sure that the army is monitoring his actions. They know that all our top leaders will be there in that one place—Vicente, Javier, Reynaldo, Esai and me. If they could set a trap big enough, they could do our cause serious harm."

Serious harm. What an interesting way of describing his own death, Brenna thought as she leaned forward to study the map. The place he had identified as the valley was marked in thin black writing as El Valle del Cielo.

"The Valley of the Sky. It's one of the highest points in our country," Andrés explained upon hearing her sound out the words carefully. "It's ringed by volcanic mountains that are no longer active. It's small, easily defensible . . . very beautiful. We'll set up camp on the western edge for the rest of the night. Your father will arrive around nine o'clock, and we'll—"

Brenna looked at him, refusing to pretend interest any longer. "Why didn't you come back to bed last night?"

He stared back for a moment, then awkwardly folded the map and put it away in the cabinet. "I slept out here so I wouldn't disturb you," he said uncomfortably. "I knew I had to get up early this morning."

"So you wouldn't disturb me?" she echoed. "Or so *I* wouldn't disturb *you*?"

He wanted to deny that, wanted to wipe away the accusing hurt in her eyes with his kiss, but he was afraid to touch her. "I don't want to fight with you, Brenna," he said stiffly.

"You just want to be rid of me, don't you?" she asked sadly. "You made that clear enough last night, but I guess I was just too stubborn to give up hope so easily." Listlessly she got to her feet and walked to the door of her room. "I'll pack my things now. Just send someone to get me when it's time to go."

Before she could go inside he was touching her, turning her in his arms, kissing her as if he might never get the chance again. "Do you know how hard this is for me?" he demanded between kisses. "For two weeks I've had light and peace and happiness in my life again. When you leave, those things will go with you. I'll lose you again—forever, this time."

"Ask me to wait for you," she whispered. "Give me some reason to believe that you'll come for me when this is over."

"I can't do that." Forcing himself to release her, he stepped back, locking his fingers together behind his back. "Don't you understand, Brenna? It may never end, and when it does, I could be dead."

"Or it could end next week and you could be very much alive. Either way, if you asked me, I would wait."

"Don't say that, Brenna. For your own sake…" And for his sake, too. He was feeling so ragged, so desperate, so needy for her, that he was ready to believe anything that would let him hold on to her.

"Do you want me to say that I'll forget you? That I'll stop loving you? That I'll go out with other men and eventually fall in love with one of them? That I'll get married and have children and live happily ever after?"

"Yes."

But that wasn't really what he wanted to hear, she thought, hearing the pain in that tiny word, seeing it in his eyes. His response had been pulled from his soul unwillingly, because he thought it was best. For her sake. Because he cared for her.

And he *did* care; she was certain of it. Maybe what he felt wasn't love, but it was certainly more than fondness, more than tenderness and lust. He was fighting it as intensely as he'd fought the need to become lovers with her, but it was there anyway.

She smiled sadly. Knowing that he cared for her was sweet and warm and eased the painful tightness around her heart, but it didn't change things. He didn't want to love her, and he was still going to send her back to Florida.

"I won't lie to you, Andrés. That was what I wanted when you left before. I wanted to hate you, but even more I wanted to forget you. I wanted to meet another man, to love him and let him take your place in my life so completely that even my memories of you would have no room to exist. But it never happened. Every man I met, I compared to you. Every one of them was competing with your memory, and none of them measured up. Not one. It didn't happen then, and it's not going to happen now. I love you, Andrés. I will always love you."

"You can't know that," he whispered miserably. "Always is a long time."

"A lifetime," she agreed.

"Too long to look ahead. Too long to promise."

"What about the war, Andrés? As long as it goes on, as long as you're able to fight, will you always fight it?"

"Yes."

"Because you made a commitment. Because you believe in your cause. Loving is a commitment, too. I believe in my love. I believe in you."

Loosening his hands, he raised one to touch her face. "But I can't make a commitment to you. Everything I have, everything I am, is tied up in this war. There's nothing left to give anyone."

"You could give me hope. You could give me your word of honor that when this war ends you'll come for me." He was an honorable man, and he would never break his word. If he said he would come, he would, and she would wait for him. Forever.

"I can't do that. It isn't fair to you."

She made an impatient gesture. "Life isn't fair, Andrés. We just have to deal with that. Tell me that when it's over you'll want me. Give me that much hope."

It was tempting. God help him, it was so tempting. It would make his life so much easier, knowing that someday they might be together again. That she might still love him, might still want him. She would heal all his sorrows, would give him hope again. But he couldn't do it. His future was too uncertain, but she would believe him, and she would wait. Life would pass her by, and he might never show up, but she would still wait. "I can't, Brenna. I'm sorry."

She hugged her arms across her chest and ducked her head. "No," she murmured. "I'm sorry. I've never begged for anything before. You made it clear that there was no future for our affair, and I promised you that I could accept that, that I wouldn't make any demands. I'm sorry. It won't happen again."

She turned away, breathing deeply to control the tears that were so close to the surface. When he touched her shoulder she shrugged him away. She didn't want comfort from him, not when that was all he could offer. "Maybe you're right.

Maybe I will fall in love with someone else. The third time's supposed to be lucky, you know. It would have to be better. I mean, how many times can God let me fall in love with someone who doesn't want me?''

He almost said it then, almost said the words that would bind her to him forever. *I do love you.* He wanted to say them over and over, until she had no choice but to believe them, until all doubt and hurt and fear were erased from her mind and heart.

But he said nothing.

He forced himself to walk away from her. "I'll let you know when it's time to go."

Brenna nodded, even though she knew from the slam of the screen door that he was gone. After a moment she went into the bedroom, closed the door and sat down on the bed. Now she would cry, would sob out all her pain and sorrow for the last time. There would be no more tears over Andrés or for herself. She had come into this affair with her eyes wide open, had known exactly what to expect. Now she would deal with it.

But first . . . first she would cry.

The sun was setting as they drove out of the village.

Instead of the old pickup truck she was used to, or the jeep, Brenna was placed in the back of a huge, lumbering truck. Andrés and Vicente sat on either side of her, while another dozen soldiers, all armed to the teeth, sat on rough benches or the wood floor. Ahead of them on the narrow road were a half-dozen jeeps and trucks; another five were behind them.

"It's a long trip," Andrés said without glancing at her. "If you can, get some sleep."

She didn't glance at him, either. The soldier was back— the cold, distant, harsh man who felt nothing, who cared about nothing but his war. Somewhere inside him was buried the man she loved, but she didn't have the energy or the courage to draw him out.

It *was* a long trip. Within half an hour her bottom was sore, then numb. When she began fidgeting restlessly, Vicente silently offered her a bedroll to sit on. It wasn't long before that small comfort, too, was as hard as the wooden floor.

"Do you ever go to Miami, Miss Mathis?" Vicente asked after a while.

She looked at him and smiled wryly. He was trying to distract her so she would forget for a few minutes how uncomfortable she was. She didn't know if any conversation could make her forget the jolting ride, but she was willing to try. "When I can. It's one of my favorite places. It's a beautiful city, and it has such an international flavor to it. When was the last time you were there?"

"A long time ago. I'm sure it's changed a great deal since then."

"Probably." She reached for another bedroll, using this one for a blanket. "Miami has a large Angeleno population, doesn't it?" Maybe that was where he'd gone to school to learn his perfect English, she mused. Maybe that was also why he'd avoided her question about his family—not because they were dead, but because while the other men's families suffered, his was living a relatively comfortable life in the States.

"Yes, it does," he replied, looking out between the side rails of the truck.

"All of them wealthy," Andrés added derisively. "And all of them pro-Romero."

That put an effective end to the conversation, Brenna thought a moment later. She huddled underneath her sleeping bag and watched the sky darken, then the stars appear. As the road climbed higher up the mountain the stars seemed close enough to touch, but it was an illusion, she sadly acknowledged. In reality they were bright, cold, distant. Like Andrés.

He didn't look at her, didn't pay attention to her, although he couldn't help bumping against her when the truck went over a particularly deep rut. She tilted her head back and closed her eyes, feeling his presence, close enough to touch but too far away to reach.

When he realized that she hadn't moved for a long time, Andrés checked and saw that she was asleep, her head bent at an awkward angle. Gently he pulled her against him, his fingers lightly massaging her neck to make the movement easier. He settled her head on his shoulder, and her body followed, snuggling closer, one arm settling around his waist, the other in his lap.

He bit back a groan and saw Vicente almost smile. "You may as well hold her in your lap," he suggested in soft English. "She'll be more comfortable. Besides, this will probably be the last chance you'll ever get to hold her."

The last chance ever. Even as he acted on Vicente's suggestion, his only thought was bleak. The last chance to hold her, to touch her, to love her.

Dear God, how could he bear it?

It was well after midnight when they reached the valley. The men jumped out of the trucks and went to work, silently performing the tasks they'd been assigned. Guards were set, ammunition distributed, a small tent set up at the edge of the trees that formed a barrier between the lush valley and the jagged mountain peaks.

Andrés watched the men work from his position leaning against the side of the truck. When the tent was up he climbed into the truck and bent down to Brenna. She lay where he had left her, wrapped in a sleeping bag, another bedroll her pillow. "Brenna, wake up." He shook her gently, turning her onto her back. "Come on, your tent is ready."

She muttered unintelligibly as he helped her down from the truck and around the obstacle course presented by the other vehicles and boxes of supplies left on the ground. The tent was old, its canvas worn thin in places, and barely high enough for her to sit upright. She crawled inside, finding a sleeping bag already laid out, and Andrés followed her. He removed her tennis shoes and helped her into the sleeping bag, tucking her in the way he might a child. He was preparing to leave when she spoke in a sleepy plea.

"Stay with me, Andrés. Keep me safe and warm."

Couldn't she understand that was what he was trying to do by sending her back alone and unfettered to Florida? he wondered in silent anguish.

Soothingly he stroked his hand over her hair. "Hush," he whispered. "Go back to sleep."

Catching his hand, she clasped it tightly against her cheek. In only a few minutes she was asleep.

He sat with her for a long time, until the muscles in his legs and back protested the awkward position. After carefully unfolding her fingers from his, he tucked the extra sleeping bag securely around her, then left the tent.

Vicente was waiting for him outside, a small radio in his hand. "Mathis and his men are spending the night in San Luis," he reported. "There's been no sign of government activity in the area."

San Luis was a town some two hours away. There were plenty of rebel soldiers between San Luis and the valley, so Andrés would be receiving constant updates once the Americans moved out in the morning. "Are the guards posted along the road?"

"Yes."

"Then I guess there's nothing left to do but wait."

Brenna awoke Wednesday morning with sunlight, bright and warm, in her face. For a long moment she lay motionless, closing her eyes against the light, feeling the numerous aches and pains that throbbed from her head to her feet. She was sleeping on the ground, she realized, in a tent in El Valle del Cielo, and the sunlight was coming through a hole in the canvas. The trade was scheduled for today.

She sat up slowly, stretching out the kinks and wincing with discomfort. She was too spoiled for roughing it like this—her body simply wasn't cut out for sleeping without soft mattresses.

"Good morning."

Abruptly she twisted around and opened her eyes, squinting through the sunlight to the shadow on the opposite side of the tent. Andrés was half sitting, half lying on the canvas floor, watching her with dark unrevealing eyes. Was it a good morning? she wondered, then despairingly shook her head. Not today. She might never see another good morning as long as she lived.

"Your father will be here soon."

She simply nodded.

"Do you want some breakfast?"

"No."

They sat in silence for a few minutes, facing each other but looking at something—anything—else. Finally Brenna struggled free of the sleeping bag and put her shoes on, lacing them tightly. "Is it okay if we go for a walk?" She needed to say goodbye to him, but not here, not in this half-light, half-gloomy shelter.

When he nodded, she crawled out of the tent, standing stiffly. She waited for him to choose a direction, then walked at his side.

They walked along the edge of the forest, keeping the camp and the narrow road that snaked across the valley in sight. Andrés kept his eyes on the ground where they walked; Brenna looked around, her attention on the view.

The valley was beautiful, as he'd said. Less than a mile wide and about twice that long, it was covered with rich green grass and—she squinted, looking closer—yes, wildflowers. They seemed delicately out of place in a country that knew so little beauty and so much horror.

She stopped beside a sun-warmed boulder, resting her hand on its surface. "This is it, isn't it?"

He stopped, too, and nodded.

"No promises."

He shook his head.

"If I write to you . . ."

"I won't read it. I won't answer it." He wouldn't lay any claims, wouldn't accept any ties that might bind her to him until he was free.

"Then . . . if I'm pregnant, I guess you'll have to wait a long, long time to find out whether you have a son or a daughter."

Against his better judgment he raised his hand to her belly, molding its flatness, tenderly cradling her. "You're not pregnant," he whispered. If there was a God in heaven, He wouldn't give him a child like this, not now, not when he couldn't marry Brenna and care for her, not when he couldn't be there to help bring his child into the world, to love and teach and treasure him. "I pray that you're not."

"I pray that I am." She covered his hand with hers, smiling at him gently. "You worry too much, Andrés. That's the biggest difference between you and me. I say I love you, and you think, 'No, I can't make a commitment to you. I can't give you anything. I can't promise you anything. I can't let you wait for me because it's not fair. I can't let you live with me because it's dangerous.'" Her smile grew even gentler. "If you said you loved me, I would think, 'I must be the luckiest woman in the world.' With love, nothing else matters. Not gifts or promises, not fairness or danger. Nothing except being together and sharing and living and loving."

Her description of his response was accurate and sounded incredibly selfish in his ears. He had never thought of himself as selfish but as the opposite. He had given up so much to fight this war, had lost so much. If asked, he would have immodestly described himself as distinctly *unselfish*.

But Brenna thought he was selfish, and so did Vicente. Maybe I'm not as noble and honorable as you, his friend had said, but then, I'm not as selfish, either.

Was it selfish to want the one person he loved more than any other in the world to be safe? Even if it meant possibly living the rest of their lives apart? Even if it meant sorrow, unhappiness and loneliness for both of them?

Was it selfish to want a better life than this for her? To want, in addition to safety and security and peace, the more ordinary conveniences of electricity and indoor plumbing, of decent schools and quality medical care? She had grown up in the most advanced country in the world; in his few short months there he'd come to rely on things like washing machines, electric stoves, air conditioners, televisions, corner convenience stores. How could he ask her to give all that up to live in his backward, third-world, war-torn country?

She pulled away from him and turned to lean back against the rock, to stare across the valley to the eastern side, where her father would soon appear. "You're so good at being the leader, Andrés, so good at judging what's best for everyone under your command. But you're not always right. Sending me back to the States like this is a mistake. I'm the best thing in your life. Giving me up is going to cost you as much as it will me."

He moved so he could stand behind her, sandwiched between the warm hardness of the boulder and the warm softness of her body. Wrapping his arms around her, he bent his head to speak into her ear, making her shiver. "You're pretty sure of yourself, aren't you?" he tried to tease, but there was too much sadness in his voice.

"Tell me I'm wrong. Tell me you're not going to miss me. Tell me you don't care for me. Tell me—"

"I love you."

He felt her stiffen, felt the rise and fall of her breasts as she sucked in a deep breath. Slowly, without leaving his embrace, she twisted around to face him, her eyes searching his. "You don't have to say that," she whispered. "Not just to please me."

She'd given him the perfect opportunity to reclaim words that never should have been spoken, but he just looked at her, his mouth closed. He shouldn't have said them, but they were true. They were all he could give her—no hope, no promises, no future—but at least she would know that he loved her.

"I don't understand, Andrés," she murmured against his chest. "If you love me—"

He brushed his hands through her hair, lifting her face so he could see her. "You *are* the best thing in my life, and giving you up is going to cost me everything, but it's for your own good. You think you love me now, but what about next month? What about a year from now, when you've been alone a long time, when you're lonely and you need to be held, to be touched and kissed and loved, and I'm not there to do it?"

"Do you think when I'm lonely anyone will do? If that were the case, Andrés, I would have gotten married a long time ago. When I need to be held and kissed and loved, I need it from *you*, not from some man who happens to be available and willing."

"How long will you need it from me when I'm not there?"

"The rest of my life. You're sending me away to spend the rest of my life alone with nothing. Lie to me. Tell me you'll send for me. Tell me you'll want me. Let me have something, even if it isn't true, to hold on to." She waited, but he said nothing. "Maybe you've already done that," she said miserably, turning away, "by telling me you love me."

He caught her arm, pulling her back. "How can you doubt my love for you?" he demanded heatedly. Didn't she know how difficult it was for him to offer even that? Didn't she know how much courage it had taken for him to say those three words? And now she was throwing them back, accusing him of lying, of making them up just to satisfy her.

Brenna looked at him, then around the valley. Trucks were arriving from the east, their engines a soft rumble underfoot. Her father was here. Her time was up. Sadly she looked back at Andrés. "I've been asking myself that same question. I say I love you, and you say I don't. How can you doubt me? I'm willing to give up my home, my job, my father, my country, to live here, to be with you. I'm willing to give up my *life* for you, yet you still doubt me. What are you willing to give me . . . besides heartache?"

He stared at her a long time, his heart aching in his chest. "Freedom," he whispered. "Safety."

That wasn't enough, Brenna thought sadly. It would never be enough.

Side by side they returned to their camp, joining the soldiers who were waiting for the Americans to reach their designated place, marked by a tall column of ancient volcanic rock a quarter of a mile away. The trucks parked next to each other, and armed soldiers jumped out. One, taller, older, marked by silver-gray hair, left the others and walked forward, covering about half the distance that separated them.

It was her father, Brenna realized, edging closer to Andrés to see better. The last time she'd seen him, his hair had been more brown than gray. He'd lost some weight since then, too—because life was harder here, she wondered, or because of the hatred that was eating him up inside?

She was unaware that she'd taken several steps toward her father until a gentle hand pulled her back. It was Vicente, who mouthed the word, "Wait."

Andrés walked forward to meet Tom Mathis. He'd left his rifle behind at the tent, but he wore the pistol and the knife, and he knew that many of his men had their rifles trained on them, just as the Americans did.

He stopped some fifteen feet away. "Where is Esai?"

Tom pulled out a cigarette and lit it, then blew the smoke into the clear air. "Bring Brenna over first."

Andrés shook his head. "You can see her. You see that she's safe."

"Tell your man to get his hands off her."

He didn't glance over his shoulder. He knew it was Vicente who held Brenna—none of the other men would willingly touch her. He also knew Vicente wouldn't hurt her. "Tell your men to bring my cousin to me now."

Tom stared at him for a long time, then dropped the cigarette to the ground and crushed it out. Without taking his gaze off Andrés, he called over his shoulder, "McCallum, Partridge, bring him out."

The two uniformed men moved slowly, not so much because of the weight of the stretcher but because of the condition of the man it bore. "I'm afraid he's unconscious," Tom said as they lowered the man to the ground beside them. "The trip was more than he could handle. My corpsman did the best he could for him, but...we both know prisoners don't get first-class treatment."

Forgetting Tom, Andrés knelt on the ground next to his cousin, lifting his hand, tasting pure rage as his gaze moved quickly over him. A heavy beard covered half of his face but didn't hide his cracked, bleeding lips. One eye was swollen shut; crusted, infected lacerations marked his cheeks, and his nose was grotesquely swollen and misshapen. There were open sores on his neck, his wrists and his feet, and one leg was bent at an awkward angle. There would be more injuries underneath the filthy uniform, Andrés knew. Injuries that very well might kill him.

With great care he replaced Esai's hand on the stretcher, then stood up and signaled to Hector. The doctor and several men hurried out to pick up their patient.

There was rage in Andrés's gaze when he looked at Tom again. "If you'd had your way, that would be me instead of my cousin."

Tom shook his head. "If I'd had my way, you'd be dead. Tell your man to send my daughter over here right now."

Andrés walked away, his muscles taut. He knew the danger he was facing in turning his back on Tom Mathis, but he walked at a steady, slow pace, his spine straight, showing no apprehension.

It was her turn to go. Brenna began backing away behind Vicente, seeking shelter that she knew didn't exist. She wanted to stay here, she cried silently. Andrés needed her— Esai and Hector needed her.

"You have to go now," Vicente said quietly. "You have to, Brenna."

She looked at him with teary eyes. "Oh, now you manage to call me by my name instead of the oh-so-formal 'Miss Mathis,'" she said, but the humor fell flat. She looked for Andrés and found him kneeling once more beside his cousin, holding Esai's hand in his, his pose prayerful. He wasn't going to tell her goodbye, she realized. He'd said all he could say.

She let Vicente give her a push. "Take care of him, will you?" she pleaded.

"Yes."

She walked across the clearing, as Andrés had done, walked right up to her father and kissed both cheeks, then hugged him tight.

"Thank God you're all right," Tom whispered, holding her in a crushing embrace. "Let's get out of here—"

She pushed until he released her, then took a step back. "I love you, Dad."

"I love you, too, babe."

"Do you?" she asked sadly.

Tom stared at her for a long time, his blue eyes narrowing on the face that was so like her mother's. "What do you mean? What's wrong? What has that bastard been telling you?"

"Did you see what they did to that man? He's practically dead. The pain, the suffering they caused him...and you would have done it to Andrés. If your plan had worked out, it would have been Andrés who was captured, Andrés who suffered."

He looked away, sighed heavily, then looked back at her, his expression hard. "This is *war*, Brenna. You don't understand."

"No, Dad, this is personal. When you involve me, it's personal." Stepping forward, she laid her hand on his arm. "I love you, Dad. In spite of what you've done, I do love you. But I can't go with you."

He grasped both her arms, shaking her hard. "It's him, isn't it? You went and fell in love with him again! Damn it, Brenna, he used you once before, and you let him do it again!"

"It's not him, Dad, it's me. He told me to go home, to forget him, to find someone else to spend my life with. I thought I could go back...but I love him. It doesn't matter whether we're both in Florida or here or on opposite sides of the world, I'm still going to love him."

"You'll get over him if you try—"

"The way Mom got over you?" She saw by the surprise in his blue eyes that she'd struck a nerve. "She loved you right up to the day she died. She kept waiting for you to realize that you missed her, that you needed her. She waited and waited and waited for you, but you never came. I can't live that way. I can't meekly go back to Florida and spend the rest of my life waiting for a man who might never come, for a love that might never arrive. I can't grow old the way Mom did, all alone and lonely and empty. I've had enough loneliness in my life for ten people. I would rather die young with Andrés than live to be a lonely old woman without him.''

''Brenna...'' Andrés stopped a few yards away. He'd tried to stay back, had tried to remain where he was, but fear hadn't let him. He'd known that when she and her father finished talking, they would climb into the trucks and leave, and he would lose her, this time forever. In spite of the danger he'd had to come out here, had to tell her that he needed her now, needed her here, to love him and care for him, to share his burdens and his life with him. He needed her sweet smiles and her gentle caresses and her tender loving. He needed her to help him to be a man—not a warrior, not a leader, not a hero, but simply a man. He needed her to live.

He'd planned to let her make her own decision. Then he'd heard what she was saying to Tom. About love and loneliness and needing and emptiness. He knew all too well the kind of life she was describing, because he had lived it for six years.

She looked at him, surprised to see him standing there. He started to reach out to her, but under Tom's fierce glare he dropped his hand back to his side. ''Don't go,'' he whispered.

Tears filled her eyes. ''I'm not,'' she replied, then laughed softly. ''I was going to stay whether you wanted me to or not. I can't go back, Andrés. There's nothing for me there without you.''

"Stay with me. Always. I'll take care of you. I can protect you." He paused to clear the emotion from his throat. "I love you."

"You can't do this, Brenna," Tom said, his voice vibrating with parental fury. "You cannot do this!"

"I have to, Dad. We don't often get a second chance at happiness, and I have to take it." She put her arms around Tom, hugging him tightly.

"Damn it, Brenna!"

Then she moved away, dried her tears and placed her hand in Andrés's. "I love you, Dad. I always will. But my life is here. My future is here." She glanced up at Andrés and smiled sweetly. "My heart is here."

When they turned to walk away, Tom called her name, his voice cracking in desperation. "Brenna!"

She didn't turn around, just tightened her hand around Andrés's and continued walking back the way she'd come. But she wasn't alone this time, walking away from her life. She was with Andrés, walking back to it.

"Damn you, Montano, I'll kill you!" Tom shouted.

Andrés glanced over his shoulder at his old friend. His new enemy. He studied him for a moment, then gave a shake of his head. "I don't think so." Because in spite of his hatred and his rage, Tom Mathis still had one worthy quality: he loved his daughter almost as much as Andrés did. He might hate her choice of a husband, but eventually he would come around, because in the long run, he wanted the same things for her that Andrés did. Happiness. Joy. Satisfaction. Completion.

Love.

The church was silent and dimly lit, the light of the candles sending flickering dancing shadows along the wall. The flames contributed to the already stifling heat in the room, but no one noticed.

Brenna had planned her wedding in a hundred different ways when she was growing up, but she had never planned one like this. Instead of white lace and satin she wore khaki slacks and a pink shirt. Instead of coming down the aisle on her father's arm she had acted more as a crutch for Esai, still barely able to walk after more than a month of freedom and the best treatment she and Hector could provide. Instead of flowers there were rifles and pistols.

But she had the groom of her dreams, she thought with a smile, turning to look at Andrés. He wasn't wearing the black tux she had often imagined but rather his everyday olive-drab uniform and heavy boots. But he was as handsome and as dear and as loving as in her dreams.

Father Hidalgo cleared his throat and began the ceremony. He spoke their vows in Spanish, and Andrés repeated them for her in English. It didn't matter, she thought dreamily. She would promise anything, would agree to anything, to spend the rest of her life as his wife.

There were no lovely gowns. No sweet-scented flowers. No flowing music. No blushing attendants. No blinding flashes from a photographer's camera to capture the occasion. No gold and diamond rings. No family but Esai, and very few friends. Just vows of love. Of eternity.

But that was the important part, wasn't it?

When the ceremony ended, Andrés raised her left hand to his lips and pressed a kiss to her bare finger. "Someday, when this war is over, I'll buy you a ring." And someday, he thought with a gentle smile, might come sooner than they had expected. The news from the States was that the government was under pressure to withdraw American troops from San Angelo and to cut off financial aid to the Romero government. Soon the war would end. Soon his people would be free, and he could forget being a soldier and concentrate on being a husband—and a father.

She smiled, too, dazed by the simple, perfect beauty of a ceremony she'd hardly understood. "I don't need a ring," she murmured, leaning forward to kiss first one cheek, then the other, then his mouth. "I already have your heart."

She was right, Andrés reflected as he drew her against him, taking another kiss, one to seal their vows. She certainly did have his heart . . . and his love . . . forever.

*   *   *   *   *

Silhouette Intimate Moments ®

COMING NEXT MONTH

#341 THE WAY BACK HOME— Emilie Richards

Ex-runaway Anna Fitzgerald had devoted her life to helping others on the run, but now just as her romance with state's attorney Grady Clayton seemed to be flourishing, her true identity and troubled past caught up with her. Could love and courage save the only happiness she'd ever found?

#342 PAINTED LADY—Maura Seger

Block Island was meant to be relaxing for vivacious photographer Petra O'Toole, but when her life was threatened, she turned to sexy Giles Chastain for help. Desire and fiery passion followed, as Petra discovered that this man would always set her heart aflame!

#343 IN SAFEKEEPING—Naomi Horton

To protect her young nephew from a major drug lord, Linn Stephen fled with him to a tiny fishing village. There she found unexpected passion in the form of securities expert Trey Hollister. Linn soon realized that Trey's "expertise" was enough to keep her safe forever—body and soul!

#344 A LASTING PROMISE— Paula Detmer Riggs

Determined to win back his ex-wife's love, John Olvera lured Aurora to his small New Mexico pueblo with the promise of a teaching position. Once she was in his arms again, John vowed to turn the disillusionment of their past into the passion of their future.

AVAILABLE THIS MONTH:

Silhouette Intimate Moments®

**Beginning this month, Intimate Moments brings
you the first of two gripping stories by Emilie Richards**

Coming in June

Runaway

by EMILIE RICHARDS

Intimate Moments #337

Coming in July

The Way Back Home

by EMILIE RICHARDS

Intimate Moments #341

Krista and Rosie Jensen were two sisters who had it all—until a
painful secret tore them apart.

They were two special women who met two very special men who
made life a little easier—and love a whole lot better—until the day
when Krista and Rosie could be sisters once again.

You'll laugh, you'll cry and you'll never, ever forget. RUNAWAY is
available now at your favorite retail outlet, or order your copy by
sending your name, address, zip or postal code along with a check
or money order for $2.95, plus 75¢ postage and handling, payable
to Silhouette Reader Service to:

Silhouette Books®

RUN-1A

A TRILOGY BY PEPPER ADAMS

Pepper Adams is back and spicier than ever with three tender, heartwarming tales, set on the plains of Oklahoma.

CIMARRON KNIGHT . . . available in June
Rugged rancher and dyed-in-the-wool bachelor Brody Sawyer meets his match in determined Noelle Chandler and her adorable twin boys!

CIMARRON GLORY . . . available in August
With a stubborn streak as strong as her foster brother Brody's, Glory Roberts has her heart set on lassoing handsome loner Ross Forbes . . . and uncovering his mysterious past. . . .

CIMARRON REBEL . . . available in October
Brody's brother Riley is a handsome rebel with a cause! And he doesn't mind getting roped into marrying Darcy Durant—in name only—to gain custody of two heartbroken kids.

**Don't miss CIMARRON KNIGHT, CIMARRON GLORY and
CIMARRON REBEL—three special stories that'll win your
heart . . . available only from Silhouette Romance!**

Take 4 bestselling love stories FREE

Plus get a FREE surprise gift!

◉ *Diamond Jubilee Collection*

It's our 10th Anniversary...
and *you* get a present!

This collection of early Silhouette
Romances features novels written
by three of your favorite authors:

ANN MAJOR—*Wild Lady*
ANNETTE BROADRICK—*Circumstantial Evidence*
DIXIE BROWNING—*Island on the Hill*

* These Silhouette Romance titles were first published in the early 1980s
  and have not been available since!

* Beautiful Collector's Edition bound in antique green simulated leather to
  last a lifetime!

* Embossed in gold on the cover and spine!

This special collection will not be sold in retail stores and is only available
through this exclusive offer.
Look for details in all Silhouette series published in June, July and August.